PIRATE'S *Mistress*
MARIANNE LaCROIX

ELLORA'S CAVE
ROMANTICA PUBLISHING

$\mathcal{W}$hat the critics are saying...

❧

CROSSED SWORDS

5 Stars "Wonderfully written story about the powerful sea Captain and his prisoner falling in love [...] If you are looking for steamy sex, that will leave you seeking your own release, look no further [...] It's perfect!" ~*Just Erotic Romance Reviews*

SEA HAWK'S MISTRESS

"Sea Hawk's Mistress was a fun blast-from-the-past for me. I used to devour pirate romances and this one looked like fun, so I grabbed it. I was not disappointed! This was a terrific, sexy little romance." ~ *Just Erotic Romance Reviews*

"If you enjoy pirate stories, step back in time and experience adventure on the high seas with this entertaining escape." ~ *Romantic Times Book Reviews*

An Ellora's Cave Romantica Publication

www.ellorascave.com

Pirate's Mistress

ISBN 9781419957437
ALL RIGHTS RESERVED.
Crossed Swords Copyright © 2007 Marianne LaCroix.
Sea Hawk's Mistress Copyright © 2007 Marianne LaCroix.
Edited by Kelli Kwiatkowski.
Cover art by Syneca.

This book printed in the U.S.A. by Jasmine-Jade Enterprises, LLC.

Trade paperback Publication March 2008

Also by Marianne LaCroix

ഔ

Beast in My Bed

Bridesmaid and the Beast

Descendants of Darkness

Ellora's Cavemen: Dreams of the Oasis III (*anthology*)

Eternal Embrace

Lady Sheba

Scorpion King

About the Author

ഔ

Multi-published author Marianne LaCroix lives in the American south in the land of cotton and mint juleps. She's an active member of the RWA in the ESPAN, GothRom, Passionate Ink, and First Coast Romance Writers chapters. She's had several recognitions for her writing including a Romantic Times BOOKClub Reviewer Choice nomination. Her tastes run to the alpha male with a dark streak in the form of a vampire, shape-shifter or other tortured-soul type. When not writing, Mari can be found with her twin toddler girls and her husband of eleven and half years.

Marianne welcomes comments from readers. You can find her website and email address on her author bio page at www.ellorascave.com.

Tell Us What You Think

We appreciate hearing reader opinions about our books. You can email us at Comments@EllorasCave.com.

PIRATE'S MISTRESS
By Marianne LaCroix

ℰℯ

CROSSED SWORDS

ℰℭ

Dedication

§

Special thanks to Sloan McBride, Stephanie Saint Blaque, Tara Greenbaum, Shannon Greenland, and Glen McCafferty.

This book is dedicated to you all…my valued writing buddies.

Five of Swords

§

The Five of Swords is the card of defeat. The seeker faces a chance of defeat if he does not work within the confines of a situation instead of trying to force his will on the situation. Hostility may come into play as the seeker puts his own interests ahead of others.

An empty victory, possibly through deceit, is at hand. Winning may not be worth the effort, or what the seeker truly desires. This card reflects a confrontation that brings pain to both sides of a conflict.

On occasion, battles have two losers. There will also be times when one has to surrender. But the worst scenario is when the winner is someone who uses an unfair advantage to win—like Captain Thorne does in Crossed Swords. To give up the fight is sometimes the only way for the battle to end…

Prologue
Caribbean Sea, 1717

&

"The Five of Swords," the gypsy announced with a low cackle.

"And what's that supposed to mean?" Captain Fredrick Thorne asked before taking another gulp of his rum. His brains had been dancing under the spicy drink's influence for over a week. He'd set to shore here in Tortuga, the pirate's haven, for his men to relax and find ways to spend the gold lining their pockets.

"'Tis the card of defeat."

"Defeat?" Fredrick sobered for a moment.

"Aye, Captain, defeat. You do not adapt to change, but instead you bend the wills of those around you. You will set your own needs ahead of others."

"Impossible," yelled a drunken Jeremy O'Connell, Fredrick's quartermaster. "Captain Thorne sets the crew's need for gold ahead of everything else!"

This garnered a boisterous cheer from the pirates celebrating nearby. Fredrick sat in silence listening to their revelry. Only those close to him knew his purpose for piracy. With every cannon blast into a British ship or port, he used piracy as a means of revenge against the British Crown, crippling the coffers of riches imported from the colonies to England. But whatever his underlying motivation, his victories were profitable not only for him but the entire crew. He kept his crew happy and rich, and in turn, they followed him without question.

Fredrick leaned forward over the gypsy's table where she read Tarot for a piece of eight. "You see, my crew comes first."

The old woman, whimsically dressed in loose, rainbow-colored calico fabric, shook her head. She placed down another card—the Queen of Cups. "No, Captain. You will think only of your own needs when you meet *her*."

"Who is she?" he asked, surprised at the notion that any woman would influence his life. He'd never let his heart get involved in his relations with women. It was strictly physical. Once he eased his lusts, he moved on.

"She is the woman who will challenge you, who will set your world into a storm to end all storms. She is a woman of love and beauty, a woman to ensnare the heart of the mighty Captain Thorne."

The men surrounding them laughed loudly.

Fredrick rose from his seat and tossed two coins to the gypsy, who snatched them up quickly. "No woman will ever tie me down. My only mistress is the sea." He laughed and turned away for another fool to be parted from his gold by the ramblings of the old gypsy. As he walked away, he called to his crew, "It will take more than a pretty face to defeat me!"

Chapter One

‍ℬ

Boom! Boom! Crash!

Arabella Prescott was shaken awake by the sound of cannon fire in the distance, then the crashing strike nearby vibrating the very walls of the governor's plantation manor.

She threw back her bedcovers and dashed to the window. Peering out into the darkness, she saw the flash of a cannon shot from a ship in the harbor.

"Milady!" Betsy, her maidservant, burst into the room from the hall. "We're under attack by pirates!"

"They would not dare attack Port Monmouth!" Despite her denials, the ship fired another cannon toward the town. Pirates were indeed attacking the British port on St. Crescentia Island.

"Milady, you must get to the cellar and hide. We have no time to lose!" Betsy darted about the room gathering clothes and other items to take with them into hiding. "They will be landing soon, and they are sure to come to the governor's residence first!"

"Bloody pirates," Arabella murmured.

"With your father away with the fleet, only a small battalion of new recruits man the fort. Untried young boys with muskets are no match for a horde of attacking pirates!"

Arabella turned to Betsy and took her cloak from the maid's hands. "Once they discover Father gone, they will look for someone else to ransom." Ransoming important people of the aristocracy and nobility, she knew, was a common pirate ploy for making money.

Betsy gasped. "Hurry! Hurry! We must hide. I cannot bear the thought of you in the hands of a pirate."

"I have no intention of becoming a prisoner." Arabella threw open the nightstand drawer and stuffed her jewelry into her pockets. She slammed the drawer shut when emptied and ran for the door. "Come, let's get to the cellar." She paused a brief moment and realized the cannon fire had stopped. "They will be here soon."

Minutes later, Arabella, Betsy and several other house servants huddled in the cramped, hidden cellar, hiding from the pirates now entering the manor. They were rowdy and loud, firing their flintlocks into the air as they rummaged through each room. Meanwhile, Arabella and the servants remained still, praying the night would end.

"Where is Governor Prescott? Where are the servants?" a baritone voice called out. The voice was steady and cultured, with a recognizable British accent.

A British pirate attacking a British port? The thought made Arabella steam with anger. How could a man attack his own countrymen?

"The house is deserted, Captain," one of the men called out in a cockney accent.

"They must be around here somewhere. Look for a hidden passage or cellar," the strong voice called to his men. Arabella guessed this was the pirate captain.

He continued to walk the wooden floor above their hiding place, and she held her breath when he stopped just above her. She could only see the shadow of his boot through the boards. He tapped his foot and dust floated down. She turned her face away, covering her mouth with her hand, fighting a sneeze.

She squeezed her eyes shut and froze, hoping he wouldn't hear them just below him.

He stepped away and she exhaled. Her body shook and the servants clutched each other in fear. Arabella looked at Betsy to see her eyes wide with terror.

Then a board was lifted away and dust filtered down upon them again. Light from a lantern illuminated the frightened group, and Arabella turned her eyes to the man now towering over her.

"Well, well, well. What do we have here?" His voice was hard but held a trace of humor.

Several of the pirates lifted away the boards covering the hidden cellar, but Arabella kept her gaze locked with the captain's.

He stood in command, a man of power, strength and dominance. He was tall, tanned and roguishly handsome, dressed in a dark brown coat with silver buttons, brown breeches, black boots that reached his muscled mid-thighs — and a flintlock in one hand cocked at her face. She gulped and found her voice. "I am Governor Prescott's daughter, and in his absence, I demand you cease your attack upon Port Monmouth immediately!"

He smirked and breathed a soft laugh. "I come looking for the governor and instead I find his daughter — hiding bravely in a root cellar." He eased the pressure upon his flintlock and tucked it into the waist of his breeches.

At least he wasn't aiming at her anymore.

He got down on one knee and offered his hand. "Allow me to assist you out of your retreat, Miss Prescott."

Loath to allow him to help her, she reluctantly took his hand and climbed out of the cellar. The warm touch of his hand was strangely appealing, but as soon as she was out of the cellar she drew her hand back as though it had been burned.

"Now what was it you *demanded*?" he asked lightly as his sea-green eyes roamed over her figure.

"Stop this attack immediately."

"Hmm." He began to circle her and she caught a glimpse of his long, pale blond hair tied back in a queue. The tail of silky hair trailed down his back, and for a split second, she wondered how those strands would feel between her fingers. "Stop the attack," he repeated, bringing her attention back to his classically chiseled, tanned face. "Not sure there is any reason to continue if Governor Prescott is not even here."

"So you will leave?" She wanted him to leave—right now. He was much too handsome and...what was that odd feeling in the pit of her belly at his close proximity? Whatever it was, she wanted it to stop. It was much too disturbing to ponder.

He stood behind her for a moment then stepped around to face her. "Oh yes, we will leave." His small smile made her heart leap. Even the scent of the sea clinging to his clothes seemed to wrap about her body, provoking a reaction she didn't want to explore.

She narrowed her eyes. No pirate would just leave so easily.

"Gents!" he called to his crew within the room. "The lady requests we leave Port Monmouth!"

They responded with vile refusals and boisterous laughter.

He turned back to her and with an evil glint in his eye, he said, "I say we leave as she asks, but that we also extend our hospitality to Governor Prescott's daughter aboard *Neptune's Sword* in place of her gallant father."

"You wouldn't dare!" Arabella ground out and stepped forward to strike him, but he caught her hand before she met her target.

"You, Miss Prescott, will be ransomed to the governor."

"You can't take Miss Prescott!" Betsy called out. She was held back by one of the crewmen.

"Take her we will." With his commanding grasp on her forearm, he pulled her to him, and she was painfully aware of his hard body against hers. The smells of the sea and his natural masculine scent mingled in her nose, and the junction between her legs ached and moisture seeped from her body. "She will be our special guest," he added in a low, husky voice.

He turned to Betsy and announced, "Tell the Lord Governor Prescott that we will ransom his daughter for forty thousand pieces of eight, and will exchange gold for her freedom in a fortnight, on the northern beach of Isla de Margarita. If he wishes to have her back, he will pay. And no tricks. Understand?"

Betsy nodded nervously.

"I am not going with you," Arabella whispered heatedly to him.

His face mere inches from hers, she couldn't help but glance at his lips and wonder what they'd feel like.

Insanity! She shouldn't be thinking such scandalous things. He was nothing but a mangy dog, unworthy of any proper lady's attention. He threatened her, and she was panting over his arm holding her steady and the powerful body flush with hers. What kind of woman was she? Certainly she wasn't a weakling who would allow such a scoundrel free rein over her fate. No, she was not weak—she must fight!

As though reading her mind, he laughed softly. "You will come with me even if I have to carry you kicking and screaming."

"You are despicable," she spat.

He leaned in, his lips a breath away from hers. "I'm a pirate, luv. That's my job."

He released her arm and she quickly moved away from him. He turned to give orders to his men and she saw it as an opportunity to run. She bolted out of the room and headed toward the entry hall. She heard the captain yell orders to catch her, but she was too quick. She ducked out of reach of several pirates chasing her. Dodging up the stairs, she ran to the only safe place she knew—her room.

Inside her bedroom she bolted the door. Turning, she scanned the room. No gun. No sword. Nothing in sight to use as a weapon. Then by the fireplace she saw the empty warming pan. She quickly grabbed it when one of her pursuers jiggled the doorknob, followed by the sound of fists pounding on the door.

There was nowhere for her to go other than out the window, which led to a steep one-story drop to the bushes below. She'd probably break her leg—or worse—attempting that.

As she considered her options, the door burst open, the bolt flying off the doorjamb with a crash.

It was the pirate captain.

She raised the warming pan in her hands threateningly.

"I'm not happy with you, Miss Prescott. Now put down that *weapon* and come along—like a calm, proper young lady." His tanned face was hard and his voice was angry.

She raised the pan an inch higher. "I told you, I will *not* go with you."

"And I told *you*, you will come along even if I have to carry you."

"I'll fight you the entire way."

He lunged at her and she swung, but he caught her arm, twisting the pan from her grasp, the metal clanging loudly on the floor. She struggled against his hold, fighting him with every ounce of her strength. He pulled her around and pushed her down upon the bed, covering her body with his, holding her forearms down into the soft coverlet as she wiggled against him, his flintlock poking into her abdomen.

"Miss Prescott, I believe you will be quite a treat to have aboard my ship. Much more appealing than any old governor with a powdered wig and a box of snuff." He adjusted his body over hers, and she realized it wasn't only his flintlock she felt against her.

"Dirty pirate!"

"Now, now. You don't even know me, luv. You may come to like me."

"Never, Captain…" She realized she didn't even know his name.

"Captain Fredrick Thorne at your service, Miss Prescott."

She spat into his face and he shook off the little bubble of moisture. "You need a good spanking, I think. You're a spoiled little wench."

"You wouldn't dare."

"Don't tempt me." His eyes narrowed and he added, "Maybe you just need a good kiss."

"I don't kiss just any man who asks."

"I'm not asking."

Before she could reply, he crushed his lips down upon hers. Nothing could have prepared her for the assault inflicted upon her senses with his kiss. Her body seemed to melt beneath him and she opened her mouth, allowing his tongue to sweep along hers. She responded to him hungrily. Her reaction was beyond her control as she gave in to his kisses.

Deep, greedy kisses. He released her hands and she curled her arms around his head, bringing him closer. He placed a hand at her waist and felt his way up to her breast. He squeezed it gently and she whimpered in response.

He drew back slightly and she moaned. She dreamily looked up at him and stared.

What exactly just happened here?

"You *did* need a good kiss," he said softly with an irritating smirk.

Her sweet surrender was short-lived as she grimaced, and with a heave of her leg, threw him off her. He laughed when she sprang from the bed.

He caught her wrist and stopped her from running again. Her senses were too jumbled to think clearly, yet she tugged at his hand. "Let me go. Please." Her voice was weak compared to only a few moments ago.

"No." Without another word, he rose from the bed and scooped her up over his shoulder. She screamed, but to no avail.

"Put me down, you dirty, vile, thieving bastard!" she yelled as she pounded his back.

"Tsk, tsk! Such language," he scolded with a light slap to her ass. "I am beginning to wonder how a *lady* knows such vulgarity." He carried her with ease out of the room and down the stairs.

"Are you inferring I am not a lady?"

He laughed and spanked her ass a bit harder. "I think you are a shrew, Miss Prescott."

She gasped in horror. "I am *not* a shrew!"

"You are, and I am about to tame you into a willing, genteel lover."

"I'll *never* let you touch me."

"Oh yes, you will, luv. You will beg for me to make love to you."

"Never!"

He chuckled as he strolled out of the governor's manor and toward the awaiting skiffs at the water's edge. Arabella looked over to the village where screams and the rowdy yells of the pirates floated across the small beach. The pirates were terrorizing the entire village.

"You didn't exactly fight me off a few moments ago," he said, breaking into her worried thoughts of the Port Monmouth citizens.

He *had* to mention the kiss. She wanted to just forget that touch still burning her swollen, tender lips. "I was taken unawares," she finally said, knowing it was a feeble excuse.

It was met with another smack on her rump and a masculine laugh. "Miss Prescott, I doubt *anything* takes you unawares."

* * * * *

"It's bad luck to have a woman aboard ship, Captain," Jeremy said when Fredrick returned to the quarterdeck after depositing the governor's daughter in his cabin.

"Aye, I know, but she is a means to get the ransom money." Fredrick scanned the returning skiffs filled with his celebrating pirate crew.

Jeremy was not only Fredrick's quartermaster and second-in-command, but also a good friend. They had served together aboard a naval frigate as lieutenants. Both had purchased their commission within the Navy and had hoped to gain much from their time at sea.

Jeremy O'Connell was an educated man, much like Fredrick, and had gone to sea to find his fortune. Many men left their homes for the sea with the same hope—to gain wealth and prosperity. Fredrick had wanted to learn the ways of running a ship to one day command the fleet in his brother's shipping company, but Jeremy had wanted to earn money in order to marry and provide his wife with a comfortable living. He and his fiancée had waited to marry until Jeremy was more financially stable.

Unfortunately, when they made port in Dover years later, Jeremy had received news of the death of his fiancée from yellow fever. Jeremy had taken it hard, turning to self-destruction. Fredrick watched over the overwrought man and helped him eventually break out of his dark mourning.

Fredrick and Jeremy supported each other through the tough times over the years. Five years ago Jeremy helped smuggle Fredrick out of England. When they were later captured by pirates, they each agreed to remain together no matter where fate may lead them. Jeremy was his confidant, his most loyal and trusted friend.

"Is it ransom that was on your mind, Captain, or was it something else?"

"Explain," Fredrick demanded.

"Remember the gypsy in Tortuga? She said a woman would be your downfall."

Surely that had been nothing but superstitious nonsense. "Don't believe what gypsies tell you when gold 'tis their purpose. They will tell you anything to get paid."

"Still…"

"I'll hear nothing more on the matter. Now make ready to sail." Fredrick gave orders to set sail as soon as the crew had all returned, then turned away from his friend and climbed down to the main deck. He'd treated Jeremy coolly, but Fredrick had no desire to hear more about the gypsy and her fortunetelling tricks.

He brooded as he stared out at the dark sky looming above the water stretching out over the horizon.

What the hell am I doing? He attacked Port Monmouth, targeting one of the king's favored nobles, Governor Charles Prescott. The plan had been to kidnap Governor Prescott and hold him for ransom. Instead, Fredrick was saddled with Prescott's shrewish daughter. Why the hell did he decide to take her? She was sure to be a pain in the ass until the day the exchange was made. He wasn't thinking clearly…or not thinking beyond the hard erection he'd gotten when he had set eyes upon her dark coffee-colored eyes hot with anger and her raven-black hair plaited into a long neat braid, lying across one shoulder and down over heaving breasts that threatened to spill out of her chemise. She looked soft and curvaceous, and when he'd pulled her body against his, his cock had hardened — painfully so.

Letting her go was out of the question. He had to have her. But then, she'd made it clear she wanted nothing to do with him. Fredrick refused to let such a trifle deter his need to sample her supple flesh.

Jeremy's reminder of the tarot reading and the warning irritated Fredrick further. He'd acted upon lust, and that is exactly what the gypsy had predicted. He'd set his own personal interests ahead of his men and their hatred for the current king of England.

No, that wasn't true. He'd taken her for revenge's sake. He would still strain the purse strings of James' monarchy with the ransom of the sultry governor's daughter. And in the meantime, he was going to slake his lusts by taking what he wanted. He brought her aboard his ship and he was going to have her—willing or not. And when he was done, he'd return her to the governor after the ransom was paid.

Thinking back to that kiss in the governor's mansion, Fredrick was sure of her eventual surrender. She would not resist him for long. She desired him, even if she denied it. She would accept him, open her legs for him and beg him to fill her. Of this, he was sure. Yes, his conquest of her body—and fighting spirit—would be a sweet victory indeed. She had a body ripe for the taking, and he was the man to do it.

After all, no woman has ever refused a chance to bed him. Why would Miss Prescott be any different?

Chapter Two

෨

"Despicable, thieving wretch." Arabella angrily paced the captain's cabin aboard the East Indiaman ship, *Neptune's Sword*. The room was large and lavish, with all the rich luxuries befitting a man commanding a band of pirates. There were chests of jewels, gold and assorted treasure. Bounty from his attacks on ships in the Caribbean, no doubt. How many lives did they cost? "Murdering pirate."

A wide window framed the large desk that dominated the room. Ledgers, maps, charts and cargo inventories were scattered on the surface. Arabella fingered a few of the papers and recognized a detailed map of St. Crescentia Island and Port Monmouth.

Had it only been eight months since she'd come to the little Caribbean port from her home in England? When her father had been appointed governor, he'd asked her to accompany him to the island paradise, where she would rejoin her fiancé, Lieutenant Nicholas Wentworth. Thrilled at the prospect of adventure and the chance to be close to Nicholas, she jumped at the opportunity.

Her engagement to Nicholas had been arranged by her father and Nicholas after a Christmas ball in London three years before. The handsome naval officer swept her heart away and she quickly fell in love. They'd courted whenever Nicholas was in port, and she'd only seen him four times before their engagement. When he asked her to be his wife, she'd wanted to marry him right away, but Nicholas insisted they wait so he could build his fortune, to provide her with a good home and a comfortable life.

Anxious to see him again, Arabella had agreed to travel to the Caribbean where Nicholas was stationed with a force of the British Navy patrolling the seas in order to control the increasing pirate activity.

When she arrived in Port Monmouth, she'd discovered her fiancé had died at the hands of pirates. Nicholas died a hero, fighting to protect the innocent from bloody, vicious pirates who thought nothing of killing.

She *hated* pirates—all of them. They were nothing but murdering thieves upon the high seas. And this Captain Fredrick Thorne was no different.

How the hell could she have kissed him? What was she thinking?

Trouble was, she hadn't been thinking. She simply reacted to his kiss. It was unlike any kiss she'd experienced before. Not even Nicholas' kisses had made her insides quiver with anticipation.

No. She mustn't think of Nicholas in such close proximity to the pirate. What if this pirate was Nicholas' murderer?

Anger flooded her and she glanced around the desk for something to throw. She picked up the closest thing, an inkwell, and tossed it at the locked wooden door. It crashed against the surface and black ink splattered as the glass shattered into hundreds of pieces. It was childish to vent her frustrations over her predicament with an inkwell, but the act made her feel slightly better.

But only momentarily.

Did this pirate think she wasn't going to fight? Her father taught her to fight from an early age. She knew how to handle a musket with apt skill, and her fencing skills were second to none. If only there was a rapier in one of those chests. Although the captain had probably made sure no weapons were within her reach, Arabella began rummaging through a few of the chests in the cabin.

Some time later, she blew at a tendril of hair that had fallen into her eyes. The chests were filled with gold coins, jewelry of all sorts—strings of pearls, diamonds, emeralds rubies, sapphires—and fine silks in rainbows of colors. No rapier. No knife. Nothing to use to defend herself against the pirate.

She began to pace the cabin, plotting her next course of action. She refused to sit back like a docile puppet, allowing some thieving bastard to take advantage of her. She glanced out the window and saw they still stood in the small inlet of Port Monmouth. Perhaps she could try to escape...

Unhooking the latch, she opened the large window behind the desk. Looking about, she saw only the massive rudder disappearing into the water below. They were still at anchor.

This may be her only chance.

She grabbed a bundle of silk, and, using the sharp edge of the chest to fray the fabric, began to rip it into wide strips. She tied the ends together, making a quick rope.

Once she'd fashioned the fabric into a lengthy rope, she secured one end to the leg of the desk and tossed the other end out the window.

Arabella stood at the window looking down at the silk rope blowing in the breeze. Now she had to actually climb down.

Hesitating, she tried to get a good grip on the rope as she climbed onto the ledge.

Just then, the lock on the door slid open and Captain Thorne filled the doorway.

"Crazy wench," he swore as he crossed the room and reached for her arm. "What're you trying to do, kill yourself?"

"Let go of me!" she yelled as he hauled her back inside the cabin and up against his body.

"Don't you realize there are sharks out there just waiting for a fine feast such as yourself?"

"Sharks? That's absurd." She struggled against his strong grip upon her upper arms. "There are no sharks here in Port Monmouth's inlet."

"Oh?" He turned her toward the open window and pointed down to the water. A dark shape broke the water—a dorsal fin. "*That*, my dear, is a shark."

Arabella felt the blood drain from her face.

He turned her in his arms and her breath caught at the warmth of his body against hers. He was big and powerful...and he just saved her from making a foolish mistake that could have cost her life.

"Thank you," she said softly.

"Next time, I suggest you think out your plans completely." His voice was gentle and understanding. It was a surprising tone, considering she had just been discovered attempting an escape.

"You know why I had to try." It wasn't a question.

"I know." Then he added in a mocking voice. "I suggest you put the thought of escape out of your mind. There is nowhere to run out in the open sea."

She renewed her resistance to his hold upon her body, against the intoxicating allure of his muscled chest rubbing along her sensitive nipples. Even through the rough fabric of his coat and her thin cotton nightshift, her skin was on fire for his touch.

What was happening to her? She shoved him away, disgusted at her own weakness. She loathed this man and all he stood for. Pirates stole her life by killing her betrothed.

"Perhaps the sharks would be better company after all," she spat.

He leaned in close to her, a small smile curling his lips. "Don't tempt me, or I will personally introduce you to the sharks."

"Swine."

He released the knot of silk from about the leg of the desk and tossed the rope out the window. "Just in case you had thoughts of climbing out again," he quipped.

She stormed over to the bed and turned on him. "You can't expect me to be happy about being a hostage."

He faced her and chuckled. "On the contrary, I suspect you are going to be a pain in the ass."

She gasped loudly. "How dare you speak to me in such a manner!"

He closed in on her. "You, Miss Prescott, are my prisoner. I suggest you come to terms with the situation."

"And you, Captain Thorne, are nothing more than a low-down, lawless pirate."

"I assure you, there are rules aboard my ship. And my rules are law upon the open sea."

"Ha!"

"I warn you, Miss Prescott. Try my patience and you will find yourself getting that spanking I mentioned earlier."

"You touch me, and I will make sure you find the sharp end of a sword through your black heart."

His face turned serious as he stared down at her. She shuddered under his gaze, fighting against the traitorous reactions of her young body. Why did she ache for this pirate's touch? Maybe it was the extreme danger that seemed to ooze from his pores that sent her heart into a frenzy. Yes, that must be it. It was the danger that surrounded Captain Thorne that made her react this way. It had to be.

"You're a fiery wench, aren't you?" he mused aloud.

"Don't call me that. I am Miss Prescott to you."

"You're a shrew—and I think your lips deny your innermost desires." He stepped closer and her breath caught in her lungs. He seemed to overpower the very space in which they stood.

"I deny nothing."

"Then why are you shaking?"

She hesitated, searching for an excuse other than the obvious. "I'm angry." She was indeed angry...with herself. How could her heart beat faster when he came near? Even the junction of her thighs reacted to his closeness. It burned for...something. She could feel the liquid heat gathering there even as she refused to acknowledge the growing desire.

He reached up to her face and a finger traced the curve of her jaw. "I think you're aroused."

Her apex throbbed. "You're imagining things."

"Am I?" He gently stroked her bottom lip with the pad of his thumb.

She closed her eyes as her quivering breath blew over his thumb. He was tempting her, testing her. Arabella was unused to men playing games with her, at least unfairly, like this pirate. He used his sexual appeal as a weapon, taking an unfair advantage over the situation. She was an unwilling prisoner of a man who stole her from her very bed...and her body yearned for something she hardly recognized.

"Don't fight it, luv. You want me, and I want you. Let's find out what it can be like." His voice was husky and she recognized the strained control.

And it made her heartbeat race faster. Even the air within her lungs seemed to still as she stood so close to this roguish man with the handsome face and muscled body, hard and completely masculine.

Pirates killed Nicholas. I hate pirates, and this man is a pirate. I abhor pirates, therefore I abhor him. I do not want him. I do not want him. She repeated in her mind, *I do not want him.*

Her eyes snapped open and she saw him lean in closer. She turned her face away in time to avoid his kiss.

"I do not want you, Captain Thorne. You're a pirate. I will not throw myself into your bed like the ladies of Tortuga who are enthralled by your lawlessness."

He forced her to face him. "Fiery little wildcat. You will learn to come to me, offering your body for my pleasure."

"Never."

"You will, luv. And your surrender will be sweeter than any wine."

He kissed her roughly—crushing, brutal, hungry. He plunged his tongue into her mouth and drank of her sweetness despite her struggles. He clamped her body against his and the contact seared her. Dear God, this was a greedy possession, nothing more. Soon, she was clutching onto the lapel of his coat as he continued to plunder her mouth. He ravaged her lips, pillaged her mouth and looted her senses.

Beneath her, her legs weakened and she held on to him to stay upright. How could she surrender to a pirate? He used his potent kisses to shut down her defenses, taking her when she was weak.

"Do you deny you desire me now, luv?" he asked in a whisper against her lips.

"No," she replied in a low hush. She couldn't deny her desire for him.

"Once we are at sea, I will return to this cabin and you will give yourself to me."

Could she? She may not be able to deny the desire burning within her heart, but she could refuse to act upon those desires. She'd saved herself for marriage. She hadn't even given in to Nicholas' pleas for intimacy before his last trip to sea. It had been hard to resist, but she had. But now, she was the prisoner of a pirate, a man used to getting exactly what he wanted.

And he wanted her.

She definitely desired him in ways she couldn't completely understand—she only knew that she burned for his touch, yearned to experience the fire between them on a more intimate level.

Could she give up her virtue, her virginity for a moment of passion?

"Give yourself to me," he repeated as he nuzzled her neck, sparking shivers down her spine in anxious excitement.

"I'm...I never..." She was too confused. Her body screamed to concede, but her heart refused to give up so easily.

"I understand." He stroked her hair, calming her with his gentle touch and softly spoken words.

Her heart raced as she thought of surrendering her body to him. She'd be ruined. Soiled. No man would ever want her, a pirate's remains. "No, please..." She pressed her palms gently against him.

He pushed her to arm's length and stood over her, a tower of strength and command. "You *will* give your body to me. You may fight me, little wildcat. However, you will not win."

"No."

He pushed her to the bed and she fell back onto it. "If you don't give me what I require," he said angrily, "then by God, I will take it by force."

And with that, he turned and strode out of the cabin, slamming the door behind him. As he slid the lock across the outside, Arabella stared after him, her own anger flaring to the surface once again.

"Only a pirate would rob a woman's virtue. But I swear it will not come without a price."

* * * * *

Rape. Was he honestly thinking of forcing the governor's daughter, his captive for ransom, into sex? Arabella Prescott was obviously a virgin, she'd indicated as much. Her inexperienced kisses were proof of her innocence. So why was he being such a damn brute—a pirate? There were rules against the mistreatment of women in the very code of conduct he'd written for his crew. Had he become so engulfed with lust as to disregard the rules he had set forth?

You will think of only your own needs when you meet her. The gypsy's words haunted him. He recalled the chill down his spine when she had turned over the Five of Swords. *You will set your own needs ahead of others.*

No, Miss Prescott was merely a momentary temptation, a fleeting infatuation with curves that tantalized, dark brown eyes that shot daggers one moment and softened with desire the next, and a fiery temper to match his own. By God, she was refreshing. She was a challenge, and he liked it. He found her courage to fight for herself downright sexy. He could almost imagine her standing toe to toe with him in a sword fight, crossing swords with him to save her treasured virginity.

It wouldn't come to that. He was sure with a proper seduction of her body through kisses and caresses, Miss Prescott would become a willing bedmate. He chuckled to himself at the thought of the wildcat in his bed. He groaned at the imagined sensation of her clawed fingernails grazing down his back as he pumped his cock deep into her wet core.

Alone in the entryway to his cabin, he released his straining cock from his pants. Holding the shaft in his hand, he thought of her sweet mouth circling his length and sucking him with reckless joy.

Fredrick stroked himself, moaning softly and climbing closer to climax. Thoughts of Miss Prescott lying naked upon his bed, pleading for his touch, drove him to increase the rhythm of his self-pleasure.

He licked his lips, imagining what she'd taste like when he feasted upon the nectar hidden between her legs. It would be sweet…delectable…intoxicating. She'd clench her fingers in his hair as he licked her little nubbin into a pert point of pleasure. He'd thrust his tongue up into her channel and lick her honeyed juices as she climaxed with loud screams of ecstasy.

He couldn't help himself. He needed release. Dealing with his prisoner was much more challenging than he'd anticipated. He wanted to fuck her into oblivion...over and over. His cock throbbed painfully whenever he touched her and when he had pressed her body to his, he felt as though he'd burst. He needed to find relief. And only Miss Prescott would do.

He continued to stroke his cock there in the dark entry stairwell to his cabin. Images of his prisoner's creamy flesh beckoning to be touched made him crazy to impale her, bury his cock deep into her heat. She'd be tight, squeezing his length with feminine muscles. And as he drove into her, she'd pant with each thrust and climax about him with clenching walls.

With the thought of her orgasm, the thought of her calling out his name with each pulse, Fredrick came. He spent his semen into his hand as he found his release, leaning back against the wall to ride the moment of pleasure.

But after his essence had been spent, he felt unfulfilled. His desire for his captive had not dissipated. He still wanted her.

There was no question as to his next move involving Miss Prescott. As he cleaned away the evidence of his pleasure, Fredrick began to plan the seduction of the feisty wildcat in his cabin. It wouldn't come to rape. He'd never raped a woman in his life, and he wasn't going to start now.

However, he was not adverse to a bit of forced seduction.

Miss Prescott would admit defeat. Eventually, *she would surrender.*

Chapter Three

ဆာ

Arabella had paced the cabin after the captain left her alone. Her reactions to the captain were hard to understand. Why did she desire him so? He threatened to force her submission and yet the idea did not appall her. She couldn't understand why.

By now the ship had sailed from Port Monmouth and was at sea. She'd watched the dawn break over the ocean, and marveled at the bright orange and red painted across the sky and reflecting upon the ocean below. It was as though the sun was a phoenix rising from the flames to greet the new day. She'd spent the entire night fighting an internal battle—virtue versus carefree abandon.

It had been hours since Captain Thorne left the cabin, and Arabella tried to sleep. His scent surrounded her, his touch was burned into her skin and his kisses were seared upon her swollen lips. Lying in his bed, she tossed and turned, unable to relax her mind enough to sleep. Her body buzzed with need, aroused by a man she wanted to hate. It was a troublesome situation for a pampered young woman of nineteen. She was used to rides in the park, afternoon tea parties and poetry readings. Certainly none of the ladies of her acquaintance had ever had to deal with a pirate, especially one as appealing as Captain Fredrick Thorne.

What would the ladies of London think of her predicament? Now that she gave the situation serious thought, her reputation would be ruined regardless, even if she managed to hold on to her virginity. No respectable man would want her—a pirate's captive.

So why should she fight her reaction to this man? If she was to live a life in ruin, why not let propriety go for several stolen moments of pleasure? It was positively scandalous to think of it, but already she was a soiled woman. She'd been alone with a pirate, a man nothing more than a black spot on society.

But there were dangers in involving herself with the captain. She'd heard tales of mistresses falling in love with their male protectors, and then being left penniless and brokenhearted. That was certainly not a fate Arabella wanted. If she were to indulge in physical pleasure with the captain, she had to keep a tight rein on her emotions. She must not fall in love with him. Her heart must remain untouched and guarded.

In the growing heat of the day, Arabella opened the wide window behind the desk to catch the cool sea breeze. She stood and leaned over the ledge and breathed the salty air deeply into her lungs. She'd always loved the sea and found comfort gazing upon the calm blue waters. She ached to be home in her own room instead of aboard a pirate ship, hostage to a roguish man and his sexual appeal.

"Beautiful," a male voice said behind her.

Startled, she turned to look upon the captain. "I wasn't trying to climb out," she said, immediately defending herself.

He chuckled. "I know. I think you may be more intelligent than that." In his hands was a tray of sliced fruit and cheese along with a pitcher and wooden goblet. "I thought you'd be hungry by now. Or are you seasick?"

"My father, as you probably know, gained his rank and favor of the king from his service in the Royal Navy."

"Yes, I know *he* can tolerate the ocean's current, but can you?"

She made a sound of frustration. "I am *not* seasick."

"Well, good, then you can eat. I have some goat's milk here too."

"You have a goat onboard?"

"Of course." Her stomach rumbled and he laughed softly. "Come, sit down and eat."

She stepped over to the desk where he sat the tray down before pouring some milk into the goblet for her.

"Why are you being nice to me all of a sudden, Captain?" she asked as she savored a bite of mango.

"I'm not. I am making sure my captive is fed so she may live to the day of her ransom."

Anger grew in her instantly. "Is that all I am, some *thing* you'll ransom for profit?"

He took a seat across from her at the desk and picked up a mango slice. "Not to be crude, Miss Prescott, but that is exactly what you are."

She took a gulp of the goat's milk and cringed. It wasn't her favorite drink, but its warmth satisfied her empty stomach. "And do you intend to keep me here locked in your cabin for the entire time until we arrive at Isla de Margarita?"

"I will take you topside for some fresh air daily, as long as you remain a good girl."

"I am not a *girl*, Captain. I am a young woman."

His eyes grazed over her breasts, thinly covered by her nightshift. "Indeed, you are very much a woman."

She quickly crossed her arms over her chest. "You're nothing but a rogue, Captain."

"Perhaps." He rose from his seat and strode to the far side of the room to one of the chests. He opened it and rummaged through the contents until he pulled out a dark blue silk overdress. "I think this may do well for you, Miss Prescott." He walked back to the desk and handed her the dress.

"From a former mistress, Captain?"

"Nay, not a mistress."

"You mean you stole a lady's dresses from a ship you attacked?" she asked in horrified shock.

His face turned hard, his mouth a grim line of barely controlled anger. "It was bought for a lady, but there was no lady aboard the ship at the time."

"Oh."

"I may be a pirate, Miss Prescott, but as I said before, I live by rules. I don't make war on women."

"You kidnapped me from my home," she countered as she stood and slipped the dress over her head.

"You have not been harmed. Have I not seen to your comfort, made sure you have food and drink?"

She cocked a brow at him. "Regardless, you threatened me."

"Perhaps."

When he said nothing further, she sat back down and ate in silence, painfully aware of him watching her. His aqua-green eyes, the color of the sea, followed every movement of her hand as she reached for several shavings of a hard cheese.

It was true. He had made sure she was well cared for. She had a soft bed—even if it was *his* bed—food to eat, goat's milk that ebbed her hunger and clothing to wear. Why was this pirate acting like...a gentleman?

"Tell me, Miss Prescott, have you ever satisfied yourself?"

She looked up at him, his smile was devilish and his gaze heated her skin. "What?"

"I mean, have you ever made yourself...given yourself pleasure?"

She wrinkled her brow. "I'm not sure I understand what you mean."

He reached over the desk and took her hand. He lightly traced the veins on the underside of her wrist with his fingertips. The touch sent chilling shivers down her spine and zeroed in on the place between her thighs. Oh dear God, she ached!

"I mean, have you ever explored your body for pleasure's sake?"

He meant sexual pleasure! How innocent she must appear. "No, Captain Thorne, and I do not wish to discuss it. It is inappropriate."

He continued to touch her wrist with featherlight caresses—making her center wetter by the second. She squeezed her thighs together to find relief, but found none.

"Have you wondered why the place between your legs makes you shift in your chair, luv?" His voice was low and husky, and its sound caressed her skin much like his fingertips across her wrist.

"I don't know what you mean."

"Tell me, do you feel yourself getting wet as I touch you?"

She gasped and closed her eyes. "Please don't."

"Don't what? Instruct you in the ways of love and passion?" She felt him kiss the underside of her wrist and she shuddered. "You are ripe for pleasure, Miss Prescott."

"Don't talk of such scandalous things." She hardly recognized her breathy voice.

Ignoring her faint pleas, he continued. "That little organ throbbing with life as I kiss your sweet pulse is your clitoris. You can try to deny its need, but not for long. You are passionate, and you will long to find out what, exactly, it needs."

"And what does it need?" she asked, lost in the sound of his voice and the gentle touch of his fingers upon her skin.

"It needs to be cared for."

Her intimate muscles clenched and she moaned.

He released her wrist, rose from his seat and moved around the desk to stand behind her. "I know how to take care of your nub." He leaned over her shoulder and lightly nipped at her neck and she gasped. "I can teach you how to touch yourself, Miss Prescott," he said in a seductive tone.

"Please, call me Arabella."

He groaned and then she felt him cup her breast, his thumb playing lightly back and forth over a taut nipple straining through the dress. "You may call me Fredrick."

He pinched the hard peak and she shifted in her seat, the ache between her thighs growing insistent for relief.

"Fredrick," she whispered.

"Mmm. I like the sound of my name on your lips...Arabella."

She was lost. There was no conscious thought while he touched her. There was no reasoning within her troubled heart as he spoke, arousing her senses. All she could do was sit and listen to his voice and lose herself in his caress.

Then he released her breast. She snapped open her eyes to watch walk to the door.

"What...?" she stuttered in disbelief. How could he talk of pleasure then leave?

"Think on what I've said. When I come back tonight, let me know if you want me to teach you the ways of pleasure."

"But—"

"You must *invite* me into your bed, Arabella. I want you as my mistress, and I will have you—willing and ready."

As she watched him leave, she took a deep breath. Her body hummed with excitement and she didn't need any time to think upon his words. She wanted everything he'd said and more. Arabella wanted to find out what it was like.

But what if she...got with child?

On second thought, the prospect of expecting the child of a pirate wasn't so appealing. Could she risk her future, her virtue and her body for a few moments of pleasure? Having a rogue's baby somehow seemed scarier than never marrying a respectable man. Could she live with the product of passion with a pirate? Maybe the consequence of sex with Captain Thorne was too great a price to pay.

However, when he touched her, spoke to her in that low, seductive voice, she couldn't think beyond the moment. She knew in her heart that surrendering her body to the pirate was inevitable. Her body weakened and succumbed to his touch each time he was near, and she was powerless to fight, especially when he kissed her into abandon.

Her body wanted to surrender, but the thought of a pregnancy made her pause. Would she have the strength to stop him when she was swept away beneath his caress? Could she stop his advances when his hands cupped her breasts and his fingers teased her nipples into sore points of aching desire?

She was so confused! The entire situation was new and exciting—an adventure. Never before had she felt such things when a man kissed her. The captain sparked desire the likes of which she'd never experienced. Her initial reaction was to give in to her desires and explore those sensations further.

But there were definitely consequences.

What would her father do if he discovered her lost virtue? Would her father demand Fredrick's life for her ruination? If she sacrificed her body to a rogue and became pregnant, her father would probably send her away then take the child to an orphanage once born. The thought of a child—*her* child—taken from her was beyond comprehension. Would she possibly come to such a fate? Could she risk it?

She squeezed her eyes shut, trying to block the horrid images from her mind. There was only one solution. She mustn't give in to her desires, no matter how much she wanted to experience the whispered promises of ecstasy. She must hold on to her virtue.

She'd keep hold of her heart and protect her body. Sighing, she thought of how he made her melt with just one kiss. How would she fight that? With a stiff upper lip, she vowed to turn her heart to stone. No man, not even the appealing Captain Fredrick Thorne, would break her spirit.

Arabella could not love a pirate. *Ever.* She wouldn't surrender her virginity to him, and most definitely not her heart.

* * * * *

"You mean she was carried aboard by that bastard?" Governor Charles Prescott asked Betsy in a rage. He'd sailed into port with his fleet of three British warships several days after the attack. Charged to protect and patrol the Caribbean Sea from pirates, Governor Prescott was enraged that one of lawless mongrels he hunted had the audacity to attack his city and kidnap his daughter.

"Yes, sir. She tried to fight him, sir. She even broke away and ran upstairs when they found us hiding in the root cellar, but the captain chased her. He threw her over his shoulder and carried her aboard his ship."

"The wretch," he muttered. Turning away from the servant, he began to pace the wooden floor of the entry. "Who was it?" he shot at her, hardly able to control his growing anger.

"Captain Fredrick Thorne," Betsy replied with a shaky voice.

"Thorne!" It was an appropriate name for the scourge of the Caribbean, the very pirate he and his fleet had been searching for over the past six months. Thorne's ship, *Neptune's Sword,* struck swiftly then disappeared faster than any vessel Charles had ever encountered. Thorne attacked Spanish and French ships, but then he also attacked British ships as well. He'd even sacked several cities and ports in the area. And now Port Monmouth was his latest outrage. He should have left additional experienced troops behind to defend the city more effectively—but even he hadn't guessed the boldness of Thorne's daring.

"They took her. *He* took her, sir. I'm afraid for her, what he will do to her." Betsy wept into her brown hands.

"He wouldn't dare touch her."

"There was lust in the captain's eyes. I saw it."

"Silence!" he yelled at the woman who cowered to her knees into a crumpled heap of hysterics. Instantly, Charles regretted his outburst. Directing the other maids standing off to the side witnessing the exchange, he said in a gentler voice, "Take her to her room. See to it she is cared for. It's been a very trying time and she must be exhausted."

The maids helped Betsy to her feet.

"Before you go, Betsy, tell me, did this rogue tell you anything of a ransom?"

"Yes, sir," she stammered in a teary voice. "He said the exchange would be in a fortnight at the Isla de Margarita for forty thousand pieces of eight."

"Forty thousand pieces of eight!" It was a king's ransom. Where did this pirate expect he could get such a sum? She nodded at his outburst. "Bloody pirate," he muttered. Then with a wave of his hand, he dismissed the maids.

He stormed to his study, tidied by the servants after it had been ransacked. Pulling keys from his belt, he searched for the special key that opened his hidden stash of brandy. Finding it, he slipped the key into the desk drawer and opened it. It was amazing those pirates didn't smash the drawer in hopes of finding more valuables. Most of his study had been stripped of trinkets he'd collected during his time of service under the king. Those mattered little compared to his greatest possession — Arabella.

He poured a glass of brandy and drank it without taking a moment to taste the fine vintage or age. That wasn't the purpose. He needed the alcohol's blessed numbing just to deal with the entire situation. His mission with the fleet had been a failure. He hadn't encountered any pirates in the six months out at sea, and worse during his mission he'd become plagued by a mysterious ailment. Not even a doctor from Barbados could help. Then upon his return home, he'd found his town had been attacked only days before—*and by the very pirate he'd hunted.* He had left inadequate defenses to protect Port Monmouth, allowing them to swoop into port and kidnap his beloved daughter.

His little girl. The pirate scum stole Arabella.

He should have never allowed her to come to the Caribbean. Danger lurked everywhere while pirates roamed the seas. And now she was in the hands of the worst sort of pirate—Fredrick Thorne. Although tales of female abduction had never been reported, the pirate had a long list of other offenses to condemn him to death. Of course, a swift death would be too good for Thorne. Once Charles captured him, he would make sure that bastard suffered the worst sentence possible.

The thought of Thorne touching Arabella sickened him. His sweet little girl would never marry well after this. She would be spoiled in the eyes of any man of breeding. Thorne had destroyed her with his piratical act.

Pouring a second glass of brandy, he began to make plans. He'd set sail immediately as soon as his ship, the *Royal Raider*, was resupplied and repaired. He'd take an additional warship with him and leave the third behind in Port Monmouth to protect the city.

"Governor." Captain William Jacobs strode into the study. "I wish to command the *Enforcer* to participate in the hunt for *Neptune's Sword* and that bastard Thorne. Arabella..."

William Jacobs was an arrogant officer who bought his commission in the Royal Navy, the second son of some obscure nobleman who had little money to spare. Charles liked his greedy drive to succeed at any price. A handsome man with long black hair and cold blue eyes, Captain Jacobs cut an imposing figure as a commanding naval leader.

Charles had hoped Arabella would take a shining to the ambitious officer. The captain was struck by Arabella and had expressed a desire to visit her in hopes of wooing her into marriage. Charles suspected the man took this kidnapping personally.

"I want to get Arabella back, and kill the pirate who kidnapped her!" His jaw clenched in barely controlled rage.

"Of course, Captain. You special skills will be needed on this voyage."

Then Charles began to cough. He pulled a lace handkerchief from his pocket, one of many he carried with him these days. His cough was harsh and draining. When he pulled his handkerchief from his mouth, blood smeared the pristine white fabric.

"Sir, are you well?" asked Jacobs, who laid a hand on Charles' shoulder.

"I am not well. But I will not let that keep me from rescuing my daughter." He tucked the crumpled handkerchief into his pocket. "I must see Arabella safe." He downed the remaining brandy in his glass and paused to let the liquid burn a fiery trail down his throat.

Jacobs strode across the room to the fireplace and paused. "I too wish to see Miss Prescott safe," added Jacobs. "In fact, I had hoped to ask for her hand when I returned, but this scoundrel dared to attack Port Monmouth. Nothing less than a torturous death will be the fate of Captain Fredrick Throne." He turned back to Charles and walked back to the desk. "I swear to you, Governor, I will hunt down that pirate to the world's end if I have to. He will pay for his piracy against Miss Prescott."

Charles smiled, his eyes glimmering with excitement. "Indeed, Captain Jacobs. We will hunt Thorne and see his piratical career concluded at the end of the hangman's rope." Then he stood and extended his hand to Jacobs. "Arabella is yours. I give my blessing wholeheartedly, Captain."

Chapter Four

🔊

When Captain Thorne entered the cabin with a tray of food that evening, Arabella was ready to fight. No matter what, she would not become a pirate's mistress. She would not surrender to a few soft-spoken words...

He smiled and turned to shut the door behind him, and her eyes roamed the length of his backside. Pale blond hair fell loose down his back, muscles straining at the fabric of his white linen shirt. Breeches stretched across his ass and wrapped tightly about thick, powerful thighs.

Her resolve weakened slightly at the thought of those thighs rubbing along hers in an intimate embrace. She shook her head to clear away such scandalous notions.

He turned back and caught her heated gaze upon his body. "Shall I undress to let you get a better look?"

She gasped. "No!" She twisted away from him and cursed herself. How could she stand there and think of this pirate as anything other than murderous?

His soft chuckle behind her only made her heart beat faster.

"I see you decided to resist your needs...and mine."

She spun to face to him. "I'll never give myself to a pirate," she spat venomously.

He sat the dinner tray on a small table. "I wasn't always a pirate, luv."

"You are now, and that is all that matters."

She watched him walk from the table toward her. "Some women think being seduced by a pirate is romantic." The room diminished in size with his dominating presence and sexual appeal.

She quickly moved away and shut her eyes, forcing her heart to slow its frantic pace. *Stay strong.* "Then I suggest you go find yourself a mistress among one of them."

He stepped behind her and gently laid his hands upon her shoulders. Heat poured from his body and seeped through the fabric of her dress. He leaned closer and his warm breath caressed the sensitive skin of her ear. "But I want *you*, Arabella. I want to have you under me, writhing with ecstasy as I fill you. I want to hear your moans as you climb higher and higher to the point of no return."

She squeezed her eyes closed tighter to shut out his sensual words, trying to find the strength to fight his allure. Perhaps she was going about this situation wrong. She needed to show her power to fight—her determination to resist.

Spinning around, she slapped him across the face. Her palm stung from the contact, but she didn't care. "Don't you talk to me like that...you dirty pirate!"

In a flash, he grabbed her and pulled her body against his. "You like me because I *am* a dirty pirate. You act the part of a proper young lady, cool and aloof, like a marble statue. However, deep inside your icy heart, you want to know what it would be like to live adventure and feel all the delights of the flesh." He traced his hand down her arm, his palm warm and seductive as he caressed her skin, pulling her body even closer into his embrace. "You like how I make you feel."

"I do not!" She denied the effect he had on her but her voice wavered.

"I make your heart beat faster." He laid a hand upon her chest. She opened her eyes and was captured by his piercing green gaze. "It beats faster when I am near, just as your breath catches and moisture gathers between your legs when I come into the room."

She gasped and tried to break away, but he grabbed her to him once again in an iron grip. He chuckled at her attempt to escape. "Do you deny I make you wet, luv?"

"You're disgusting."

His low laugh vibrated through his chest. Her breasts were crushed against him so tightly, he was sure to feel the tips harden at the contact.

"I excite you. And you excite me, Arabella."

"Don't talk to me like that."

"I want to make love to you," he continued.

"I am not excited by you," she said flatly.

"Yes, you are. You want to know what it is like to lie with me naked in my bed." He pressed his hips against her and she was painfully aware of his rock-hard erection.

"I don't want to know about *anything* that involves you." Her voice cracked. God, why did she want to grasp at the hard bulge in his pants that he continued to rub against her?

"You want me to pleasure you as you open your legs for me."

The muscles between her thighs clenched and a jolt of excitement pumped through her body. "No, I don't," she denied. The urge to pump her hips against him was hard to resist. She squeezed her thighs together to try to shut away the building tension, but it did little to ease her torture.

"Yes, you do. I feel your body react to mine." He cupped her buttocks and pressed her into his erection and guided her to move against him in a natural rhythm she seemed to instinctively know. "You're ripe to be loved, Arabella."

Her mind raced for an answer, then she blurted, "I'm afraid of you. This is fear you see."

He chuckled again. "Fear? You? That is not fear, it is desire—raw desire."

She shook her head, not trusting her voice to deny his accusations. The delicious movement of his hips was driving her insane. How could she fight him when he assaulted her body with such wondrous sensations? And what was this powerful ache building between her legs?

No, she had to fight this. Fight *him*. Deny her feelings. Refuse to admit her growing desire. Reject his advances. Remain true to her heart and protect her virtue. Fight her awakened passion.

He added in a soft voice, "I see desire reflected in your eyes—especially after I kiss you."

"No," she denied once again. Her lips tightened with anger at her weak voice.

She turned her face from him but he forced it back with his hand. Then he crushed her lips beneath his own. He held her head tightly with his hand as he plundered her lips with forceful, bruising kisses.

Any fight that coursed through her body melted away as he took possession of her mouth with his skilled lips. She sighed and leaned into him and he took advantage of the moment. His tongue swept into her mouth and he drank of her. She gripped at his shirt to steady herself, but it was unnecessary. He held her tightly against his body, hard and unmoving like a great marble pillar. Ruthless in his assault upon her senses, he forced her conscious thoughts to give way to carnal reaction.

Still holding her in an iron embrace, he eased his mouth from hers. He lightly kissed her swollen lips then he spoke softly. "Can you deny that you want me now?"

She opened her eyes and looked up into his stormy green gaze. Desire and passion swam in their depths—*reactions she invoked in him*. The knowledge excited her, and even though she wanted to refuse to believe any sort of attraction, she realized fighting this seduction was a losing battle. Struggling against her overwhelming need was futile. She was lost.

He kissed her gently, and she responded by kissing him back.

"Do you admit defeat, luv?" he asked in a whisper against her lips.

"Sometimes the only way for the battle to end is for one to surrender."

He leaned back his head farther and cocked a brow. "Surrender the battle?"

She inhaled and then slowly said, "I will give myself to you tonight, Captain." She wrapped her arms about his neck and stood on her toes. "Now kiss me again."

With a devilish grin he murmured in a husky voice, "I'll be doing more than kissing you this night, Arabella," before lightly pressing his lips to hers.

In response, she groaned and melted into his kiss.

* * * * *

Fredrick intended to relish every moment of her sweet surrender. She admitted defeat to the moment, but not to her situation, and that was not lost on him. Arabella Prescott was a woman of courage and beauty, and both those qualities drove him to seduce the little spitfire and sample her delights. She'd given in to his demands with a little persuasion. She melted in his arms when he kissed her, but her kisses were different from those of the women he'd known before. They were curious…innocent. Her kisses were sweeter than any wine he'd ever tasted and her naïve reactions and unpracticed responses inflamed him.

He craved her.

He was even more certain now that she was a virgin. Was it the fact that she was untouched that made his cock so hard he couldn't stand the pain any longer? He restrained the urge to plunge deep into her immediately when she'd surrendered. This was to be her first experience with a man. He wanted to take care of her during this night.

Odd that he wanted to be gentle for her first time. Since when did Captain Thorne think of anyone's comfort other than his own? Normally he would punish himself for that weakness, but Arabella brought out a protective streak in him. He vowed to make this as pleasurable as possible.

He kissed her gently, holding her body to his. She'd opened her mouth and her tongue darted out against his, testing his reaction. The innocent swipe of her tongue drove him wild with need as did the perfect fit of her curvaceous body against his.

"I need to feel your flesh," he whispered against her ear as he began to gather the material of her dress in his hands. "I want to see your beautiful breasts when I kiss them."

Her whimpered reply had him quickly pulling the blue dress over her head, leaving her shivering in her thin chemise.

"Don't be afraid, luv," he softly reassured her.

"But I've never—"

He placed a finger across her lips. "Shh. I know."

She raised her gaze to his, striking him breathless at the simple beauty of her innocent yet silent plea.

"Tell me how much you want me to touch you."

She hesitated.

"Tell me, Arabella. I need to hear you tell me that you want me."

"I...I want you," she offered quietly.

"You want me to touch your body."

"Yes, Fredrick, I want you to touch me."

He slowly gathered a length of her shift into his hands. "You want me to make love to you—to kiss you everywhere, taste your sweet skin and run my hands over every part of you."

In a breathless whisper she said, "Yes...I want you to...do all of that."

He lifted the thin chemise over her head and tossed it to the floor. She immediately tried to cover her breasts and her thatch, but he grabbed her hands gently and pulled them away. "Don't ever feel you must hide your body from me, luv."

She shook slightly but obeyed by forcing herself to drop her arms to her sides. She kept her face turned away from him. A rosy blush crept up her neck to inflame her cheeks.

He took a step back and slowly drank in the sight of her naked flesh. He had been correct—her body was ripe for love. Her skin was smooth and flawless with a hint of a light tan from living in the tropics. Her slightly rounded abdomen and her shapely hips were well proportioned with her full breasts. She was well nourished and curvaceous, but not overly so. His mouth watered looking at her feminine form.

Her breasts were tipped with pink, perfect nipples that were tight and pert for his touch. He reached out to her breasts and caressed the outside curves. Her quick inhalation of breath drew his eyes to her face...a beautiful face that many men could fall in love with at one glance.

He cupped her breasts in his hands and then stroked the taut nipples with his thumbs. She whimpered, and his cock jumped in reaction. He was ready to plunge into her, take her soaring into a rocking climax, but he hesitated. He wanted her to enjoy this. He wanted her to feel pleasure when he finally entered her and took her maidenhead.

Fredrick released her breasts, then bent and lifted her into his arms. She instantly wrapped her arms about his neck and leaned into him. Yes, he'd won her surrender, and tonight, he was going to enjoy every moment he could while she was so responsive.

There was no tomorrow. There was only tonight. He didn't want to think of how she'd react in the morning.

He laid her on his bed then rid himself of his clothes. He couldn't strip away the material separating his skin from hers fast enough. Never taking his eyes from her figure, his heart raced wildly in anticipation. His cock jutted out from his pants when released from its confines. He gripped the hard length in his hand and stroked it briefly. No self-pleasure tonight. He would pump his essence deep into Arabella.

She watched him closely as he touched his shaft before reaching out with gentle fingers and lightly caressing the engorged head of his cock. When he sucked in a sharp breath she drew away her hand, but he caught it.

"Did I hurt you?" she asked quietly.

"No, luv." He guided her hand back to his cock and instructed, "Touch me."

She wrapped her fingers about his length and he sighed, fighting the urge to just plow into her like a rutting bull.

"Ahh, Arabella, you keep touching me like that, I'm afraid my plan to woo you *slowly* into passionate ecstasy may not happen."

She pulled her hand away and gazed up to his face. He read her nervousness in those cocoa-colored eyes.

"Don't be afraid, luv. I will take care of you."

She lowered her gaze shyly.

His heart swelled with emotions...sensations he'd never experienced before. He wanted to protect her, drive away the fear in her eyes, hold and comfort her through this night and the next. "Trust in me," he said as he leaned low over her luscious body.

Without another word, he captured her lips in a kiss. Succulent and intoxicating, she immediately opened to him, and he plundered her mouth with his tongue. He swept his tongue along hers and he moaned into the kiss at her innocent response to building passion. He slowly climbed on the bed and lay upon her, his hands charting the new territory of her naked flesh.

He palmed a breast and marveled at the firm perfection. Her nipple was already hardened into a tight, berry-like invitation. He broke their kiss to sample the luscious texture of her nipple. She groaned and threaded her fingers through his hair as he stroked the tip of her breast with his tongue. He caressed and savored her breast, sucking upon the pink peak.

Her body moved beneath his, and he was conscious to not lean his full weight down upon her. She writhed with awakening desire and it was hard to control his building need to fuck her into complete oblivion. He had to remind himself to take it slow and easy. This was not a bar wench used to opening her legs for any man who paid the price for her company. Her excitement was not an act to please—it was born of natural, carnal response.

"Fredrick," she whispered, tightening her grip in his hair.

His name on her lips robbed him of control momentarily. His thoughts scattered and he savagely devoured her breast, aiding her into a helpless surrender.

He switched his attention from one breast to the other, his hands stroking her sides and learning each soft curve of her feminine form. His cock was hard and painful, aching to end this torture, but he held the reins of control tighter and continued to lavish upon her breast.

Once he tasted both nipples, he decided to sample more of her body. He held her firmly in place and licked her from the valley of her breasts to the dip of her belly button. She whimpered and pushed his head lightly to continue his venture further. In her innocence, her cries of pleasure were melodious to the pirate captain.

Firmly gripping her hips, he moved lower to the dark thatch of hair at her apex and breathed in the feminine perfume of her arousal. There was never a more stimulating scent than Arabella's sweet fragrance of sexual hunger, and his cock surged with increased need to fuck her quickly, forgetting all sense and gentility.

Her legs were slightly parted, and when he tried to guide her to open them farther, she resisted.

"Luv, open your legs for me. There is nothing to fear. I only want to look upon your pink lips, all wet and luscious."

She groaned and reluctantly obeyed.

Fredrick was greeted by the most beautiful sight of her labial opening. Honeyed cream slickened the little opening he yearned to know intimately. His cock ached to explore her channel, but he needed to sample her juices first. He was sure they would be finer than the most expensive French wines he'd tasted in his travels.

"Draw up your knees, and then let your legs fall open," he gently instructed. She followed his hands with her own as he guided her to lie in the position he desired.

"Beautiful," he said in a soft voice. He leaned down close and inhaled her perfume deeply. "Completely delicious."

"What are you going to do?" she asked in a wavering voice.

"I am going to sip of your juices and take you on a journey."

"What?" she asked, but he ignored her plea to answer further as he closed his mouth around her engorged clitoris. Her questions and protests fell silent, and she began to moan and gently buck her hips.

Suckling the pearl between her legs was only the beginning of the things he wanted to do to her. She tossed her arms above her head and gripped the bars upon his headboard. She rode out the sensations he created, and her building excitement and pleasure urged him to continue. She tasted delightful and utterly scrumptious, and when he dipped his tongue along her slit, drinking of her honey, she cried out his name.

"Oh, Fredrick...oh my! Oh...oh!"

He continued to lap at her juices as she bucked more wildly, and he steadied her hips with his hands to keep from missing one drop of the delectable tastes of ecstasy. He reached his tongue up into her sheath as far as it could go, and then moved his hand to cover her thatch where he could easily stroke her clitoris with his thumb. Within a few light caresses, she screamed in orgasm. He licked at her cream and teased her nubbin further as she shattered, thrashing her head from side to side against the pillow, still gripping the headboard bars.

Fredrick was ready to explode hearing her climax, the melodious sounds as she cried out in pure passion.

It was time. As she quivered from her climax, he climbed upon her body and marveled at her face—her eyes were wide with sensual discovery and her lips were parted, still panting from her release.

His heart swelled again as he looked upon her, flushed and breathless from his loving. And yet it was only the beginning.

She instinctively hugged his hips with her legs and it was the breaking point of his control. He needed to be inside her—now!

Yet he hesitated in forcing his path into her virginal sheath. He paused and cupped her cheek with a hand. "This may hurt at first, but I promise, you will be screaming again in passion soon."

She nodded and he leaned down and kissed her gently. Slowly, he pushed his hard cock into her. He groaned at the glorious fit of her wet, tight walls about his length, deepening their kiss as he thrust deeper. She cried into his kiss, and he paused in his movements to allow her body to adjust to the feel of a man inside her for the first time.

When her cries turned into moans and she wrapped her arms about his shoulders, he began to move within her. He kept it slow and luxurious in pace, enjoying every moment of her slick walls hugging his cock as he pumped in and out and back again. He broke their kiss and held her face between his hands as he entered her. He watched the amazement on her face at the sensation, then he pulled back to hear a disappointed whimper. He slid into her moist heat once again, and she gasped in bliss.

The sounds of sex filled the cabin as sweat-slickened bodies rubbed together with each thrust of his hips. The smell of her arousal filled his nostrils and the glorious feel of her flesh surrounding his cock drove all cares for gentleness out of his mind. Lust and desire for the woman writhing beneath him stimulated his senses into acting upon his needs. He pumped faster and she clutched her legs about his hips tightly, taking him in to the hilt. She moaned with each thrust and found a shared rhythm. She was perfection, matching his moves by bucking her hips upward to take him deeply inside.

He grasped her wrists and held her arms above her head to the bars again. She wound her hands around them and he laced his fingers with hers. His chest rubbed along her breasts, the tight tips taut and pert. She fit against his body like she had been created just for his pleasure.

He watched her face as she came closer to her release. Such beauty overwhelmed him as he made love to this fascinating and exciting woman. He could come to love her in time...

"Oh Fredrick...it's happening again!"

When she hit her climax, he thrust into her wildly and joined her in release. Explosions of color filled his vision as hot seed shot deep into her channel. He cried out with each wave and pumped his seed into Arabella.

As the climax receded his muscles relaxed and the frenzy calmed. Fredrick lifted his body from hers and lay next to her on the bed. He gathered her close and she clung to him willingly. He held her in silence as their breaths eased to a normal rate. He stroked her hair and reveled in the soft waves of raven-wing black.

She lay with him without speaking a word, and he began to worry. "Was I too rough on you, luv?"

"No. Not at all," she replied quickly.

Silence.

He waited a beat then asked, "Do you hurt much?"

She moved her hips closer then said, "I'm a little sore."

Her innocent movement inflamed him once again. She thoughtlessly touched the hair on his chest, fingering the golden curls.

"Too sore to try again later?" he asked.

She paused then leaned up on his chest to look down at his face. "You're asking me to...do that again?"

He was asking for more. He needed to hear her say that she wanted him. "Yes, I am *asking* you."

She stroked his chin with her fingertips. "You're a strange man."

"Why?"

"Because I am here as your hostage, and yet, you are asking for permission to make love again."

He threaded his fingers into her hair and held her head. "Remember, you are here in my bed of your free will."

"I was seduced."

He smiled. "True."

She stared down at him and traced her fingers over the swell of his bottom lip. "And how many other governors' daughters have you seduced in your career?"

"Including you, luv?"

She nodded.

"Only one, luv. Only one."

Chapter Five

✖

Fredrick stood on the deck of *Neptune's Sword*, gazing out over the sea, pondering what exactly happened last night. He'd set forth to seduce Arabella in order to cleanse his mind of her sweet innocence and her unplanned responses to his touch. Instead, after a night of tasting her flesh and losing himself deep within her tight sheath, Fredrick was inflamed further, desiring her more now than before their night of ecstasy.

The gypsy's words from months prior haunted his memory. A woman would come between him and his pirate life. Could Arabella be the Queen of Cups, the one to make him forget his business responsibilities for his own desires?

No, this was purely lust...lust for a beautiful woman. Once Arabella was ransomed and off his ship, he would forget her. And last night would become nothing more than a few stolen moments of ardor with a woman—a woman who answered his passion with a hungry need of her own. Arabella had taken him to previously uncharted waters of sexual fulfillment.

Licking his lips, Fredrick still tasted her upon his tongue. She'd opened her body to him, allowed to sample her most intimate parts with his lips, tongue and fingers. Her flesh was sweet and luscious, and her juices were intoxicating and addictive. He wanted to drink of her, quenching his thirst for her tantalizing aphrodisiac. *Absolutely delicious.*

Even after he'd sipped her nectar she had writhed with untapped passion, moaning and pleading him to fulfill her body's demands—even the taking of her final barrier of innocence.

She gave her virginity to him, her cherished pearl of maidenhood. What sort of woman would give such a prize to a pirate? Fredrick was practiced in the ways of love and sex, but never had he taken the maidenhead of a virgin.

Words from his youth echoed within his memory, teachings of a long-dead mother whose love was cut off by a cruel king and his lust for power.

He'd ruined Arabella. She was a lady of fine birth and he had destroyed her chance for any marriage of good standing in society. As a man formerly in high standing, his actions were nothing more than that of a mangy dog. If he were any sort of gentleman, he would marry Arabella. But he was no gentleman.

You are nothing more than a low-down, lawless pirate.

Arabella was so right. He was nothing but a pirate. Not that he was sorry for the way he'd spent the last several years, forced into the career of a buccaneer upon the high seas through desperate circumstances. Why should he be sorry for choosing to live lawlessly rather than dying in a London gutter, cold, wet and hungry?

And his passionate act against her body, robbing her of her maidenhead, was the pinnacle of his piracy. Only a true pirate would leave a woman ruined for life.

His guilt ate at him as he scanned the horizon, watching the sun rise over the waves. How could he make up for his behavior toward Arabella? Marriage would be the answer if he were back in London. But they were not in England, nor did he ever plan to return there.

Fredrick pondered this and was so deep in thought that he did not hear Jeremy walk up behind him.

"The crew is concerned, Captain," he finally said.

"Explain," Fredrick replied without turning to the man.

"Governor Prescott is a hard man. Kidnapping him is one matter. Kidnapping his *daughter* is another."

Fredrick realized he'd thought little regarding his crew and the consequences for kidnapping Arabella.

Jeremy continued. "When he finds Miss Prescott has been taken, he is going to hunt us down with the entire British fleet here in the Caribbean. He will stop at nothing to see her safe, and her kidnappers punished."

"I take full responsibility for the lady. She is my concern."

"Permission to be frank, Captain?"

Fredrick gazed at him then turned to him fully, one hand on the grip of his sword. "Jeremy, you know you may speak to me anytime. You do not need permission."

"Aye. Sorry, Fredrick." Jeremy nodded and sat on a nearby barrel and pushed a hand through his wavy black hair. "I'm afraid that if the girl has been...compromised, the revenge could mean death to us all."

"Jeremy, we all have death warrants on our heads already."

"But you have tainted the daughter of Governor Prescott. He will hunt you down...it will be a personal vendetta to see you hang, along with your crew."

"Then we will lead him on a merry hunt," he said, a plan beginning to form in his mind.

"Captain?"

"Perhaps it is time we change our hunting grounds while we hold Miss Prescott as our hostage."

"That should keep Prescott guessing where we are—until the day of the ransom."

"It should keep the fleet scattered throughout the Caribbean."

Jeremy's face lit with enthusiasm. "Scattered and divided."

"On the day of the ransom, they will gather about Isla de Margarita thinking to spring a trap on us. Instead, we will have left a message to deliver the ransom to Tortuga. Once delivered, Miss Prescott will be returned a fortnight later to Port Monmouth."

"And how do you intend to return her to the stronghold of the British fleet?"

"After they deliver the money in Tortuga, I will escort her home. I have a few debts to collect in Tortuga, and I will get us passage on a ship to Port Monmouth. We will sail to the far side of the island and take a dingy to the beach. I will guide Miss Prescott across the island to her home. Meanwhile, you and the crew will take the ship to the Dutch West Indies for a month then return to Tortuga. Once I join you in Tortuga, we will set sail for the Indian Ocean. I think it may be advisable to put some distance between us and Governor Prescott."

And Arabella, he added to himself. Once she returned to Port Monmouth and her father, Fredrick must put the memory of her sweet sexual surrender out of his mind.

"How can you be so sure they will pay the ransom?"

Fredrick smiled. "We will leave a little piece of Miss Prescott behind to encourage their cooperation."

Jeremy nodded understanding. "And what if you are captured in Port Monmouth?"

Fredrick placed a hand on Jeremy's shoulder. "Then I will hang."

* * * * *

Arabella awoke when Fredrick left the cabin. She lay still, pretending to be asleep, not wanting to face the man who had performed such feats of pleasure on her the night before. Surely, no gently bred man would do the incredible things Fredrick had done. The thought of his mouth upon her nipples brought a blush to her face—a mild reaction, also, to the memory of his tongue awakening her body with each sinful swipe across the little nubbin between her legs. It was a part of her she'd had no idea existed until the moment he touched it with his fingertips. And what a glorious sensation stroking that nubbin created. Surely to feel such pleasure was a sin.

Her heart leapt as her stomach churned. *Sin.* She had committed a forbidden act for an unmarried young lady. She'd had sex, and now fear rolled through her at the consequences of her weak resolve. She was no longer a maiden, and her marriage prospects had decreased with the loss of her virginity. And what if she'd gotten with child? Was one night of bliss enough to plant the seed of motherhood? She prayed it was not. If Arabella arrived home after this ordeal carrying the child of a pirate, she was sure her father would send her away, possibly back to England to a country estate for confinement.

"Oh God," she murmured, momentarily shivering at the notion of having a baby out of wedlock.

She placed a hand upon her belly, closed her eyes and tried to relax. She inhaled and released her breath slowly, trying to calm her frazzled nerves.

Fredrick. Who was Fredrick Thorne back in London? Before turning to a life of piracy on the high seas, he had surely been a man of wealth and rank judging by his educated manner of speaking and certain cultured mannerisms. Even his clothes spoke of a man of fine tastes rather than some lowly, ignorant commoner who happened to become captain of a band of pirates. What drove a man of advanced social standing into a life of bloodshed and lawlessness? Who was the man behind the rugged image of the devil-may-care buccaneer?

She imagined another place, another time—in London at a grand ball, and she spotting Fredrick across the dance floor.

She could see him in her mind's eye, tall and handsome in a dark gray coat and breeches. His hair would be neatly tied back into a queue and his tanned skin glowing with the health of a man who loved the outdoors. He'd smile and her heart would leap within her chest. Fredrick would cut a fine figure in a tailored suit and she'd be the envy of every maiden in the room as he crossed the dance floor to introduce himself and ask for a dance.

Arabella sighed at the images in her mind, swirling about the dance floor in his strong arms, his attention unwavering from her smiles and flirtatious small talk. He would be completely under her spell.

Then out of the crowd, a man yelled, "Pirate!"

It was her father.

And in his hand he held a saber, poised and ready.

Her eyes snapped open at the disturbing image that crept into her daydream. There was no way to blot out how Fredrick lived his life. He was a pirate, and Arabella had given her body to him for a night of passion.

The hours passed and Arabella took to pacing to work out her emotional distress. Dressed in his breeches and a very loose white linen shirt, she was beginning to feel as though he surrounded her with his scent, imprisoned her with his power and controlled her with his intoxicating touch. She impatiently marched back and forth in the cabin like a caged animal, hoping to push away the sexual yearnings of her body.

So much had happened over the course of the past few days—she'd been kidnapped and held for ransom by a handsome, sexy pirate, she'd lost her virginity to that same pirate and now she may be carrying his child. If she were to ever return to her father, he would surely never look at her the same again. Was momentary desire a good enough excuse?

Fredrick's kisses brought her heart to a standstill. The earth shuddered and quaked beneath her feet and she was helpless to resist the attraction of the rogue and his seductive lips. He'd played upon her inexperience and newly awakened feelings to lure her into sensual surrender.

In a flash, she stopped her pacing. Would sex with Nicholas have been as wonderful? Somehow the image of his face was blurred by the handsome features of Captain Thorne. Arabella pressed her wrist to her forehead, trying to squeeze away the pirate's face from that of her lost fiancé, but she couldn't. She relived the moments of ecstasy—Fredrick gazing down at her as he mounted her body and plunged his length deep within her channel. Her stomach lurched with renewed desire at the thought of the glorious memory of his cock, thickly veined and hard as an iron pike, stretching her walls and filling her channel. Nothing could compare to the painful delight of his cock deep inside. Even now, standing alone in his cabin, her intimate muscles clenched in need of him to fill her to capacity once again.

When Fredrick finally entered the cabin in the late morning, Arabella was determined to tell him what passed between them the night before could not happen again. She didn't want to take too many risks in getting pregnant. The more she engaged in sex with the handsome captain, the more chances she took. She couldn't bear the idea of her father's disappointment...or the shame of having a bastard child.

"Did you sleep well, Arabella?" he asked in a lighthearted voice when he closed the door behind him.

"I did finally sleep a little, Captain Thorne," she said coolly.

He frowned.

Unable to look at him, she moved to the open window and gazed out over the sea. How did he think she would act the morning after her seduction? Did he think she would be the accommodating lover?

"Has your heart turned to ice again so quickly, luv?"

She turned on him. "I wish you'd stop calling me that."

He stepped toward her and she spun back to the window, squeezing her eyes shut and fighting the urge to throw herself into his arms. Regardless of the risks, her traitorous body wanted him again.

Fredrick stood behind her, mere inches away, yet he did not touch her. She silently wished for his embrace. She couldn't deny her attraction to him, helpless against the achy need for his kiss...his touch. She longed for his naked body to slide along hers as he sent her senses reeling out of control.

"I'm sure this morning your mind has been mulling over scattered worries and thoughts of our night together. I admit, I have been giving it thought too."

He thought of her beyond the bedroom? This admission surprised her. "You have?" She cocked her head to peer at him out the corner of her eye. He stood with his hands clenched in fists at his sides. His face was tight and a muscle at his jaw twitched slightly as though fighting an inner battle. Tanned and handsome, his pale blond hair tied back neatly, he was the figure of a commander, a true leader. Yet softness reflected in his eyes revealed the kinder, gentler man she'd glimpsed hours before.

"I came down to ask if you wished to take a walk on deck. But perhaps I was wrong—"

She faced him quickly and broke in, "Oh yes, I would love that very much." She rested her hands on his chest, and through the layer of linen she could feel the steady beat of his heart.

He gazed down at her face and she thought he'd speak, but he stood silent. Then he caressed her cheek with his fingertips.

Her breath caught at the tender touch. She sighed and closed her eyes. He kissed her softly, gently, and she was lost within the power of his intoxicating kisses. Her lips melted into his and she clung to his shirt as he pulled her closer within his embrace.

Time lost meaning as his lips danced with hers in melodious unison. How can a man have so much control over her senses with the simplest kiss? It was not demanding or urgent, yet it absorbed her and conscious thoughts escaped her mind. She was lost when he kissed her, not matter how deeply or hungrily.

When he broke their kiss, they were breathless. She released her grip on his shirt but he held her against him a moment longer before backing away.

"Come and take a walk with me, Arabella." His voice was low and controlled.

"But...but I am not dressed to be seen," she said, indicating the oversized linen shirt and breeches she'd found among his trunks. The waist was cinched with a large belt, and upon her feet she wore the delicate slippers from the night of her abduction. She lifted her hands to her loosely braided hair, tendrils falling loose about her face. "I look like...like..."

"You look beautiful, luv. Never doubt that for a moment." He smiled and lifted a hand to her. "Come with me."

Chapter Six

ℬ

Fredrick escorted Arabella up the stairs to the main deck. His men stilled in their work to gaze upon her. With a disapproving scowl from Fredrick, they quickly turned back to their work.

The late morning sun kissed her face and he stood in awe of her glowing beauty beneath the Caribbean rays. She closed her eyes to the breeze and inhaled deeply. He couldn't help but ache to cup her breasts as they thrust forward when she breathed in the warm air.

"Come, let me show you around," he said, taking her hand, guiding her.

He led her to the quarterdeck where Jeremy stood at the helm. With him was the ship's surgeon, Bruce McGregor.

Bruce was a ship's surgeon before fate led him to join the crew of *Neptune's Sword*. He was a naval officer turned pirate as well. Fredrick had met the man in Tortuga and after a night of bed sport with a few tavern wenches and numerous mugs of rum, Bruce agreed to sign on for the next venture. Bruce could withstand an inhuman amount of rum in one night without a trace of adverse effects the next day.

Fredrick introduced Arabella to his men. "The dark-haired fellow with the charming smile is Jeremy O'Connell. He's been with me right from the beginning. We'd be lost at sea without him."

"Nice to meet you, Mr. O'Connell," she greeted sweetly.

Jeremy paused and took her hand. He lifted her hand to his mouth and kissed the back of her palm. "A pleasure, my lady."

"Thank you." She giggled and Fredrick fought the rising desire in his heart. He wanted to shield her from his crew's eyes, but he stood firm against the irrational jealousy.

"And this scholarly looking fellow here," Fredrick said, indicating the aging Bruce sitting close by, "is Doc Bruce McGregor, a Scotsman who is versed in all the herbal remedies you could possibly dream of."

"Aye, milady. But I do much more around here than mix up tonics," he said in a thick brogue.

"I'm sure you do, Dr. McGregor."

"Ahh, I haven't heard myself called *Dr. McGregor* since I left Scotland three years ago. They all call me Doc Bruce."

"Don't you miss your home?" she asked.

"Och, no. My wife is dead and I had no children. I'm much more useful here with these scurvy fellows than back on the farm dealing with cows." He shook his body in mock revulsion. "I hate cows. Stupid, dirty animals."

She laughed and her eyes danced with humor. Both Jeremy and Doc Bruce were not immune to her charm and beauty.

He led her onto the main deck where he pointed out the parts of the ship, and found she was a quick learner and asked many questions.

"An East Indiaman ship is intended to facilitate shipping and trading. We customized her into a pirate warship with forty cannon. We could carry more, but we cut it down to save room for the crew and cargo we'd acquire during our adventures. We added several swivel guns for added firepower." He gently caressed the railing. "She's served me well over the past few years. We often intimidate our enemies without firing a shot."

"How much of a crew is needed to man such a ship?"

"We have a hundred and fifty-three men aboard. We can easily carry up to three hundred."

"Where was *Neptune's Sword* built?" she asked.

"Holland. The Dutch are some of the finest shipbuilders in the world. I captured her on a voyage two years ago when in the Mediterranean. I changed the name in honor of the Greek god of the sea. Anyway, the Dutch put up a good fight, and sank my craft, the *Black Manta*, but they lost the battle when I killed their captain."

Her smile faded and she turned away from him.

He placed his hands upon her shoulders as they stood at the railing. "I can't change who I am, Arabella. I'm a pirate."

She swatted his hands away and stepped out of his reach. "You murdered a man. How can you justify that?"

"He was transporting slaves who were ill-fed and sick. Hundreds of men and women were stowed below like cattle. It was inhumane. So yes, I killed a man...a bad man who deserved to die a thousand times over."

She softened her defense and turned away, but not before he saw the tears in her eyes.

"Arabella, I wasn't always a pirate. But as captain of this ship, I make the rules and I expect my men to follow them. My word is law. When my men break my rules, there are consequences. I attacked that ship because I was looking for gold and treasure, but instead I found black ivory—human cargo from Africa. The conditions those people were forced to endure—chained together so they couldn't move, the dead left to rot and fester, the living barely surviving on what little they had to eat, and most of that was spoiled and bug-infested. I faced the captain and demanded an explanation, but he did not wish to parley. He chose to fight. I let the end of my rapier ultimately pass sentence. I saved hundreds of people from the cargo hold and future victims from being treated worse than beasts of burden."

"I'm sorry," she croaked through her tears.

He stood watching her. He wanted to offer comfort, but refused to move.

Eventually he sighed and moved next to her at the rail. "I was a gentleman once, if you can believe that."

Sniffling, she asked, "You were?"

He nodded. "Aye, I was the second son of a rich man of good social standing in London society. Obviously, Thorne is not my real name. I adopted the name when I decided to become a pirate."

"Do you have family still in England?"

"My father died before I went to sea. My older brother Malcolm, according to law, inherited the estate and the business, Thorndike Trade & Shipping Company. I was fine with him taking over as I had no head for running a merchant business. He wanted me to command the small fleet of three merchant vessels, but I had no knowledge of how to run a ship or lead a crew of men. So, Malcolm paid for my commission in the Royal Navy, and I went to sea to learn how to be a seaman. That is where I met Jeremy, during my service in the king's Navy." He paused as a tear threatened to spill down his cheek. "Later, I discovered my brother and two younger sisters were accused of treason against the Crown and put to death."

"Oh! I'm so sorry, Fredrick," she declared sincerely, laying her hand upon his. "That must have been horrible to bear while away from home."

"I discovered what happened when my ship docked at Dover. I was immediately arrested and charged with treason. However, the soldiers sent to arrest me did not deliver me to London. I escaped with Jeremy's help. I made my way out to sea again, but this time on a merchant vessel to the Americas. I spent most of the time drunk and in torment. After several months at sea, we were attacked by pirates. I joined their crew, vowing revenge for the death of my brother and sisters."

"But I don't understand, what was their treason?"

He smiled and turned to her. "I've never been able to find out after all these years."

"Are you so sure they were put to death?"

"That's what the soldiers told me when I was arrested. They described in detail how my brother was sent to the block, and how my sisters were raped repeatedly before they were hanged."

She stared at the horizon, shaking her head in amazed wonderment. "You must have lived a nightmare after hearing that."

"You might be able to now understand why I turned to piracy. I wanted revenge against the country that murdered my family. My brother and sisters would never commit any crime to warrant their brutal deaths."

"You should find out if the reports are true, Fredrick. And if so, discover the reason. I can't believe an entire family would be put to death like that without some sort of trial and written reports."

He cocked his brow. "Why are you so interested?"

"Because..." she stammered. "Because their deaths should not be in vain."

"I can never return to England now. Perhaps if I was rational five years ago, I could have stayed and hunted down the truth, or even visited my family's estate, but I did not. I avoided further chance of arrest and smuggled myself out of England...forever."

She stood in silence holding his hand. Her grip tightened then she asked, "What were their names?"

"My brother was Malcolm Thorndike, and my sisters were Abigail and Amelia. Abigail was seventeen, and Amelia was fourteen. My father cared for all of us after our mother died shortly after giving birth to Amelia." He paused then asked, "How old are you, Arabella?"

"Nineteen."

"Mmm." He nodded. "You are about Amelia's age...or at least, *if* she had lived."

She absently stroked the back of his hand with her thumb.

"During the five years since I left England, I avenged their deaths. I was a man driven by anger."

"And now?"

"I'm not angry anymore. I live with my pain."

"But I don't understand. Your family was executed, yet you take your revenge on those who probably had nothing to do with their deaths. I don't believe it's all because of a thirst for revenge." Her voice grew tense and angered.

"Because I am a pirate, luv. I'm free to live however I wish. I don't live by a set of rules dictated by a bunch of wigged politicians. I make my way in this world by taking from those who can afford a bump in their purse's weight."

"You make your adventures sound like a Robin Hood of the sea."

He chuckled. "In a way. However, the *poor* I give to is myself and my crew."

"You are a rogue, Captain Thorne."

"A rogue? Hmmm. I like the sound of that."

"I don't know how you can joke." Her voice was straining for control.

"I've lived with my ghosts and memories for five years," he started in a soft, tender voice. "There is not a day that passes that I do not think of Malcolm, Abigail or dear Amelia. They are always with me."

She touched his face gently and he saw the anger turn to compassion. "Fredrick."

He gazed into her eyes and saw her caring soul reaching out to him, and then he lowered his lips to hers. He kissed her lightly then leaned away. She was an unusual woman, unlike any he'd known before. The littlest kiss made his body burst into flames of overwhelming need and desire. His cock hardened, his heart began to race and his craving to taste her flesh increased. Having her last night had simply whetted his appetite for Arabella and her luscious body. He wanted more.

He grasped her hand and placed it on the bulge straining in his pants. "You touch me, luv, and I find I have an incredible appetite for your body to be beneath mine, writhing in passion." He guided her hand over his cock that grew harder by the moment. He groaned at her gingerly touch over the spongy tip and along the shaft.

She moved in closer and lightly massaged his cock further without urging. "I want to..." Her voice broke as she reluctantly pulled her hand away.

Still the innocent, he mused.

* * * * *

Fredrick had endured a difficult life, a life harder than Arabella could imagine. Her heart had ached as he'd revealed the story of the circumstances that drove him to piracy. She began to understand a little, however, she couldn't understand why he refused to discover the truth of his family and their deaths. If she ever returned to England, she would set out to discover the real tale behind the Thorndike family. If a wealthy family of good lineage was suddenly accused of treason, it would surely be a story that spread among the whole of London. *Someone* had to know the details.

At the moment, Fredrick led her below to the cabin. Touched by his painful story, she wanted to comfort him, caress him—make love to him.

When she'd touched the massive erection through his pants, her heart had begun to race and wetness gathered between her legs. As a woman who now knew the intimacies of sex, she'd instantly wished his hard member were inside her sheath.

Inside the cabin, he closed and bolted the door. She backed into the bed, the mattress against her calves.

He turned and smiled at her. "You look like a pirate's wench." He stepped closer and began to peel off his shirt to reveal the perfectly sculpted muscles of his chest and arms. He was breathtaking in form, and when he reached for her, she willingly stepped into his arms.

He held her to him and she placed her ear against his chest and listened to the steady thump of his heartbeat. It was the sound of humanity. She inhaled deeply the scent of the ocean— sweat and a hint of salt—that coated his skin.

His chest was perfectly smooth and she grazed a palm over the surface, testing his reaction to her touch. At his quick intake of breath, she smiled. He was just as affected by her touch as she was to his. Her fingertips lightly stroked his nipple and he gasped softly and tightened his hold about her body, the hand behind her head tenderly holding her.

When she pinched the tip of a nipple, he chuckled then kissed the top of her head. "I like it when you touch me like this, luv."

"I thought if I enjoy you pinching mine, you may like it too."

"Aye. I would like it *more* if you kissed me there." His voice was breathless.

She shifted in his arms and lightly kissed his erect nipple. "What else do you want me to do?"

"Stroke your tongue over the tip. Suck on it. Go with your instinct from there."

She lightly kissed his nipple again, her lips gently encircling the tip. She tested his flesh with her tongue and he moaned. She liked to hear his reactions to her movements. She grew bolder and pressed her lips together about his nipple. His fingers gripped her hair more urgently. She teased his nipple with her teeth, grazing the surface. He grunted and cupped her ass with his hands, pulling her hips closer. She felt the hard rod of his erect cock through his pants and she instinctively moved her body, rubbing his member. He let out a frustrated breath and he began to push her back onto the bed behind her.

"No, Fredrick."

He stopped. "What is it?"

"I want to undress you."

His green eyes glowed hot with desire and he smiled. Her heart raced when he nodded approval then added, "Take off your clothes first, luv."

She took off her too-loose shirt and pants and stood before him naked. She liked the way his eyes roamed possessively over her body. A blush warmed her skin and he fingered her chin, tilting her gaze to his. "Don't be embarrassed. You're beautiful."

"I'm afraid I don't know what to do first."

"Take off my pants to start."

She sheepishly smiled and then knelt, his crotch level with her face. Carefully she unfastened his belt and unbuttoned his pants. When she accidentally brushed her hand over the large bulge of his erection, he moaned.

Slowly she lowered his pants and the magnificent cock was released. She'd never seen a man's member this close before. The shaft was long and thick, and the tip was large and purplish. A tiny clear droplet of fluid escaped the small opening and she licked her lips. What would it taste like? Would he think her strange for wanting a taste?

He cupped her head and she gazed up to his face. "Put me in your mouth," he instructed.

She looked back to his cock and gently reached for it with her hand.

"Wrap your fingers around it," he said in a barely controlled voice.

She obeyed and was rewarded with his moan. She tested the organ with her hands, moving her fingers over the silky skin covering hot, iron-hard flesh. It was unlike anything she'd ever seen before. Small droplets glistening upon the tip of his cock and she tasted them with her tongue.

He exhaled loudly with a groan and held her head securely. "Put me in your mouth," he repeated, begging.

Slowly, she closed her lips about his cock and he pushed his length deeper inside. She suckled upon the length, licking the salty fluid from his skin.

"Oh yes, sweet Arabella," he groaned. He began to move his hips. She opened her mouth wide and took him in as he pumped slowly at first, gradually picking up speed. She twirled her tongue over his cock and he continued thrusting into her mouth.

Still wanting to explore this unbelievable control over the powerful captain, she lifted a hand and touched the sac under his cock. He yelled out in pleasure and pumped faster as she tested the weight and shape of his balls.

Arabella glanced up and marveled in the masculine beauty of his face lost in ecstasy. With his head tossed back he looked like a Nordic god finding the point of no return within his lover.

Then he commanded in a husky voice, "Touch your clitoris. Make yourself come with me."

Her nub already tingled, excited at her mastery over his body. Seeing Fredrick lost in sexual bliss, she obeyed willingly. She reached down and her honey covered the tips of her fingers. She touched her nubbin and fingered the sensitive surface. The pleasure of her strokes across the little button vibrated throughout her body. Each pass of her finger sent pulses of delight coursing through her veins. She increased the pressure of her touch and quickened her strokes as she climbed higher to her final destination. Then she shattered, her body convulsing in rhythmic spasms.

She screamed about his cock as he stilled and cried out with his own release. Salty fluid filled her mouth and she swallowed in between her own pants and cries. He pulled out and continued to spurt his fluid over her chin and chest as she slipped a finger, then a second up into her. Muscles squeezed in rhythmic spasms and she arched her back to take her fingers in deeper.

As her climax began to calm in intensity, she slipped her fingers out of her body and lowered her bottom to the floor. She wiped his white essence from her chin and smiled.

So that was how to bring down the powerful pirate.

He stood towering over her, gazing down at her body. "Thank you, luv." His voice was thick with tenderness, and then he smiled.

She chuckled when she touched more of the white fluid on her neck. "Seems like I have to clean up."

In a flash he strode to the table and splashed some water into an accompanying basin from a pitcher he always kept there in the room. He wrung out a clean cloth left for her to bathe, and returned to her side. He crouched down to the floor on the balls of his feet and wiped away the liquid substance.

"Looks like a pearl necklace," he commented as he continued to clean away his ejaculate.

She scrunched her lips with distaste. "Nothing like the pearls I've ever seen."

"One day, I will give you a strand of real pearls to adorn your beautiful neck."

She reached up to his face and traced the outline of his jaw. What could she say to such a promise? Was he considering an affair beyond an onboard encounter? Could she even fathom a real relationship with Fredrick beyond a pirate captain and his female captive lover?

The reality hit her—hard.

She was indeed a *pirate's* lover.

Chapter Seven

ഇ

The fleet of three British warships, the *Enforcer*, the *Golden Harpoon* and the *Royal Raider*, stood at anchor for the evening. Governor Prescott stood in his cabin aboard the *Royal Raider* discussing the plan to capture Captain Thorne and save Arabella. "Thorne must be caught," he started. "But without cannon fire. I do not want my daughter hurt in a sea battle."

"But sir, how can we take *Neptune's Sword* without engaging the pirates in an attack?" asked Captain Jacobs in frustrated anger.

"Watch your tone, Captain," he warned Jacobs. "I want to surround him in such a way he will have no choice but to surrender," answered Charles.

"Sir, I mean no disrespect," started Captain Nelson. Commander of the *Golden Harpoon*, a ship from a neighboring port, Nelson had agreed to join the hunt and aid the governor. "However, we would need more ships than the three we have. Pirates are known to show no fear even when admittedly outnumbered."

"We will sail to Isla de Margarita and trap his ship in the inlet, cutting off his escape," Charles explained.

"Sir, he most likely expects us to try such a tactic." Captain Nelson tried to reason with him, but the governor grew angrier—and weaker—each day. Charles Prescott was not a man who dragged his daughter into political affairs...or dealings with pirates. Poor Arabella must be suffering at the hands of that bastard Thorne.

Charles slammed his palm down on the oak desk where charts of the nearby islands lay. "I want the man stopped, damn it! I don't care how we do it, I want my daughter back."

"Perhaps what we need to do is think like a pirate," Captain Jacobs offered. "Think like Thorne."

"Go on." Charles thumped down onto a nearby chair, anxious to hear what the conniving captain had in mind.

"Thorne will know we will want to capture him. He told us where to go for the ransom to be paid, knowing we would try to trick him."

"I'm listening."

"He won't be at Margarita knowing we will be there in force."

"Then where will he be?"

Captain Jacobs shuffled through the assorted charts on the desk and when he found the one he sought, unrolled the parchment and smoothed the wrinkled surface. "Where do pirates go to feel safe from the law in the Caribbean?" The captain dragged his forefinger over the chart and stopped upon a tiny island. "Tortuga."

*   *   *   *   *

Arabella lay in the darkness, listening to Fredrick's steady breathing. The ship rocked with the current. The night was still except for the sound of the few night crew members on duty, the boards creaking beneath their feet as they slowly went about their tasks.

She sighed and turned over in bed, her back to her lover. In the few days she'd been aboard *Neptune's Sword*, she had become a weakling to carnal desire. She was a sinner, a wanton woman—a pirate's wench. Even Fredrick had said she looked like one. At this moment, she felt like one. What had she done to her life in a few short days? She'd become the very thing she swore to avoid. She was a pirate's harlot lover.

"What's the matter?" Fredrick's voice cut through the darkness. He turned, curling his body along hers and wrapping his arm about her body in a possessive embrace.

"I hate pirates," she blurted.

He stilled.

She lay in silence then confessed, "I should have fought harder."

"You *did* fight."

She pulled away from him, taking the sheet with her to cover her naked body. "Not enough," she said, tears filling her eyes as she sat on the bed, unable to face him.

He didn't answer. He reached out to touch her arm, but she quickly jerked away.

"You've ruined me." She stood, her back still facing him. "I can never marry now."

"Don't be foolish. Of course you can."

"No. I can't."

"Arabella—"

"I do not wish to be a pirate's wench. I do not want anything to do with pirates. Pirates are horrid, bloodthirsty men who have no care in this world other than their own greedy needs."

"I am not bloodthirsty, Arabella. Nor am I greedy."

"You admitted to stealing gold for yourself and your crew. You killed one captain and could justify his death with his crime. But how many others have you killed and without reason, other than your covetous need for treasure?"

Fredrick lunged out of bed and reached for his pants, shoving in one leg and then the other. "I don't have to justify anything to you. You are nothing more than a spoiled, heartless wench."

She refused to argue. If he believed she was heartless, so be it. If only she was unaffected by his cutting words and accusations. Despite her aching heart, she continued to push him away. He was getting too close. After last night, Arabella was afraid of actually coming to care for him.

"You care about no one but yourself," he added venomously.

"You kill men for your own glory. What about the families they leave behind? What sort of explanation do they get? How are their wives or lovers to go on knowing a pirate killed their men?"

He paused, his tanned chest muscles glowing in the shadows from the pale moonlight filtering in through the window. "Who was it you lost?" he asked in a strained voice.

Tears threatened to spill from her eyes as she met his gaze. "My fiancé."

"Did you love him?"

She debated her response. "We were engaged."

"That's not what I asked," he snapped. "Were you in love with him?"

She hesitated then said, "Yes."

He scowled, grabbed his shirt and boots, and stomped for the door. Without another word, he left the cabin with a slam of the door behind him.

Tears began to rush down her cheeks as her heart shattered into pieces. She had indeed gotten too close to caring for him, and now, she'd driven him out of her bed, but she had to protect her heart, even if it hurt beyond all reason. If she let her affair with the captain continue she would surely fall in love with him. How would she ever live if he was captured and hanged for piracy?

Once again, she worried about her father discovering her predicament. He would surely send the fleet after Fredrick—if they weren't already hot on his trail. Fredrick would hang for his crimes. There would be no leniency, no forgiveness.

She walked back to the bed and sat down on the edge, wishing this was all just a dream and she'd wake up to find herself safely tucked in her bed in Port Monmouth. Closing her eyes, she imagined lying in her soft bed, warm and secure.

Then at her back, heated flesh grazed her skin and a possessive arm encircled her body. *Fredrick.*

Goose bumps rose along her arms at the thought of him lying in her bed at home. She shook her head and tried to clear away the erotic thought of his powerful form cradling her body. Had it only been moments before that he'd held her here in their bed?

Their bed. Odd that she had begun to think of it thus.

She had to stop thinking such things. She had to drive him from her mind, shut him out of her heart.

Then suddenly he barged back into the room, slamming the door behind him. His shirt was open and disheveled and his hair wild about his shoulders. His face was tight and red-hot rage flashed in his eyes.

"You think I'm a ruthless pirate. Now I'll show you how much of a pirate I can be!"

She jumped up from the bed and tried to run, but he caught her arm and ripped the sheet from her body.

"No! Don't—"

Her pleas were cut off by his ferocious kiss. He plunged his tongue into her mouth, branding her with searing heat and scorching her senses. His strength overpowered her as he held her in a steel grip. She tried to fight, but her struggles were fruitless. He commanded her body as well as her responses. In her heart, she did not want to fight him. She *wanted* him to take her—dominate her body and conquer her heart.

He pulled away from her mouth breathlessly but never eased his hold upon her. He gazed down at her, and her heart skipped. Her body was aflame with desire at his greedy possessiveness.

"Get on the bed," he ordered in a stern yet husky voice. He pushed her to the bed and she fell upon its softness. She stared at him, shocked at his savage yet reined strength. His anger was violent, yet he did not hurt her.

"Turn over onto your knees." She didn't move until he added a stern, "Now, wench!"

Arabella nodded and obeyed. She felt exposed and perverse as she lifted her rear upward to him. She felt her juices cream and lubricate her sex. By God, he excited her with his mastery!

She crouched on the bed in silence as he moved behind her, opening his pants to release his cock. She wished she could turn and look at the large member surging with need, but he tugged at her hips, pulling her body closer to the edge of the bed. He stood behind her, keeping his hands upon her hips.

She felt his cock slide through her juices and she moaned.

"You want my cock inside you, don't you, wench?" he asked harshly. "You want me to fuck you." His cock glided through her seeping moisture along the opening to her channel. "Answer me," he commanded.

"Yes!"

"You will address me as 'my lord Captain', wench. I am lord of your body. You belong to me. And for the remainder of this voyage, you will succumb to me and my wishes without argument. Do you understand that, wench?"

"But—"

Smack! He swatted a buttock and it stung. She screeched, only to have him swat her buttock once again.

"Answer me or I will make sure you get a true and painful punishment."

"Yes, I understand, my lord Captain."

"Very good."

His hands on her ass, he thrust his cock inside her sheath with one hearty push. She screamed and grasped onto the sheets beneath her.

"You are about to learn what it is like to be fucked by a pirate." He began to quickly pump in and out of her, and she

83

held on to the sheets for dear life. The orgasms she'd experienced before took time to build. But now, as he fiercely ravaged her, she felt her climax building quickly. He held her hips steady as he rammed into her then retreated, only to repeat his wild lovemaking.

He massaged the puckered entrance to her rear with the tip of his finger and she moaned.

"Don't want to be a pirate's wench? I think not. You are, luv, moaning like a true mistress." His voice was harsh with rage and desire.

Arabella was lost in the growing climax as he plundered her body. She couldn't resist the violent need to fulfill the moment with a crashing release. She was close, so close to her breaking point.

Smack! He spanked her reddened buttock. "Tell me, wench. How do you like a pirate fucking you?"

She was surprise how the feel of the hot flesh of her ass only seemed to excite her further. "I...oh Fredrick..."

Smack! He struck her buttock again and it almost tumbled her over into climax. Almost.

"You love being fucked by me, a bloody pirate, don't you?"

"I love it! I love being fucked by you, my lord Captain."

His pace became faster and he gripped her hips fiercely as he pumped into her wildly.

It was more than she could bear. Her orgasm washed over her in one ferocious wave into another. Her body quaked and shook with the intensity as she rode out the spasms starting between her legs and radiating out through every cell. He yelled aloud with his release and thrust into her deeply with each flush of heated semen.

Once emptied, his cock beginning to go limp, Fredrick pulled out of her sheath and she adjusted her position on the bed. He reached down for the discarded sheet then gently covered her body.

When he did not join her in bed, she leaned up to see him securing his pants about his waist. He hadn't even undressed! He still wore his pants and shirt!

Instantly she was enraged, but said nothing. Her body hummed and she was too weak to move to fight him. She had already surrendered to him, promising to obey his every command.

He moved to the door and paused to look back at her. "You are mine, a pirate's wench. Learn to accept it, luv."

He closed the door behind him with a resounding click, and she growled. Grabbing a pillow, she tossed it at the door. "Pirate bastard."

* * * * *

Fredrick stormed to the quarterdeck, buttoning his shirt. Rage had provoked him to force her to submit—anger over the mention of another man, her fiancé. It was enough to send him into a jealous rage.

Jeremy stood behind the helm, keeping the ship on course. An expression of concern etched the man's features. Bruce sat on a nearby barrel, drinking rum out of a wooden mug, dribbles of the drink trailing down his graying beard.

"Captain," Jeremy greeted him.

Fredrick tucked his shirt into his pants. Being disheveled was unlike him and Jeremy continued to watch him as he sat on another barrel and put on his boots.

"How is Miss Prescott?" Bruce finally asked when Fredrick sighed and covered his face with his hands.

"She's the most aggravating, spoiled female I've ever met."

"She's a lady used to having her way, and I'm sure this type of living does not suit such a woman of fine breeding," Jeremy commented, never taking his eyes from the horizon.

"She knows exactly how to get me angry with her sharp tongue. She drives me completely insane."

Jeremy laughed softly. "We can all see that, Captain."

Fredrick dropped his hands to his lap and shot him a questioning glare.

"You're besotted with her," Jeremy laughed.

"I am *not* besotted. I am..." *What?* He didn't even know how to explain his feelings.

"In love," Bruce finished.

"In love? No, no, no. I am *not* in love with that wench."

Jeremy smirked and raised an eyebrow in disbelief. Bruce took another gulp of his rum.

"I may be *infatuated* with the little spitfire, but I'm not in love with her."

"If you insist, Captain," Jeremy teased.

"I admit to having a certain...regard for her. Her body enflames me, and her beauty is beyond compare. *However*, her insistence to fight me every moment we are together..."

"*Every* moment, Captain?" Jeremy seemed to enjoy watching him struggle.

"The only way to stop her infuriating arguments is to kiss her senseless."

"Aye, bloody infuriating females," Bruce chuckled drunkenly.

Fredrick looked up at Bruce and then Jeremy. Could they be right? Was this becoming much more complicated than a dalliance with a female hostage?

"What are you going to do when it comes time to give her back to her father?" Jeremy asked, breaking into his thoughts.

"Return her, of course."

Bruce shook his head. "And what if Miss Prescott discovers she is with child?"

Fredrick blinked. Arabella with child? What would he do if she was indeed pregnant? Fredrick hadn't given this possibility any thought and suddenly felt sick.

He felt like the worst sort of cad. He was an evil-to-the-core pirate for not even considering the possibility of impregnating her. He was only concerned with sating his lust. He wasn't remotely a gentleman, he was an irresponsible rake. How could he not think beyond his own desires and needs?

It's like the gypsy had predicted...

He lowered his face into his hands once again and moaned in distress.

"Her father will make sure you are hung out in the bay to greet all visitors to Port Monmouth as a warning to those who engage in piracy. He'll hunt you down until you pay with your life for soiling his daughter and giving her a bastard child."

Fredrick glared at Jeremy. "Are you two trying to make me feel better? If so, it is not working."

"We're trying to get you to see things from her point of view," Bruce started in a slurred brogue. "It's possible she has grown feelings for you, and the only way for her to protect herself—to protect *you*—is to push you away."

"She mentioned a fiancé. He was killed by pirates," Fredrick admitted solemnly.

Jeremy nodded understanding. "A good reason to hate pirates—and you."

"Ahoy below!" called a man from the crow's nest. "A ship to southern!"

Fredrick jumped up and reached for his spyglass, gazed out over the black sea to the horizon. There stood the outline of an approaching craft. "Can't make out who it is," he said as he kept his eye on the faint shadow in the distance.

"Could it be Governor Prescott?" Jeremy asked from the helm.

"Possible." Fredrick lowered his glass. "Make ready for battle." Then he added with a smile as he faced Jeremy, "Let's go on over and introduce ourselves."

Chapter Eight

ဢ

Arabella had just drifted to sleep when the sound of cannon fire startled her awake. She heard the men on deck running to their stations, preparing for battle. She lunged out of bed and hurried to the window. She saw nothing on the horizon in the early morning light.

She quickly tossed away the sheet and scrambled for her clothes—loose pants and an even looser shirt. Once dressed, she tired the door, only to find it bolted from the outside. Damn him!

"Let me out, you bastard!" she yelled, banging her fists upon the door.

It was no use, she was trapped inside. She ran back to the window and strained to peer out the sides to capture a glimpse of the other vessel.

Then she saw it—a British merchant vessel. She spotted the red, white and blue flag of her country as *Neptune's Sword* turned to fire broadside.

She watched in shock as the pirates fired upon the British ship, followed by cheers of glee when their shots struck the craft. It listed to one side and a roar of shouting rolled over the ocean surface. Amid the celebration she heard the order to prepare to board the ship.

The warship moved out of sight as *Neptune's Sword* turned and closed the distance between the two crafts, pulling alongside to board the ship and engage in hand-to-hand combat. The pirate craft was intimidating compared to the inferior merchant vessel.

She stormed to the door and began to bang on it again. "Fredrick, you bastard, I'll kill you for this!"

The attack incensed her.

All her conclusions were correct. Captain Thorne was no different than any other pirate. Bloodthirsty bastard! He was exactly like all the rest—like the men who killed Nicholas.

She'd sullied her body and actually believed she cared for Fredrick. No! Fredrick wasn't one ounce of the man Nicholas had been. How could she dishonor his memory by making love with the pirate? What must he think of her now as he gazed down from heaven?

Harlot. A pirate's wench.

Arabella became enraged at her weakness. She could not let him command her again so easily. Or at least she had to disconnect her emotions from the physical sex. He did not feel tenderness when he took her that last time. She may have agreed to obey during a moment of ecstasy, but she had no intention of complying. Her body's reactions were weakened by the handsome pirate...but she had to stay strong and defend her heart. It was her last line of defense. If he took her again, she had to disconnect herself from the overwhelming flood of...

She gulped. She couldn't utter the label for what she'd begun to feel. No, she couldn't even think it. Fredrick Thorne was a no-good dog, undeserving of her affection—even if she'd suspected growing tenderness in his heart for her at one time. A man would not force the woman he loved into sexual surrender.

Would he?

No, the answer was clear. She would be a marble statue, cold and unfeeling. He may force her body into submission, but he will never conquer her heart.

Hours later the sea quieted as the battle finally ended. Arabella sat at the window watching the last remnants of the merchant vessel sink into the sea. Scattered upon the waves were various pieces of wreckage. Bodies floated about before getting dragged down to the depths by feasting sharks. She refused to close her eyes to the carnage but instead sat there in sad mourning for the brave men who died in the service of England.

The sun dipped behind the flat horizon and she waited for Fredrick to appear. She was sure the man would come as he did each night.

At what seemed like midnight, he unlocked the door and strode into the room.

"Keep away from me," she ground out at him, trying to control her anger.

"Luv, you are mine. You will do as I say, remember?" His voice was slurred from obvious celebrating. "I've had a hard day. Many of my men were wounded in the battle, not to mention some damage to my ship that needs repair. I'm in no mood to argue with you."

"You sank a British ship!"

"Aye, but not before we salvaged tons of cargo. It will bring us a good price in trade. A profitable day indeed." He flopped onto the bed and lay back fully clothed. "Now come here and take off my boots."

"No."

He leaned up onto his elbows. "What did you say?"

"I said no. I am not undressing you. You can take your own boots off. In fact, get out and take them off elsewhere."

"Always the fighter, aren't you, luv?"

"For the final time, stop calling me that!" Her voice was losing its restraint, but he tested her patience.

"I said, come here and take off my boots," he commanded sternly.

"And I said *no*." She crossed her arms over her chest and stood firm. Her glare was strong and she refused to let him melt her spirit.

As long as he doesn't kiss me…

He lay back in the bed and heaved a great sigh then mumbled under his breath.

"I told you to leave," she reiterated.

"I'm not going anywhere, luv." He sighed again then sat up on the bed. "In fact, I think it is time I teach you a lesson in obedience." He stood, the room suddenly shrinking beneath his overpowering form.

She shivered, fear and sexual awareness coursing through her body. "You already spanked me," she said as she began backing away from his approach.

"You need another spanking...to start."

"What do you mean?" she asked as she scurried backward.

"Worried, luv?" he asked in a mocking tone. "Afraid I might tie you up and have my way with you?"

"You wouldn't dare tie—"

"On second thought," he interrupted as he caught her and shoved her body against the wall. He pressed his body against hers, his lips a breath away. "I think you need to be shown *never* to question or make demands of your lord Captain. You need to be thoroughly punished."

She squirmed but it only rubbed her body along his enticingly. "Leave me alone." Her voice cracked.

He kissed her face and nuzzled the sensitive skin by her ear. "I'm going to make you beg me to fuck you, to end the torture. But I won't, I'll just tease you more. Your body with scream with need only I can fulfill. You're going to want to come so badly, you will plead for me to end your pain." Then he added, "You, my dear Miss Prescott, are about to learn the punishment for disobeying me."

Before she could struggle, he captured her wrists in his strong hands.

"Don't do this, Fredrick," she pleaded as tears began to fall.

"Oh, it's Fredrick now? Too late, luv." He quickly whipped off his belt and wrapped it about her wrists tightly. "You call me 'my lord Captain'."

"Please don't." He tugged her toward the bed.

"Sit on the bed," he commanded and secured the loose end of his belt to the headboard.

She whimpered as she watched him move about the cabin to one of the sea chests. He rummaged through the contents and pulled out a blood-red silk scarf. "Perfect. This will do nicely," he commented in a low voice. He turned and strode back to the bed.

He sat next to her and brought the scarf up to her face.

"What are you going to do with that?" she asked nervously.

He smiled devilishly. "Blindfold you, luv."

She jumped and pulled against her restraints, but it was no use.

He leaned in to her and she stared up at him with wide eyes. "I won't hurt you. You must trust me," he said softly.

She stilled. Indeed, he wouldn't harm her. It was with shock that she realized she *had* grown to trust him. When the whisper of the sleek fabric covered her eyes, she inhaled deeply. The scent of the ocean clung to his body and it affected her intensely. Her little nubbin tingled and a familiar wetness gathered between her thighs. She felt the bed dip beneath his weight.

"You say I am a heartless pirate," he started in a stern voice. "Perhaps you are right."

She gulped down the lump in her throat.

"How do you feel, bound to my bed and blind?" he asked.

"I feel…helpless."

The sound of his low chuckle rumbled in his chest. "Precisely. You are helpless to my whim."

She shifted on the bed as the ache increased within her sex. Inhaling sharply at his barest touch across her nipple, she gasped when he suddenly pinched the tip into a hard peak.

"Does that excite you?"

Her body shivered with a pleasant warm heat of arousal as she imagined his eyes grazing over her breasts. She opened her legs a little, hoping he'd be tempted to touch her further.

"Mmm. I can see that it does. You want to deny me, refuse to accept you are indeed a pirate's lover, yet here you are, offering me the opportunity to sample your sweet juices."

When she moaned, he placed his hand over a breast. He cupped the globe and squeezed it gently at first, but then his touch became rougher, more abusive.

And she liked it.

"Please..." she whined, tugging on her restraints.

"No."

She paused her pulling on the belt.

Then he rose from the bed, the mattress moving beneath her body.

She strained to listen to his movements about the room — and the opening of the door. Without another word he left, and the ominous click of the lock followed his departure.

She lay in bed bound and blind, and completely in shock. Why did he leave her like this? What could he possibly gain from treating her thus?

"Pirate," she venomously whispered.

The sound of the ocean lulled her to sleep as she waited. The ship rolled with the tide as it cut through the waves, and eventually, she gave in to exhaustion. What seemed like moments later, her eyes snapped open. *Darkness.* The blindfold still covered her eyes and face, but she was aware of movement in the room.

But first she needed to take care of another necessity.

"Fre—I mean, my lord Captain?"

He paused in his movement. "You may speak."

Pausing, she worded her request carefully. "May I use the chamber pot?"

He sighed. "Yes, of course." His tone was kinder than before.

He released her wrists and when she lifted her hands to pull away the blindfold, he stopped her. "No, luv. This is all about trust. You must learn to trust me. I will help you." He guided her off the bed and to the pot. He helped her sit and her face blushed as she tried to turn away.

She listened to him move about the room and she relaxed. Once she finished, he guided her to the bed.

"Give me your right hand," he instructed. She gently eased out her hand and he took it. Wrapping a soft fabric about the tender flesh, he secured her wrist above her head. Then he repeated the movements and tied her other wrist.

Then he grasped her leg and he tied some fabric about her ankle, securing it to the bed.

"Why are you doing this?" she cried in a panic.

"Because to you, I am nothing but a pirate."

She fought him as he reached for her other ankle, unwilling to be bested so easily—or without a struggle. "You are!" she ground out when he caught her kicking leg within his steel grip.

He wrapped another piece of soft fabric about her other ankle. "No, luv. I am much more than just a lawless sea rover."

Tied spread-eagle on the bed, she concentrated on her breathing. "Why do you care what I think?" she asked, her voice choked with tears.

"Because..." His voice trailed off and she heard his breathing deepen as he considered what to say. Then he rose from the bed, leaving the room, but only briefly.

When he returned she strained to listen to his movements. What was he doing? How could he treat her like this? She thought he had begun to care for her. Tears burned her eyes.

Nothing but a pirate.

He stilled and the room fell silent for a moment before he spoke. "You are mine," he growled.

She whimpered.

"I can have you whenever I wish." His voice sent jolts of hot pleasure to her sex. She writhed against her bonds.

"Your lips deny me, but your body betrays your words." A cool object touched the taut peak of her nipple and she groaned.

"You want me to fuck you, but you refuse to admit it." He traced the curve of her breast with something hard and smooth. Her body began a needful rhythm as she flexed her hips gently.

"You need to be punished for denying your lord Captain."

Cream oozed from her slit and ran down between her buttocks. His voice vibrated across her skin, sensitizing the surface.

"I should use the lash upon you like any other crew member who causes trouble onboard this ship. How would you like that, luv? Your ass would be red and pulsing from the vicious whipping."

She fidgeted, and he continued. "I'd dip my fingers deep into your sopping-wet cunt only to pull away before you find your release." He grazed the smooth object down the valley of her breasts. "I'd let you calm before starting all over again, maybe spanking your reddened ass cheeks first and then fucking you with the handle of my lash as you cry out for mercy."

"My lord Captain." She breathed the soft plea.

The mattress gave under his weight when he climbed upon the bed near her feet. She closed her eyes and lay still, waiting for what came next.

The hard object he held was cool against her heated skin. He teased her mound with the curved object and her hips continued to move against it in a tantalizing rhythm.

It dipped down through her folds and passed over her throbbing clitoris, then slowly he swirled the end through her juices.

"What are you doing to me?" she asked as the object teased the entrance of her sheath.

"Torturing you like a captive," he replied then pushed the object into her heat. Hard and smooth and deliciously wide in girth, she panted as he paused to allow her body to adjust.

"Oh God," she whimpered as the object filled her.

The tip caressed her inner walls and Arabella's climax threatened to break…if only she could urge on his torture with the flex of her hips. "Hold still," he commanded as he pulled the object out a little only to push it back into her. "I will tell you when you can come, and you cannot come yet."

"Fredrick." Her voice was hoarse. She grasped the restraints in her hands and held on tightly, fighting her body's building excitement.

He pushed the object in and out and she squealed, her grasp fiercely tight and her legs straining to open wider. But the restraints held her securely.

"You know what this is that I am fucking you with, luv?" he asked as he increased the speed of his thrusting.

"No!" she called out when he stopped suddenly.

He chuckled.

"Do you like it?"

She groaned in frustration, wishing he'd stop talking and just make her come.

"What is it, luv? Tell me."

She hesitated but then cried out, "Don't stop!"

"Hmm." He refused to move the object, but the size excited her, stretching her walls snuggly, almost painfully.

"Please…" she moaned.

"What, luv? Tell me what you want."

She flexed her hips, taking in the object a bit farther, and she gasped.

He moved on the bed and when he straddled her thigh, she was confused. He moved the object within her once again, but this time in tempo to another noise.

"Mmm, sweet Arabella. I like seeing you tied down and helpless on my bed." The noise continued—the sound of slapping skin.

Then she realized that Fredrick pumped his cock in his hand as he thrust the object up inside her.

She wept, helpless to do anything but ride the tempestuous sensations he created.

She wanted to come, but he stopped thrusting the object and commanded her to resist. She was so close to completion.

"Do not come yet, luv." His voice was tight. Then in the next heartbeat, he yelled aloud and a heated fluid tickled over her belly.

Bastard. He pumped seed onto her body and refused to complete her climax.

He moved off her and left the bed. The object still remained in her channel, hard and unmoving. Torture.

Then he grasped her arm and a tearing sound echoed through the cabin.

Her arm dropped to the bed. Stunned, she lay in silence as he sliced through the other restraint about her wrist. She moved to remove the blindfold, but he caught her hands. "No," he said softly.

She lowered her arms to rest upon the bed.

Then he cut through the bonds at her ankles.

But he did not remove the object so snuggly tucked into her sex.

"Turn over and raise your ass in the air," he said in a gentle but stern tone.

She obeyed and when she crouched onto her knees, her inner muscles sucked upon the object within her. She groaned as she tilted her ass upward.

The mattress dipped as he climbed onto the bed once again. The object jerked when he touched the exposed end and began to turn it within her. What *was* the object deep inside her, giving her so much pleasure?

He moved behind her and his thighs pressed against the back of hers. If he was going to enter her, shouldn't he take that hard object out first?

Then he pressed a finger against the puckered hole of her anus.

"Oh!" she shrieked. A wave of thrilling euphoria swept through her body. She shook at the intensity of pleasure radiating from his stroking thumb over her anus. He coated his fingers in the juices flowing from her body about the object.

"A virgin once again," he commented in a low voice as he pushed a finger past the circle of muscle. She screamed at the pain. He stilled and after a few moments, the pain was replaced by a delicious fullness.

Gently Fredrick moved his finger in and out of the little hole and Arabella moaned loudly. Never had anything felt so sinfully wonderful.

"Not yet, luv," he reminded her.

"When, Fredrick? I need..." She sounded panicked even to her own ears.

His finger retreated and she protested with a whine.

Then he pressed his thighs against her once again. He poured something cool and slippery over her anus and she jumped with a gasp.

"Relax, luv. You're so tight there, I don't want to hurt you."

Confused, she was about to ask what he intended to do when he pressed something against the puckered entrance. Slowly he pushed into her and stretched her muscles. Then as she realized he pushed his cock up into her rear, he began to move the object within her sheath. The sensation was almost too much to bear. Arabella tucked her head down and tried to breathe as the sensations coursed through her body in crashing blissful waves.

"You may come, Arabella," he said, huffing with each thrust of his cock.

Colors splayed before her closed eyes despite the blindfold. There was no separation of her body from his. They were joined as one. She bound her soul to his in these moments of ecstasy. The joy overwhelmed her as the first tingles of orgasm began.

She had no control. Her body convulsed with each spasm of her muscles about the object and his cock. Her thoughts scrambled as he came inside her. She screamed in joy as her first orgasm exploded into another. Heated semen filled her rear and he yelled out with every pump of seed.

When her body climbed down from the precipice of sexual wonder, Arabella crumpled onto her stomach, her legs turning to mush. He pulled the object from her sex and she sighed in blissful contentment.

She hadn't the strength to move as he climbed off the bed. In the darkness of her blindfold she heard him move about and then the door opened.

Her thoughts jumbled for order as her mind raced. Why would he leave her after the most intense sexual experience they'd ever shared?

When he returned moments later she heard water splash into a basin.

"Come, turn over," he instructed gently as he helped her move.

Then he placed a warm, wet cloth on her thigh and began to wash her. He stroked her skin in silence and with each pass of the cloth along her skin, even in her fatigued post-climactic state, her awareness of his masculine power hummed through her veins.

Curiosity ate at her. "What was it that you...that object that felt so good?"

He continued stroking her body. "A belaying pin. A smaller-sized one. I always thought it would make a good dildo."

"It did." She smiled at the creative use of a simple piece of the ship—a part of something he loved.

He stopped for a moment. "How do you feel toward me, Arabella?"

"I..." She did not know how to answer. He'd shown her the most earth-shattering pleasure moments before. Did that change things?

When he dipped the cloth across her sex, she moaned. It was erotic without being overtly sexual. She was ready to burst into flames once again.

"Why do you deny me?" he asked softly.

The question sobered her senses a little.

"You insist on shutting me out of your heart." He sounded disappointed.

"I can't...I just can't..." Grief filled her shaking voice.

He left the bed again and she heard him rinse out the cloth. "You are fooling yourself," he finally said.

"No." She tried to sound strong.

"You want me in your bed. You want me to make love to you. Your body screams for mine. You surrender to my kisses, you whimper at my touch."

"I can't let myself…" Her voice faltered.

"What?"

She didn't want to say it. She turned her head from his voice. "I don't want to discuss it."

Strong fingers gripped her face and he ripped off the blindfold. He forced her to look at him. "You will tell me," he demanded, anger growing in his voice.

"I don't want to love you!" she yelled.

He released her face as though he'd been burned. "Afraid to love a pirate? Or is it that you are afraid to love *me*?"

She shook her head, thoughts and emotions colliding in a confused frenzy. He was a pirate. She couldn't love a pirate.

Love. Oh God, no. It couldn't be. The realization hit her and she began to sob. She looked at his face, searching for any sign of tender emotion…but she found none. Anger etched his handsome features and his eyes changed to an icy stare.

"Fredrick?"

He snubbed her entreaty and rose from the bed.

Her mind scrambled to stop him. "My lord Captain?"

He paused, his back facing her. "Yes?" His voice was void of emotion.

"What do you plan to do with me now?"

Watching him move to the door, disappointment and sadness filled her heart.

"Nothing. You are no longer my captive. I will no longer burden you with my presence," he replied flatly. Without a backward glance, he left the cabin.

He had freed her. He did not even slide the lock in place at the door.

Arabella curled her body into a fetal position, hugging her knees to her chest. Tears fell unchecked from her eyes as her heart broke. She hadn't avoided falling in love. It happened despite her denials, and now she felt utterly defeated—and completely trapped. Her heart was bound, utterly in his possession, more securely than any physical restraint. She was still a hostage—a prisoner of unrequited love.

Chapter Nine

ᔕᔑ

The next morning, she awoke alone and sat up in bed. She glanced about her and no trace of the previous night's activities could be seen. No blindfold of scarlet silk. No torn silken bonds. Only her sore body bore evidence of their night together. Her heart ached with renewed pain.

She rose and took care of her toilette and washed with the water and basin left there for her use. Once dressed, she felt a little better. But only a little.

Thinking of the sensations Fredrick had created warmed her. He was a pirate to the world, but in the privacy of his bed, he was a man yearning for love. He awakened her soul to yearn for a love she'd had no notion existed. Her body hummed beneath his touch. She had to blush at the memory of her bound to his bed, writhing with desire as he slipped the belaying pin into her channel. Even when he threatened her with a spanking or the lash, her sex throbbed with need.

But Arabella could not ever admit her love to him. Fredrick was a man with an unstable future. His lifestyle would catch up to him some day. If she openly gave her heart to him, where would she end up once he was caught and tried for his crimes? A lasting relationship beyond this moment in time was impossible.

A knock on the door startled her. Fredrick? Her heart jumped with hopeful anticipation.

"Come in," she said, trying to seem calm.

It was not Fredrick.

Jeremy opened the door and smiled, his blue eyes shining like bright blue jewels against his tanned complexion. His black hair was tied neatly back and his coat of navy blue was neatly pressed. In his hands he carried a tray of fruit, milk and biscuits. "I thought you might be hungry, and then once you've eaten, we can go for a walk on deck."

"Oh...yes, thank you." Confused, she asked, "Where's Fredrick?"

"The captain is otherwise detained from spending time with you this morning. He's asked that I care for your needs."

Once she ate a small dried biscuit and a cup of milk, she was ready to take a walk in the sunshine.

As she stepped up the stairs to the deck, she asked lightly, "Is your best coat something you normally wear, Mr. O'Connell?" She hid her pain behind a forced smile.

He held out his hand to her and smiled. "I wanted to impress you."

She giggled at his easy humor. "I see."

Jeremy walked slowly at her side. "Did I succeed, Miss Prescott?"

"Indeed, Mr. O'Connell. I am very impressed." She giggled again. It was nice to laugh at the man's flirtations.

Then at the bow she saw Fredrick. He stood facing the sea, the wind blowing his blond hair behind him as he gazed out over his domain. He lifted a spyglass to his eye and scanned the horizon. Her breath caught at the simple majesty of his commanding pose. He lowered the glass and gripped a rope, seemingly lost in thought.

"Miss Prescott?" Jeremy said.

"Oh, I'm sorry." She was startled by the vision of Fredrick, the powerful captain on duty, a man with the entire well-being of his ship and crew in the palms of his hands. It was unlike the man she'd known in the privacy of her cabin.

"I asked if you needed anything to make your voyage more comfortable below. As you know, women onboard are not the norm around here. I do hope we make you as comfortable as possible while you endure your situation."

Fredrick turned toward her and their gazes locked. A jolt of awareness shot through her veins. Even at a distance, she recognized the pain within his eyes. In a flash, the responsible captain transformed from the cool leader to a vulnerable man.

Then he turned away, twisting his back to her.

Rejection.

Her heart sank. Pain stabbed her belly.

"Please, Mr. O'Connell, I wish to return below," she said weakly, grasping his arm and heading back to the cabin. "I suddenly find myself not feeling well."

* * * * *

Excitement rang out over the deck of the *Enforcer* as they pulled aboard a man floating upon some wreckage. Half dead from sun exposure, the man mumbled incoherently with fever.

"Who did this to you?" Captain Jacobs demanded of the sick man.

"Pirates," he said. "*Neptune's Sword.*"

"Ah, Thorne." His mind reeled with worry. "Did you see a woman on his ship?"

"A woman? No," the man replied in a slurred voice.

He was weak, but William needed to know more before letting the man rest and recover. "Tell me, what direction did Thorne sail after he attacked your ship?"

"Southeast, sir. Though I cannot be sure."

William waved at the crew to take the man and give him medical attention. He turned to his first mate. "Southeast."

"Aye, Captain. Right to Margarita."

"I wonder if our pirate friend plans to meet us at Margarita after all." William gazed up at the sails. "Add more canvas. I want to catch up with Thorne quickly. This latest outrage will not go unavenged."

"But sir, we're at full sail now."

William faced the man, anger brimming over to rage. "Thorne sank a British vessel. He's kidnapped the governor's daughter, my future wife, and put her in harm's way. I don't care if you have to use handkerchiefs, I want more speed!"

The first mate saluted and mumbled, "Aye, Captain. More speed it is."

William stepped to the railing and smiled. "Once we catch this pirate, he will pay for every crime he's ever committed. I'll peel away his skin and cut off his fingers one by one. And if he soiled my Arabella, I will make sure his cock is the first part to be fed to the gulls."

* * * * *

"Jeremy," Fredrick called when he saw the man return to the deck after escorting Arabella below.

"Aye, Captain," Jeremy called as he strode over to him, still standing at the bow.

The sun rode high in the late morning sky, promising a hot tropical day upon the sea. Fredrick stripped off his coat and laid it over the railing. "I've been giving Miss Prescott some thought."

Jeremy tucked his folded hands behind his back. "As I can imagine."

Fredrick shot him a scowl. "Plot a course for Barbados."

"Sir?" Shock registered on Jeremy's face.

"I mean to take her to the nearest British settlement."

"But sir…I don't understand. What about the ransom?"

"I will not hold her for ransom any longer. I was wrong to take her from her home." Fredrick smirked and added, "It was indeed bad luck to bring her aboard."

"But Fredrick, I don't understand. Why the change in plan?"

Fredrick turned to gaze to the sea. His heart ached painfully. Arabella's words echoed through his memory. *I don't want to love you.* They pierced deeply into his heart with bleeding viciousness. What did he truly expect? He'd taken her virginity, and last night he had bent her to his will utterly. He'd fucked her unlike any other, and somehow, the movement of her hips, the whimper in her voice, the gentle pleading for more ate at his heart. As he came deep within her, Fredrick realized he loved her. He wanted to yell it to the world, but he hesitated. He wanted her to love him in return.

After the explosive climax they'd shared, he'd cared for her, washing away the evidence of their love. He had wanted to tell her what was in his heart. He'd yearned to confess his love, yet he probed her with questions.

Arabella had mentioned a fiancé. She loved him. Killed at sea by pirates. He was a pirate, guilty as the men who actually murdered her love.

"It's time to face the consequences of my actions." Fredrick sighed. He'd thought little of what Governor Prescott's vengeance would entail. He refused to put his ship and crew in danger for his own selfishness. As they approached the day of the ransom exchange, he was sure death lay in store for all of them. "We sail for Barbados. I will take a dingy to shore and escort Miss Prescott to the governor's mansion."

"You'll be captured!" Jeremy stepped forward anxiously, worry clouding his eyes.

"It is better than putting the entire crew at risk of capture in Margarita."

"But Fredrick—"

Enraged, Fredrick pushed at Jeremy. "I said change course to Barbados! Make speed there."

Jeremy straightened, stunned at the shocking behavior of the normally coolheaded captain. "Aye, sir. Speed it is."

Meanwhile several crew members stopped working to stare at Fredrick. He scanned the faces of the men who'd voted him as their captain and guilt wrapped about his heart. He'd displayed weakness to his crew because of a woman. It was unforgivable. As they continued to stare, Fredrick angrily ordered, "Get back to work!" The men scrambled back to their duties.

Fredrick watched Jeremy march across deck and up to the quarterdeck to make his calculations for the new heading. Fredrick almost followed to apologize to his friend, but instead turned back to the sea. In moments, *Neptune's Sword* changed course.

* * * * *

Arabella felt the swell of the ocean beneath her as she lay in the cabin. They were turning. She jumped from the bed and ran to the window. They were indeed changing course. But why?

She bolted out the door and up to the deck. The wind kissed her face and she breathed in the salty freshness as she scanned the deck. There, still at the bow overlooking the sea, stood Fredrick. She stormed across the deck to his side. "What are you doing?"

He slowly turned to her. "I'm taking you to Barbados. From there you can send word to your father."

"But why? I don't understand."

He reached for her face and cupped her cheek. "Because I was wrong to take you."

Tilting her head, she examined his face. He loved her. She knew it in her heart. "Fredrick, I —"

He pulled is hand away and reached into his pocket. "I have something for you." He pulled out a small black bag and handed it to her.

She gingerly opened the bag and poured out the contents into her palm. "Pearls," she gasped in shock.

"A pearl necklace," he said, taking the extraordinarily long strand from her hand and stepping behind her. "I told you I would give you one someday."

She fingered the smooth texture of the pearls he wrapped about her neck. "But I can't possibly take this." She faced him, her eyes searching his face.

"I want you to have them. And when you wear them, may you always remember me and our time together." He once again touched her face. She closed her eyes and inhaled his masculine scent.

He dropped his hand to his side and she snapped open her eyes to watch him back away from her. Her sadness overwhelmed her.

"This is for the best, Arabella. I'm a pirate, and you are a lady. We have no chance of a future together."

"No matter how much...?" Her voice faltered. She couldn't reveal her heart. It would only make the pain worse.

"No matter how much," he repeated dismally, the unspoken words ringing loudly within her mind. *No matter how much we love each other.*

He smiled sadly and turned away. She stood in silence, looking after his retreating figure. Her heart reached for him, urging her to run after him and beg him to love her, but her better reason held her at bay. She could never tell him her heart.

Touching the strand of exquisite pearls wrapped three times about her neck and dipping down past her cleavage, she turned to face the open ocean before her. The vast beauty of the blue-green waves against the blue sky was breathtaking. But it had little impact upon the anguish within her heart.

Then as the ocean winds caressed her face and stroked through the long length of her hair, she whispered, "I love you, Fredrick. Always."

Chapter Ten

ಐ

Days passed slowly onboard *Neptune's Sword* as they sailed to Barbados. Arabella should have been happy, but she was not. Since the day Fredrick had given her the pearl necklace, he'd remained at a distance. She walked the main deck with Jeremy on a daily basis just to see him. He'd watch her with a heated gaze, but then turn away coolly. Her body shivered with need each time before slumping in disappointed rejection.

Each night, Arabella cried into the pillow that smelled of him. She curled into his shirts, hugging the fabric to her skin as his clean ocean scent surrounded her. She pined for her lover, the pirate who stole her heart.

Heartache ate at her, and just when she thought she could no longer bear another moment, Fredrick burst through the cabin door.

"Fredrick!" she cried out, tears of joy in her eyes.

"Get dressed, Arabella." His tone was flat and unemotional.

She scooted to the side of the bed. "What is it?"

"There is a British warship on the horizon. I do not intend to face off with a warship. Not only are we outmanned and outgunned..." He paused then added in a low, tender voice, "I will not risk hurting you by engaging in an attack."

She quickly rose from the bed and scurried to find her dress. "But what are you intending to do?"

He straightened his posture. "I will escort you to the British."

She stopped and faced him. "What? But Fredrick, you'll be arrested on sight."

"Or shot."

"No, Fredrick, you can't. Just put me in a dingy and they will pick me up at sea. Don't risk your life for me."

He raised an eyebrow and his mouth softened. "Why do you care about what I do?"

"Because…" She stammered. Then she reached for him and touched his arm. He quickly covered her hand with his. The heat of his skin seeped into her.

"Why, Arabella?"

She lightly squeezed his hand. "I—"

Boom! In the distance, the ship shot a warning shot, jolting Fredrick to release her hand and step to the door. "Get dressed. Two minutes, you must be ready."

He left the cabin and Arabella shook. She quickly slipped her gown, the gown he'd given her, over her head and put on her slippers. She flung a cloak about her shoulders and as she fastened the frog, Fredrick returned.

He escorted her on deck to the awaiting rowboat. Jeremy stood somber as the boat was lowered into the water. "I do not approve of this, Captain."

"I will not endanger the entire crew for my acts." Then to Arabella, Fredrick said, "Come now, let me help you down." He assisted her into a miniature lift seat and the crew lowered her to the awaiting rowboat. Fredrick climbed down a rope ladder and helped her off the lift and into the boat.

"Captain, what are your orders?" Jeremy called down to him.

"You're captain of *Neptune's Sword* now. I suggest you sail the hell away from here. That warship is bearing down fast."

Fredrick picked up the oars and began to row away from *Neptune's Sword*.

"They are leaving you behind?" she asked.

He chuckled. "Pirate's code, luv."

Over the waves she heard Jeremy shouting orders to make sail and change course. "I can't believe they will just leave you," she said in wonderment.

"They aren't leaving me. I am leaving them."

She sat in silence as Fredrick rowed their little boat closer to the warship now bearing down on them. She looked back at *Neptune's Sword* and marveled at the speed with which it sailed away.

Moments later she was lifted onto the deck of the *Enforcer*, one of the ships commanded by her father. Captain William Jacobs stood on deck, watching with a stern expression upon his handsome face and a ramrod-straight stance. He was the image of a British naval officer with honor and loyalty to the Crown. Not a man to be lenient on pirates.

"Captain Fredrick Thorne," Captain Jacobs mused with a tilt of his mouth. "I had hoped to see you as my prisoner some day, but I did not expect to have you surrender, and so easily."

Fredrick stood straight and towered over the British officer by an inch or two. "Life is full of surprises, Captain."

"Aye, indeed." Jacobs stepped forward to stand toe to toe with Fredrick. "And despite this circumstance, you remain arrogant to the last."

"Call it a character flaw."

"I pray Miss Prescott was not harmed during her stay aboard your ship?" The men stood their ground, two titans measuring each other's strengths and weaknesses.

Fredrick smiled devilishly. "Perhaps you should ask her. After all, I am a pirate. I could lie about it."

Jacobs nodded and slid his gaze to her. She shivered under his scrutiny, never liking the man from the time her father introduced them upon her arrival in Port Monmouth. "I was treated well, Captain Jacobs."

"You appear fit, Miss Prescott, despite your time with the pirates and away from proper society." Jacobs faced Fredrick once again and scowled. "A circumstance that should've never happened."

Fredrick lifted a brow. "It was unfortunate Governor Prescott was not present to accept my invitation to join me aboard my ship."

"Instead you kidnapped his daughter, ruining her reputation."

Arabella felt her face burn with a heated blush. How could he say such a thing as she stood nearby?

"You, Captain, forget the lady is in your presence," Fredrick commented in a tightly controlled voice. She recognized his growing annoyance at Jacobs. She looked up to his face and nodded her silent appreciation for defending her honor.

Captain Jacobs turned to her and reached out a hand to her arm. "Forgive me, Miss Prescott. Sometimes seamen forget the delicacies of young ladies while aboard ship."

"Sounds like a *reasonable* excuse to me," Fredrick quipped.

Jacobs flung about and jabbed Fredrick in the belly with his fist. "Pirate, you insult me for the last time!" Then as he watched Fredrick crumple to the deck, gripping his middle, Jacobs yelled to his crew, "Take him below and clap him in irons. It is past time this pirate pays for his crimes."

Arabella watched in horror as Fredrick was roughly dragged across the deck by several men. She squeaked when they kicked Fredrick in the sides and he curled his body to protect himself from the onslaught of abuse. They laughed louder and Arabella stood in shock, biting the heel of her palm to keep from screaming.

"Come now, Miss Prescott," Captain Jacobs started as he encircled her shoulders with an arm, guiding her away from the spectacle. "I will take you below where you may refresh yourself."

She pulled out of his grasp. "What do you intend to do with Fredrick?" His brow rose at her familiar term and she quickly corrected herself. "I mean, Captain Thorne."

"We will sail for Port Monmouth and he will be tried for his crimes there. I'm sure your father will see to it Thorne pays with his life for kidnapping you." He lifted a finger to her cheek and his touch repulsed her. "Tell me, Miss Prescott—did the pirates take liberties with you?"

She jerked her face away from his touch and her hand flew across his face in a resounding slap. "How dare you! And you say *he* is the pirate!" With that she marched across the deck to where she assumed the captain's cabin was located. But before she climbed down the steps, she turned to the stunned British officer now cradling his face from her attack. She smirked and then said, "Pray I don't mention your behavior to my father, Captain. I do not think he would be pleased in the least."

* * * * *

Fredrick lay in damp straw that faintly smelled of mildew. He adjusted his body to the sounds of his chains clanking. His body rhythmically rocked with the swell of the ship cutting through the waves, closing the distance between him and his execution.

It hurt to move once the crew finally deposited him here. He was sure a few ribs were cracked and one eye was swollen shut. At the corner of his mouth, blood trickled. His teeth had cut the inside of his mouth when they kicked his face. He tried to move his arms, only to send a sharp jolt of pain coursing through his body. His stomach ached from the numerous kicks. For a moment, he doubted if Jacobs would let him live to arrive in Port Monmouth. Then again, perhaps Jacobs hoped his injuries would heal by the time they made port—to be tortured once again.

None of it mattered. Arabella was safe. He'd give his life for her. He'd realized his true feelings that night he bound her to his bed. He loved her, truly *loved* her.

How it had happened, he couldn't determine. But somehow, he wanted much more from Arabella than her physical surrender. He yearned for her love. When she proclaimed that she could never love a pirate, he had been crushed. He'd set about to free her immediately. He couldn't bring himself to keep her a moment longer than needed. No ransom, no pile of gold or chest of treasure, could ever replace her in his heart.

As Fredrick swam between blissful unconsciousness and raw reality, he heard the hatch open and someone climb down the ladder. He wanted to move his head to see who'd come to look upon the once-proud pirate captain.

"Oh God, Fredrick!" a sweet familiar voice caressed his ears as she flung herself down to his side. Gentle fingers probed his injured body. "Fredrick, can you hear me?" Arabella asked.

"Aye, luv," he answered in a croak. "Forgive me if I don't hug your precious body against me. I'm a little sore to move much."

"Brutes," she spat. "They ought to be horsewhipped for this." She nudged him to roll upon his back from his crumpled position.

Daggers of hot steel jabbed every muscle in his body as he straightened. The manacles about his wrists scraped his skin and the chains weighed down his arms. He yelled out in pain and she was there to speak softly to comfort him.

"Do you think anything is broken?" she asked as she unbuttoned his coat.

"My ribs. I think a few are cracked."

"Dear God, your face." She touched his swollen eye and he grabbed her hand. He inhaled sharply at the splitting agony.

"I know you mean well, luv, but do you think it wise to be here with me, caring for a pirate?" He continued to hold her hand.

She brought it to her face and kissed the back. "I don't care what they say."

"Your father might. After all, I kidnapped you, forced you aboard my ship…" Then he added softly, "I seduced you into my bed and stole your virginity. I am the worst sort of pirate, Arabella."

He tried to open his eyes but could only see faint shadows in the darkness. She leaned over him and touched her lips to his. She kissed him gently and his senses reeled.

"I was too weak to resist you, Fredrick."

"You are not weak, luv."

"But I was when you kissed me. I was lost beyond that."

His breath caught. "What are you telling me?" Could he even hope a change in her heart?

She stroked his face and kissed his lips again, tender and soft. Then she drew back and whispered, "I love you, Fredrick."

His mouth went dry and he wondered if this was a mirage brought on by the pain. "Arabella…say you love me again. I must be dreaming."

She giggled yet tears splashed onto his face. "I love you."

It hurt to smile, his split lip ripped open but Fredrick didn't care. He reached his arm around her and pulled her to him. "You've made me a very happy man, luv."

"Do you love me too?" she asked in earnest.

"Aye, luv. My heart belongs to you. I love you more than I even thought possible."

Suddenly a clapping behind her startled them. "So heartwarming. The pirate and the governor's daughter declaring their forbidden love. Too bad this is not some sort of sensational novel. Perhaps you both would have hope for a happy ending."

Arabella pulled away from Fredrick and gasped. "Captain Jacobs."

"Sorry to disturb such a tender moment. I only planned to question the pirate, and here I find a romance in bloom." The captain chuckled like a demon. "I wonder what your father would say, Miss Prescott."

"Leave her alone, Jacobs," Fredrick growled, wishing he had the strength to knock a fist across the man's jaw.

Instead Fredrick was rewarded with a swift kick to his side. Stars blared behind his eyes. The bastard hit a cracked rib.

"Stop it, you beast!" Arabella yelled, flinging her body at the man.

"Tut, tut, Miss Prescott. Don't let your emotions run away with your better sense."

Fredrick glared up in the direction of the man and saw him clutch Arabella in his arms.

"Hmm, perhaps the best way to destroy the pirate is to taint his lover," Jacobs chuckled sadistically. "I could take her right here, Thorne, and you wouldn't be able to stop me," he said. "Yes, I think I like that idea very much."

Arabella struggled against the man as he backed her against the wall, pressing his body into hers.

Blinded by rage, Fredrick gathered his last ounce of strength and rose from the floor. He could see shapes, and that was enough. His body screamed but he ignored the pain. He had to save her.

Fredrick grabbed the captain's shoulder and shoved him off Arabella. The man fell to the floor. "Touch her, Jacobs, and I'll kill you here and now."

"You dare to threaten me, an officer of the Royal Navy?"

Fredrick widened his stance, placing his body in front of Arabella. "Yes, I do," he proudly proclaimed.

Just when Fredrick thought Jacobs would rise and attack, a call from deck sounded. "'Tis the *Royal Raider*! Ahoy, Captain! 'Tis Governor Prescott's ship off the port bow!"

Jacobs scrambled to his feet and closed the distance between them. "This is not over, pirate. I'll see you dead before long." Then with a mighty tug to his chains, Jacobs pulled Fredrick back to the pallet of damp straw. Fredrick fell onto his knees and then crumpled to the floor.

"And you, Miss Prescott, shall see the day when I will be the one to make your heart beat faster with passion." He grasped her arm and pulled her toward the hatchway.

"No! Leave me alone," she cried, fighting the man bravely.

He swung his palm and struck her face.

Fredrick felt the bile rise in his stomach.

"Be nice to me, wench, and I won't inform your daddy about the little scene I witnessed."

She stilled. Fredrick watched as she straightened and thrust out her jaw. "You can't threaten me."

"Indeed I can, Miss Prescott. Remember, your lover is aboard my ship. It would be a shame if he met an accident before reaching Port Monmouth."

Like a knife in my chest, thought Fredrick as they left him behind. He lay in the straw, mildew filling his nostrils, nausea roiling his empty stomach and pain racking his body. He couldn't protect Arabella from the beast Jacobs. Rage shook Fredrick as he cursed his body's weakness.

Jacobs and Governor Prescott would make sure he suffered to the maximum extent. There would be no mercy. No kindness. No reprieve. He wanted to die. He moved and the daggers of torment ripped into his flesh. Perhaps death was the only way for the pain to end.

But then her words echoed in his brain. *"I love you, Fredrick."*

His heart swelled with happiness. She loved him! She risked everything to come to him. Her bravery and tender words renewed his strength and motivation to carry on. Perhaps there was indeed something to live for, to fight for.

If he could escape this bloody situation alive.

Chapter Eleven

℘

Arabella watched the *Royal Raider* pull alongside the *Enforcer* and her stomach sank. Captain Jacobs stood at her side, his presence ever-threatening. She peered at him out the corner of her eye, and shivered at the memory of his mouth grazing her face. She'd never liked him, unable to label the reason why. Within her heart, she knew his character was merciless and cruel, and now she'd witnessed his savagery firsthand.

"Your father will be happy to see you are well, Miss Prescott," he said, never taking his eyes from the men working with the ropes, securing the vessels.

"Indeed."

He turned his face and she was struck by the cruel lines about his eyes and mouth, deep indications of his true nature. His blue eyes were cold and his mouth curled in a devilish smirk. "I wonder how he will punish your pirate lover. Will it be a quick thrust of a dagger to the gut? Or something more prolonged in suffering, like the hangman's noose."

"Don't bait me, Captain Jacobs. I know what you are trying to do." She looked away from his icy gaze.

He chuckled. "You are ruined by the pirate for any decent man to have as a wife, yet I find the idea quite appetizing."

She gasped and faced him in horror. "What do you mean?"

He turned to her and placed his hands upon her shoulders. "I asked your father for permission to marry you."

"He'd never agree!" She backed away out of his light grasp.

"He jumped at the prospect. Think about it. You have lain with a pirate. Even now, you may carry his bastard child."

"And you mean to save me from bearing a child out of wedlock." She sarcastically added, "How noble."

He stepped closer and shook his head. "No, my dear. You misunderstand."

She cocked her head. What was this blackguard up to?

"If you discover you are with child, I will see to it that an accident ends the situation."

Her mouth dropped open. "You *bastard*. How could you?"

"It would be for your own good. Do you want your father to know you are no longer pure? I am offering you a way out. Imagine the disappointment…the sorrow…the heartbreak."

She hadn't wanted to tell her father of the affair with Fredrick. She loved her father, and she loved Fredrick. She couldn't betray one man for the other. "I won't do it, Captain Jacobs."

"Don't decide now. Wait. Greet your father. Think about my offer of marriage. I assure you, it is the best offer you will ever have. I am not without wealth and connections. My time in the Navy has served me well."

"I will not consider your offer. Do not linger for me to change my mind."

"We'll see."

The boarding plank was set in place and her father crossed onto the *Enforcer*. Her heart sank as she looked upon him for the first time in six months. He'd been gone to sea several months before her abduction, and many changes had occurred to his appearance. His face was tanner, more deeply lined with wrinkles, and his frame was much thinner than she remembered. Despite his fashionable clothes and wig, Governor Charles Prescott did not appear to be a well man.

"Arabella!" He called to her and she gladly met him after he set foot on deck.

"Father! I am so glad to see you!" She welcomed his embrace but was shocked at his weakened stature.

He set her at arm's length. "Please, tell me. Are you well? Did the pirate harm you in any way? I couldn't bear it if you were hurt, my precious daughter."

She choked down a tear and forced a smile. "I am well. Put your mind at ease. I am well."

He sighed relief and hugged her again. Her heart broke for worrying him so terribly.

"Good afternoon, Governor Prescott. You'll be happy to know the culprit of your daughter's abduction is below—in chains." Captain Jacobs announced from behind her.

Her father released her and greeted Jacobs. "Good work, Captain. I shall write to the king of your capture of the rogue. One less pirate scoundrel in the Caribbean. Well done, well done indeed."

"Thank you, sir. The man surrendered to us without a fight in delivering Miss Prescott to our ship. I believe we frightened the pirates. Their ship turned and ran at the sight of our sails."

Arabella sniffed at the idea of the crew of *Neptune's Sword* being frightened by any ship in these waters. Her contempt was not unnoticed by her father—or Jacobs. She lowered her head and wiped her face with her gloved hand as though crying.

The ruse worked and the men turned away from her.

"I want Thorne to be taken to Port Monmouth for trial," her father announced. "There he will face the fate of piracy."

"Will you hang his tarred, dead body in the harbor as a warning to the fate of pirates?"

Arabella raised her head and glared at the smiling Captain Jacobs. The horrid image of Fredrick dead and put on display turned her stomach. Her eyes darted from Jacobs to her father.

"The idea has merit, indeed," he commented while scratching his chin. He seemed to consider the prospect!

"Father, come and dine with me now. No more talk of the fate of the pirate captain. This discussion is hardly fit for my ears." The part of the delicate female seemed to put an end to the discussion.

Her father nodded and took her arm. "Indeed. Arabella is right." He looked up at Jacobs. "Transport the prisoner to Port Monmouth and there we will discuss his fate. Tether the ships together tonight. We shall set sail to St. Crescentia Island in the morning."

As she began to walk with her father to board the *Royal Raider*, Captain Jacobs called out to her. "Arabella." She paused at his use of her given name, and he stepped to her side. He took her free hand and brought it to his lips. "My offer stands," he whispered low for only her to hear.

He released her hand and a clammy sensation wrapped about her body.

"Come, dear Arabella. I missed you so. I wanted to destroy that pirate for taking you."

"Yes, Father."

As she walked across the plank to her father's ship, Arabella thought of what Captain Jacobs had said. *"I am offering you a way out."* She clutched the bony hand of her father and was humbled by his endurance to hunt for her through the Caribbean in his condition. She loved him dearly, but she also loved Fredrick.

She was torn by love for two men—two men who were sworn enemies.

That evening Arabella sat at a grand table aboard the *Royal Raider* after dining upon an elaborate feast of broiled fish, boiled potatoes and assorted fruits. Her father sat next to her and picked at his plate, nibbling at the delicious foods set out on fine bone china. He was not well, and she'd resisted broaching the subject of his health for most of the evening.

"I'm dying, Arabella," he finally blurted. "I went to see a doctor in Barbados, one known about the Caribbean for being the best in treating all sorts of ailments."

"And?" she asked, setting down her spoon next to her tea cup. The silver clanked against the saucer sharply.

"I have consumption."

Her eyes widened in horror. "Consumption," she repeated softly.

"I have trouble sleeping at night, waking up drenched in my own sweat. I can't seem to tolerate food anymore. It hurts to breathe at times. I have days when I am taken with a fever and unable to rise from my bed."

"Why didn't you return to Port Monmouth and tell me? You needed to be home and taken care of."

"Because I did not want to be cared for. I only felt the symptoms on occasion. But I admit the past month has been difficult."

She moved to his side and took his hand in hers. It seemed so frail and weak compared to hers. Tears burned her eyes. "Father, what would I ever do without you?"

He patted her hand. "You will go on. I think you should marry and perhaps return to England. It is too dangerous here for you alone."

Alone.

Her father was dying from illness. Fredrick would be hanged for his crimes.

"My dear, are you well? I worry..." His voice trailed off. He heaved a ragged sigh then asked, "I hesitate to ask you. But...what happened aboard Thorne's ship?"

She met his sad gaze and her heart wept. She couldn't hurt him, not when he was so fragile. "I was treated well." Her tone was hesitant.

"Did he…touch you?"

Gathering strength to comfort him, she smiled and shook her head. "No, Father."

His brow rose over his gray eyes. "No?"

"No."

He stared at her in silence.

"What was Captain Jacobs so secretive about?"

"He…oh…well…" She stumbled to find the right words. She certainly couldn't tell her father she'd been threatened with blackmail. "Nothing. Captain Jacobs seems to have taken a fancy to me. That's all."

He smiled. "That warms my heart. Captain Jacobs is a fine man and an excellent soldier." He patted her hand and a glimmer of joy reflected in his eyes. "He asked for permission to marry you, and I granted it wholeheartedly."

Inside she screamed in horror. She forced a smile.

"Will you accept his proposal, Arabella?"

Gazing into the frail man's eyes, her heart sank. "Yes, Father. If that will make you happy."

"Blessed be, I must speak with him at once." He stood weakly from the table and reached for a nearby cane. "To see you well wed is one dream I shall not miss before I die."

As he marched out of the cabin, Arabella was left alone. Tears burst from her and she sobbed not for the coming match with the evil Jacobs but for the man chained in the hold of the *Enforcer*. If only there was something she could do to change the wheel of fate…

Escape.

Fredrick must escape. And she would help him do it.

* * * * *

Fredrick heard the hatchway open and footsteps descend. He lifted his head from the straw and squinted his eyes. He could make out two shapes in the faint light of the lantern they carried.

"Here is the scourge of the Caribbean, Captain Fredrick Thorne," Jacobs announced mockingly.

"Dear God, what happened to him?" the other man asked.

Jacobs chuckled. "My men had a little fight with the mighty captain in getting him down here."

Fredrick chose to be silent, unwilling to bring upon himself more punishment. His body ached and throbbed already.

The other man crouched by Fredrick's head. "My daughter says you treated her well. That you did not touch her." He sounded unconvinced. "I ask you, pirate. Did you spoil my little girl?"

So it was Governor Prescott. Fredrick remained silent.

"You were asked a question, pirate." Jacobs moved closer then kicked Fredrick in the shoulder. Renewed pain shot through his body and Fredrick moaned in agony.

"Wish for me to kick you again?" Jacobs asked with a growl.

"Why ask me? Why trust the word of a pirate?" Fredrick finally asked in a strained voice.

"Because we want to know if I should wed her now rather than waiting to reach Port Monmouth."

Fredrick stilled and forced his lungs to fill with air. He slowly released his breath and asked, "You will marry Arabella?"

"'Tis no concern of yours, pirate!" Jacobs yelled. "Just answer our question. Did you touch Miss Prescott?"

Fredrick's mind raced. What would they do to her if he told the truth? Would they put her through an exam to make sure? She'd lied already, denying their involvement. Surely, if he revealed the truth, Arabella would be swept into a marriage with that ass Jacobs. If he lied, he would give her time to return to Port Monmouth. Then what?

Escape. Arabella had to escape. But how?

"Answer!" Jacobs demanded.

Fredrick sighed heavily. "I did not."

Governor Prescott released his held breath. "Good." He straightened and moved to the hatchway. "You will be taken to Port Monmouth for trial. I assure you, the fate for piracy is hanging."

"And in Port Monmouth, I shall take the lovely Miss Prescott as my bride," Jacobs added.

Fredrick heard footsteps ascend the ladder, but Jacobs lingered behind.

Then in a low voice, Jacobs said, "'Tis a pity I can't have her sooner. I know you touched her, you lying bastard. But when I do, I will make sure it is my name she cries out in ecstasy as I fuck her every night. Perhaps I should thank you for breaking her in. She was too innocent before. I can see she has bloomed into her sexuality. I will wholeheartedly enjoy taking what was yours and making it mine." Jacobs moved to kick him in the middle.

Fredrick anticipated the man's cruel act and caught his ankle. Knocking Jacobs to the floor, Fredrick slugged the man in the face. Jacobs pushed him off and scurried to his feet and out of reach.

"Son of a bitch," Jacobs spat as he held a hand to his aching jaw.

"At your service," chuckled Fredrick as he watched the man leave with the lantern, plunging the hold into darkness once again. His hand stung from hitting Jacobs, but some pain was worth the price.

Chapter Twelve

ക

Arabella paced her bedchamber in Port Monmouth, trying to think of a way to stop Fredrick's hanging. His trial was set for the morrow. So sure of Fredrick's sentence, the gallows were built in the village square. Fredrick's trial and sentence would prove to be swift and merciless. They had waited several days for her father's condition to improve before proceeding. With pressure from Captain Jacobs, there would be no more delays. His execution would be a spectacle for the entire village to witness and an example of the penalty for those practicing piracy.

There had to be a way to enter the prison undetected and break Fredrick out. If she had managed to delay her nuptials to Captain Jacobs, then she was sly enough to help Fredrick escape before the trial in the morning.

When the fleet had returned to Port Monmouth ten days ago, Arabella asked to see Fredrick but her father and Captain Jacobs refused. She then pleaded a headache and took to her room. Luckily, her monthly chose that moment to start, giving her the perfect excuse to remain in her room—away from Captain Jacobs. She was a little relieved she was not pregnant. She would've loved to carry Fredrick's child, but Jacobs would make sure it would never survive. She shuddered to think of Jacobs' evil cruelty.

He called for her each day, but she denied him entry. Her father pleaded with her to allow her fiancé to sit at her bedside, but she refused. Again, the demure female act helped her get her way. However, she was sure Jacobs would not be so easily fooled.

Back and forth across her rug, she tried to brainstorm ideas. If she didn't do something, Fredrick would die. She'd address the upcoming marriage to Jacobs later. Helping Fredrick escape came first.

Darkness had fallen over the island as night approached. The last sunset Fredrick had to live. Tears burned her eyes.

A knock at the door startled her. "Come in."

Betsy strode in with Arabella's nightshift flung over her arm. "Ready to dress for bed, milady?"

"No." Arabella padded over to the balcony and pushed back the curtain. The night was black as pitch, not even the moonlight danced across the inlet where once stood *Neptune's Sword*. It seemed eons ago when she had so rashly decided to try to escape and Fredrick saved her from becoming food for the sharks.

"Is it the outlaw, milady?" Betsy asked as she moved about the room.

"Yes. I can't help but…" Arabella turned to Betsy. "I can't help but love him."

Worry etched the black woman's face. "I was afraid something like this would happen."

"He's not a bad man, Betsy. I know him. He lives the life of a pirate, but inside beats the heart of a gentleman."

"How can you say that? He kidnapped you, carried you over his shoulder onto his ship. He's a pirate through and through."

"I think when he finally realized he loved me, he set me free. That's why he surrendered to Captain Jacobs. He didn't want to harm me."

The woman sniffed in contempt. "Captain Jacobs is a pirate in disguise." She paused then added, "I was surprised to hear of your engagement to him."

Arabella strode back to the bed and sat upon the soft mattress. "I did it to make my father happy." She sighed heavily and glanced up at Betsy. "He's so sick and frail. I couldn't hurt him by telling him my secret."

"That the pirate about to hang stole more than your purity?"

Arabella gasped. "How did you know?"

The woman chuckled and began to turn back the bedcovers. "Because I saw the look in his eyes that day he took you away. I've seen that same look many times before from my own man."

"Father would be disappointed if he knew." Arabella stood and let Betsy undress her for the night. "I don't think he could take the truth."

Betsy unlaced the bodice and pulled the gown over Arabella's head. "I think the governor suspects already."

Arabella twisted about. "What do you mean?"

Betsy turned away and laid the gown upon the back of a chair. "He asked if you had your monthly. Actually, Captain Jacobs asked and your father sat nearby at his desk."

"What? When did this happen?"

"Yesterday. They called me to the governor's study and asked me of your health. I told 'em that you was in bed with pain in your head and you could hardly eat. That's when they asked about your monthly."

They asked about her monthly suspecting she'd lied. The betrayal hurt her. Jacobs surely surmised the truth and told her father. She couldn't even turn to him for comfort.

Betsy slipped the nightshift over Arabella's head and helped her into bed. It was nice to have Betsy with her again, but Arabella missed the intimacy of the ship—and Fredrick in her bed. After tomorrow, he would be gone from her life forever. Tears slowly ran down her face. Her love would be put to death, and she would remain behind to pine in heartache.

She laid her head back into the downy pillow and let the tears fall. "I feel alone."

Betsy placed a comforting hand on her forearm. "Don't lose hope. Maybe a miracle will happen."

"No, it's hopeless. Nothing can save Fredrick."

BOOM!

A scream outside in the distance caught her ears. Then a loud crash shook the house.

Betsy and Arabella exchanged startled glances and then they raced to the window and threw back the curtain to see a flash of cannon fire from a ship in the inlet.

An attack.

"Pirates?" Arabella whispered in hopes it was Jeremy with *Neptune's Sword* come to help Fredrick escape.

"I don't know." The ship was joined by two others in firing upon the town. A flare of return fire flashed from the ships in the harbor, the *Enforcer* and the *Royal Raider*, and the fort.

Just then Arabella's father burst into the room. "Go! Take my daughter away from here into the sugar fields. Hide her!"

"But Governor, the cellar—"

"Go! Not the cellar. You were found before. I will not have my daughter captured again, and this time by the Spanish."

"The Spanish?" Arabella asked in astonishment.

He grabbed her arm and began pulling her toward the door. "Come now. I will give myself up to them to delay any notion to search for you."

Arabella tugged her arm from his weak grip. "But why is the Spanish attacking?"

He stopped and faced her. "They call this the Spanish Main and have right to claim every island in the Caribbean. Even if we are not *officially* at war, Spain is at war with the world."

She gasped. Another round of cannon fire rained upon the village.

"Now go!" he yelled.

Betsy and Arabella wrapped themselves in cloaks and ran out into the darkness with several other house servants. They ran toward the sugar cane fields to conceal themselves until the Spanish departed.

Arabella ran behind Betsy who seemed to know where to go. Then out of nowhere, someone grabbed her from the side, pulling her off her feet. She struggled until she heard a familiar voice exclaim, "Stop, Miss Prescott. It's me, Jeremy."

She stilled. "Jeremy?" Then she saw his face and he smiled. "Jeremy!" She couldn't contain her joy and hugged the man covered with soot and dirt.

"We haven't much time," he said, pulling away from her embrace.

"The Spanish. They're attacking."

"Aye. I know. We saw them sail in."

"You knew?"

"Not until a few hours ago."

"But—"

He shook her lightly. "I'm sorry I couldn't give you warning, but we needed this diversion to help Fredrick."

"Can you get him away from Port Monmouth?"

"Aye, that's the idea. Come with me," he said.

"Where are we going?"

"We are going to blast our way into the prison and get Fredrick out. *Neptune's Sword* awaits us off a northern beach."

"And when the smoke clears, they will think it was a Spanish cannon that destroyed the prison walls."

"Smart girl," he chuckled.

"But where are your men?"

"I left them to watch for an opportune moment. I wanted to come and make sure you were safe. I may be a pirate without a country, but I was born British, and I have no love for the Spanish."

They ran in the night into the streets of Port Monmouth. Men and women dashed with carts and wagons filled with possessions, racing from the city to hide. Children cried and women screamed as cannon fire exploded nearby, walls and buildings toppling into rubble.

At the prison, she instantly recognized several of the crew.

"Doc Bruce!"

"Ah, lass, good to see ye!" he called to her.

Jeremy laughed at the Scot holding a tankard of ale in one hand. "Had time to stop for a mug full, I see."

"Aye, couldn't let a night like this go by without a bit of celebrating."

"Let's save the celebrating until after Fredrick is free." He turned to her and said, "Miss Prescott, stay here with Doc Bruce. We'll be only a moment or two." The men about them laughed loudly. Drawing his sword, Jeremy yelled to the men. "Ready, lads?"

They all answered in a resounding "Aye!"

"Light it!" he called and one man used a lantern to light an explosive. He tossed it at the prison and in an instant the crash of the explosion shook the walls, breaking a hole in the side.

"Give 'em hell, lads!" Jeremy led a charge toward the prison guards, cutting the men down without hesitation.

Arabella watched in horror as Doc Bruce held her back out of harm's way. "Come, lass. I'm to take ye to the rendezvous point." He took a large gulp of his ale and then smashed the tankard to the ground.

He tugged on her arm and she followed blindly.

"The Spanish seem to have stopped firing. Means they are gettin' ready to come ashore. We want to be gone before then."

She wanted to turn about and run back to the prison and to Fredrick. She was denied her request to visit him, and she yearned to hold him, to find a few moments of comfort in a life that had spun out of control.

After what seemed like hours, Arabella and Doc Bruce walked along a beach where she recognized *Neptune's Sword* offshore.

"What now?" she asked, sinking to the soft sand.

"We wait for the crew to return." He sat next to her with a harrumph. He reached into his coat and pulled out a small flask. Flipping the cap, he said, "I don't suspect we will have long to wait. Fredrick won't want to linger long near the gallows. That rope almost had his name on it."

She said nothing, unable to get past the fear pumping in her veins. Did Fredrick survive the explosion? Would he be struck down as he fought his way through the guards?

Did he know of her engagement to Captain Jacobs?

Minutes passed and she worried, her hands wringing the fabric of her nightshift into a ball on her lap.

"Ah, there they come." Bruce pointed to the edge of the trees as he struggled to rise onto his unsteady legs.

She stood and scanned the men walking toward them. For a split second, her heart paused when she couldn't spot Fredrick. Then she saw him. Raising her hands to her face, tears spilled from her eyes. She blinked, but her vision blurred. She wiped away her tears and began to run toward him. "Fredrick!"

The group of men parted for her to pass as she lunged into Fredrick's arms. The wounds on his face from the beating he'd received onboard the *Enforcer* had almost healed, yet he moved with calculated care. His clothes were tattered and torn and in his hand he held a sword covered in blood. His hair was unkempt and across his cheek bled a new cut that oozed.

"Fredrick, I thought I'd lost you." She wept as he held her to him.

He chuckled and then kissed the top of her head. "You can't keep a pirate worth his salt locked up for long."

* * * * *

"Come with us," he pleaded with her as he held her hand.

Most of his men had returned to the ship and a second boat awaited Fredrick, but Arabella refused to leave. They stood on the beach, hand in hand.

"I can't go with you. Believe me. I want nothing more than to be with you."

"You can," he said.

She shook her head. "No. Not when my father is so ill. If I left him, it would kill him."

"If you stay, will you marry that braggart, Jacobs?"

Sighing, she let her hand drop from his grasp. "I have little choice."

He reached for her and shook her shoulders. "No, you *do* have a choice. Come with me, live with me on *Neptune's Sword*. I will show you the world. We are off to the Indian Ocean, a new hunting ground, a new beginning. It could be our new beginning together too. I want to explore the world with you at my side. There's so much to see and experience, and I want you there with me."

"I cannot go with you."

He released her, disappointment sagging his shoulders. "I offer you everything I have, Arabella. And yet, you still deny me."

"No, I don't deny my love. I do love you, Fredrick. More than I ever thought possible. But I also love my father. I have a responsibility to see him live out his final days with me by his side. Would you deny a man the presence of his beloved daughter, the only family he has left, to hold his hand as he lay dying?"

He gazed down at her with sadness in his eyes. He touched her face with his fingertips. "I ought to carry you over my shoulder kicking and screaming in protest."

"But you won't."

Her chest tightened at his nod in agreement. "You will be with me no matter where on earth I may go." He lifted a hand to touch her face. He stroked her cheek and said, "No other woman will fill my heart like my sweet Arabella."

"I love you." Tears began to stream down her face.

He brushed away the wetness with his thumb. "No tears, luv. I don't wish to carry with me the vision of you crying." He fingered the pearls at her neck and smiled. "Too bad we didn't have more time to explore those pearls more fully." She cocked a brow and he smiled devilishly. "I know a thing or two about pearls—and their secret uses."

She wrapped her arms about his neck and smiled through her sorrow. "Perhaps you will come back someday and show me."

"Aye, that sounds like a good plan to me."

Then he dipped his head and kissed her. Her tongue swiped along his and she moaned into his mouth. His lips were warm and welcoming as they molded to hers in a sensual dance. He tightened his hold about her waist and brought her closer. He deepened his kiss, delving into her mouth. He was hungry, and she was the tempting delight that could satisfy. She answered his rising passion with a sigh as he broke their kisses to nuzzle her neck.

"I love you, Arabella," he whispered against her skin.

"Fredrick…" Her knees weakened as he assaulted her senses with his skillful lips, tantalizing the sensitive flesh behind her ear. Shivers ran down her spine and goose bumps rose along her arms.

"Captain! Ahoy!" one of the men called.

Fredrick turned toward the man who pointed to the British warship in the distance making a turn about the island. "Looks like Captain Jacobs figured out our plan." Most of the ship was hidden by the island rocks jutting out into the ocean, but the large mast and sails were unmistakable.

She gasped. "Go, Fredrick, before it's too late." She pushed at his shoulder. "Go, please. Now."

He faced her and quickly kissed her lips. "Until we meet again, luv. Don't marry that ass."

"I won't."

"Promise me."

"Go now," she said pushing at him.

He resisted moving. "Promise me, Arabella," he insisted.

"I promise! I promise!" She was frantic for his escape. "Now go!"

He kissed her again and then turned for the dingy. He pushed the small boat into the water before climbing inside.

She stood alone on the beach watching Fredrick row out to his waiting ship as the *Enforcer* turned to attack. The chase was on as Fredrick climbed aboard *Neptune's Sword* and made sail. The *Enforcer* opened fire upon the pirates, only for the shots to drop into the sea. The pirates were out of range and increasing in speed every second.

"Goodbye, Fredrick," she whispered as she saw his ship sail toward the horizon with the *Enforcer* in pursuit.

Chapter Thirteen

ഗ

"I want Captain Thorne dead! By God, I want *Neptune's Sword* at the bottom of the ocean!" yelled William in a tirade as the *Enforcer* circled about the island, spotting Thorne's ship.

Making ready the ship was hard considering the damage the Spanish inflicted. Luckily, the tides turned in the battle once they manned their posts and returned fire. The Spanish lost one of their crafts and the other two ships were crippled and their crews captured. It was a victory for him, but at the news of the pirate's escape, he immediately made ready to sail. He knew the pirates were close.

"Captain, there is someone on the beach there," called the first mate, handing William the glass.

"Arabella." His immediate reaction was rage, but then why didn't she leave with Thorne? "Interesting."

He turned and gazed across the waters to *Neptune's Sword*. They hoisted sail and the chase was on. So close…so close. Fredrick slipped from the hangman's rope, but he would not be so lucky for long. "If I had my way, that bastard would have died days ago. Trial…he needed no trial. Thorne is as guilty as hell." He faced his first mate and ordered to make all speed. "I will not let him get away!"

* * * * *

Fredrick shouted orders to his crew. "We must make all possible speed. Lighten our load. Throw overboard whatever we don't need."

"Sir, the cargo?" Jeremy asked, yelling from the hatchway to the hull.

"I said *everything*. We encounter Jacobs, none of us may live after today."

They dumped barrels of spices and crates of sugar over the side. When Fredrick spotted a crewman passing with a crate of firearms, he grabbed the man's arm. "Not those. We will need those before this day is through."

Despite their attempts, the increased speed did not help them outrun the *Enforcer*. "Damn it," Fredrick whispered.

Jeremy ran to his side, grime and dirt sticking to his sweat-drenched skin. "He's gaining on us. I don't understand how."

"Because he wants us dead and will stop at nothing to get what he wants." Fredrick faced his friend. "You shouldn't have come after me."

"The crew decided upon it. They all voted to go after you."

Fredrick scanned the men now gathering about, looking to him to lead them out of the hornet's nest. These men who stood at his side through many battles had risked their lives to save him. "I couldn't ask for a more loyal crew. Thank you, lads. Thank you. But I'm afraid that decision may have condemned us. Captain Jacobs is determined to see us all dead—especially me."

"We'll outrun 'em," called one man.

"No ship can match the *Sword*!" another yelled.

"And no captain can match wits with Captain Throne!"

A cry of rowdy agreement rang out on deck in a boisterous chorus of support.

Fredrick glanced at Jeremy. "Outrun them," he said softly. "No! By God, we won't run anymore."

"Sir?" Jeremy asked, enthusiasm etching his face.

"I say we give Jacobs what he wants. Turn about. We'll cut him down with a frontal attack. We'll board the *Enforcer* and take her!"

Within moments, the ship had sharply turned about and headed to encounter the *Enforcer*.

"Load the cannons!" he called out to his men. "Cripple them! Bring down the masts! Show them that we are not just thieves — we are skilled seamen and efficient marksmen! We will not go down without a fight!"

The men on deck loaded the cannons and when Fredrick ordered to fire, both ships exploded in cannon fire. Fredrick strode up and down the deck where men loaded the cannon and shot at the *Enforcer* at will.

"Head into her!" he cried to Jeremy at the helm.

Fredrick grasped his sword, drawing strength from the cool metal. Either he would die, or Jacobs. There was no escaping. Rage stoked within him at the thought of Jacobs touching Arabella, striking her into submission, threatening her with promises of painful humiliation. Clutching the sword, he swore to kill Captain William Jacobs.

Within moments the ships collided in a crash of splintering wood and heart-wrenching power. Fredrick held on to a rigging rope to stay on his feet, a disadvantage when the British crew began to board. He righted himself as the men poured aboard over the railing, cutlasses swinging and flintlocks firing. The men Fredrick cut down were of little importance. Only one man mattered. Jacobs.

Then Fredrick spotted the man's black hair and fine blue uniform with gold buttons. The men paused and glared at each other then returned to their fight. Fredrick grabbed a rope and swung over to the captain. Landing, he faced Jacobs.

"This has been long in coming," growled Jacobs.

"I'm sure you have dreamt of the day you died many times."

"I'll not be the one dying this day, Thorne." Jacobs thrust his sword, but Fredrick anticipated the rash move and parried the strike.

Flashing metal, strike and thrust, parry and deflect, the two enemies dueled to the death. Neither intended to surrender. Only skill and speed would see each man through.

Fredrick slashed at Jacobs, striking his face. Blood oozed from the wound, but it only enraged Jacobs further. He attacked with a vicious brutality, and Fredrick answered each thrust of his sword with a perfect deflection.

"When you die, she will be mine," Jacobs said in a hysterical voice.

"She'll *never* be yours." Fredrick awaited the next advance.

"Tell me, did she whimper like a whore when she was beneath you? She did with me. Doesn't seem to matter who she rides now — thanks to you. She just wants to get fucked."

"You lie!"

"And the calls of pleasure when she comes..." Jacobs sharply inhaled and smiled wickedly. "Like music of an angel. I'll enjoy hearing her scream every night after we are married."

Anger overtook Fredrick and he attacked the man. Jacobs had hoped for the opening and dug the tip of his sword through Fredrick's right shoulder. Fredrick fell to the deck onto his knees as Jacobs pulled his sword from the wound.

"I will kill you now, pirate. I will drag your carcass back to Port Monmouth and have it dipped in tar and hung at the end of the docks as a warning to those who consider piracy in the Caribbean." Jacobs stabbed Fredrick's left shoulder with his sword. "Not so proud and strong, are you? I wonder how Arabella will react to seeing your body on display. Perhaps her stomach will turn at the sight of your blackened flesh rotting a little more each day."

"Do you make it a habit to talk your enemies to death?" Fredrick asked as he eased his hand to his boot.

"I find that this day will prove to be the greatest of my life. I want to enjoy it."

In a flash Fredrick pulled the dagger from his boot and flung it into Jacobs' chest. "It *is* the greatest day of your life—the day you died at the hands of a pirate."

Jacobs fell to the deck and his breath gurgled as blood bubbled from his mouth. His eyes wide in fear as he gasped for breath, he clutched at the knife and then fell over dead into a growing pool of blood.

It was then Fredrick realized the fighting about him had stopped. Both crews stood in shock at the fallen figure of the British officer bleeding out his very life. Yet none moved to help.

Jeremy stepped to Fredrick's side and helped him rise.

"What do we do with the *Enforcer* and the crew?" Jeremy asked as he assisted Fredrick.

"See if any of the crew wants to join us. Set ashore the ones who don't and sink the *Enforcer*."

"Sink her, sir?"

"Aye," Fredrick breathed weakly. "Sink her." Then unable to stand any longer, he collapsed against Jeremy.

Darkness crept about him, engulfing his senses into a painless void.

* * * * *

Six months later

Arabella stood near her friend's family, watching the couples dance at the latest ball during the winter season in London. She had returned home weeks before and had taken residence in her father's former London townhouse. She reentered London society as a widow, introducing herself as Mrs. Thorndike.

So much had happened in her time in the Caribbean. She'd lost Nicholas, her father and Fredrick. Not since the day of Fredrick's escape had she heard any news of his whereabouts—if he was even alive.

When the men from the sunken *Enforcer* had come ashore with the news of Captain Jacobs' death and Fredrick's collapse, she'd been racked with worry. The men reported Fredrick had been wounded in a duel with Jacobs, and many surmised his imminent death. She refused to believe Fredrick was dead. However, why hadn't he returned to Port Monmouth for her?

Her father was incensed by the loss of not only Captain Jacobs but the *Enforcer* as well. The fact the notorious Captain Thorne had escaped did not help the matter. He'd sent the *Royal Raider* out on the hunt but returned only days later due to his ill health.

For the next three months Arabella had sat at his bedside, nursing him to the best of her ability. It was difficult to watch her father deteriorate before her eyes. All the while, her heart yearned to learn any scrap of news of Fredrick. As much as she believed he was alive somewhere, no news, not even of attacks at sea, were ever reported. It was as though *Neptune's Sword*, and all aboard her, had disappeared.

She hoped the lack of any news was due to his plan to sail to the Indian Ocean. However, she wished for more than speculation.

As the weeks passed, her father grew weaker, each breath labored and crackled. It took all his strength to just fill his lungs with air. Toward the end, he'd refused to even take the broth she offered, too weak to eat or drink.

When he took his last breath and drifted into the silent peace, Arabella had sighed in relief. At last he felt no pain. His suffering had finally ended.

With her father's death, Arabella was forced to make a choice. Should she stay in Port Monmouth or return home to London? What was left for her in the Caribbean? All those she'd loved were gone. Even if Fredrick lived, he'd not returned to Port Monmouth. Her heart ached to know of his fate, and if she had remained there, she'd never move beyond mourning for the loss of her love. Better to live in London with the many diversions of society—the theater, operas, evening parties and balls—than to stay in Port Monmouth surrounded by memories and pain.

A sad smile played at her lips. She'd begun a new life in London, but forever in her heart will live the memory of her lost love—her pirate lover.

"Excuse me, Mrs. Thorndike." Lady Cassandra Mitchell, the young wife of Lord Fitzwilliam Mitchell, leaned to Arabella's ear and whispered, "I must say, I admire your string of pearls."

Arabella's hand touched the polished surface of the pearls Fredrick had given her. She wore them always. "Thank you, your ladyship."

"May I ask where you acquired them?"

"My husband. He gave them to me during our brief time together in the Caribbean."

"I heard he was lost at sea. I am so sorry to hear of your loss," Lady Mitchell said as she placed a hand on Arabella's. "It must have been horrid, especially when your father was dying."

"Thank you. I stayed with my father until he died. It was indeed hard. After losing him and my husband, I couldn't remain in Port Monmouth."

"Please, allow me to introduce you to some of my friends, Mrs. Thorndike." Lady Mitchell led Arabella by the elbow to a group of ladies ranging in ages. "I wish to introduce you all to Mrs. Thorndike. She's just returned from Port Monmouth. She's the daughter of the former governor there, Governor Charles Prescott."

Three of the ladies of comparable age greeted her coolly.

"How do you do, Mrs. Thorndike," said one lady whom Arabella presumed to be in her fifties. "I am Lady Russell. Would you be related to the Thorndike family?"

Arabella raised an eyebrow. "I have never actually met any of my husband's family." Her heart began to hammer in her chest. Could Fredrick's brother and sisters still be alive? She had dismissed the possibility when taking his name, parading as a widow. No other name seemed to fit but Thorndike—Fredrick's real last name.

"Some years ago there was a scandal involving Fredrick and Malcolm Thorndike," the woman began, and Arabella's breath caught at Fredrick's name. "The one brother joined the Navy and disappeared at sea shortly thereafter, while the older brother, Malcolm, ran a shipping business. Turned out the business was forced into fronting some sort of smuggling ring."

Arabella gasped. "Goodness. What happened once it was discovered?" Smuggling. So that was the treason.

"Yes, I remember this," added Lady Mitchell. "Malcolm helped the Navy set a trap for the smugglers. They were all caught with cargo holds filled with slaves."

The ladies who had dismissed Arabella now listened intently and gasped in horror.

"So Malcolm Thorndike wasn't hanged?" Arabella asked.

"Bless me, no," declared Lady Russell. "He was hailed as a hero. He's now in the Navy as a commander."

"But what of his shipping company?"

"Apparently there was more money in capturing Spanish vessels in the Caribbean...and pirates. I believe he is part of Governor Rogers' fleet to stomp out all pirate activity."

Arabella's mind raced. Fredrick believed his brother dead, but instead, Malcolm was part of the British Navy hunting pirates.

He was Fredrick's enemy.

"The most delicious part is the appearance of Fredrick, thought to be lost at sea." Lady Russell smiled. "I imagine there was quite the family reunion when he arrived home with

Malcolm two days ago. Fredrick hadn't seen his two sisters in years."

Arabella wavered as her head swam.

"Are you well, Mrs. Thorndike?" asked a concerned Lady Russell.

"Please excuse me, I suddenly do not feel well." Arabella stumbled from the group, but Lady Mitchell followed.

"My dear, what is wrong?" Lady Mitchell asked, taking Arabella's arm to assist her to the door.

"I...I must go home." Fredrick was alive. *Alive*. Months of fear and sorrow slammed into her, and Arabella was left drained and on the verge of hysterics. She couldn't lose her composure here. It would be better if they all believed she was ill.

"Of course. Please, let me escort you home. I can leave Fitz here. He's in the back room playing cards with some of his gentleman friends anyway."

Arabella welcomed the woman's company. "Thank you, Lady Mitchell. You are too kind," she said as they walked out into the night air. Arabella breathed a sigh upon leaving the crowded room.

Lady Mitchell was a pretty, youthful bride to her older husband. She seemed happy and chattered on about her honeymoon in Scotland. Her dark auburn hair was expertly coiffed into a mass of curls and held by hairpins of sparkling gemstones. Her white skin was creamy and flawless, and Arabella instantly liked her friendly manner and warm smile.

They climbed aboard Lady Mitchell's coach and gave directions to the driver to Arabella's townhouse. Within moments the coach lurched forward with a jolt.

"The buzz all over London is the return of the Thorndike brothers. Malcolm left four years ago or so, to join the Navy," she said with a flutter of her feathered fan as she sat next to Arabella in the coach. "I must say, I always liked the older brother Malcolm. I had a crush on him while growing up. My family owned the neighboring estate."

"Is he handsome?" Arabella asked.

"Oh yes, tall and strong, and of course the Thorndike blond hair."

Memories of Fredrick's hair falling across his chest as they lay in bed together skittered across her mind. Her heart warmed at the pleasant memory of his naked body hot against hers after making love. She smiled, a blush creeping across her cheeks.

"I couldn't help but notice your sudden illness at the mention of Fredrick."

Arabella's cheeks warmed hotter.

"I must admit, Mrs. Thorndike. I sought you out tonight."

Arabella quickly turned to her. "You did?"

"Forgive me. My curiosity was aching to meet the woman who shares the same name as my former neighbors."

Perhaps letting Lady Mitchell escort her home wasn't the best of ideas. Now Arabella was cornered. She remained silent.

"As I mentioned, I had a special affection for Malcolm as a girl. I thought he was the most handsome man I'd ever seen, and Fredrick was a close second. But Malcolm used to treat me special, with little gifts when the family would visit." The woman glowed, lost in thought to happy memories. "One time he gave me a single red rose on my fifteenth birthday. This was before their father passed. Malcolm promised to marry me someday."

"But you're married to Lord Mitchell."

The light happiness faded from her face. "I had little choice. It was an arranged marriage." She smiled sadly. "Fitz is not a bad man. He treats me very well and indulges me, so long as I let him play his cards without complaint."

"Do you love him?"

Lady Mitchell cast down her eyes to gaze at her hands holding the maroon feathered fan. "There is only one man I love."

It wasn't hard to recognize of whom she spoke. "Malcolm," Arabella whispered.

Lady Mitchell grasped her hands. "Please do not tell Fitz...or anyone. I do not know why I opened my heart to you just now." Tears filled her eyes. "Perhaps it was how you reacted to Lady Russell mentioning Fredrick..."

"I do not know him." Arabella pulled her hands from the woman's gentle grasp.

"I'm sorry to have burdened you with my woes, Mrs. Thorndike."

Arabella faced Lady Mitchell and smiled. "Please, call me Arabella."

"And you must call me Cassandra," she offered with excitement comparable to that of a giddy young girl.

The women hugged and Arabella said, "Thank you. You're the only friend I have here in London."

Sniffing, Cassandra straightened with a giggle. "We will fix that immediately. Come to my home Saturday evening. We are holding an evening party with dinner, music and cards. Please come as my special guest."

Chapter Fourteen

ഇ

Saturday evening arrived and Arabella climbed from her chaise outside the Mitchell's home. Since meeting Cassandra days before, the woman had been a daily visitor and the friendship had grown quickly. Never before had Arabella felt such a connection to another woman. It was nice to talk to another female. However, Arabella kept her heart guarded — as well as her past. Cassandra had known Fredrick years ago, a circumstance she hadn't expected when she started going about as Mrs. Thorndike. She scolded herself daily at the rash idiocy of her choice of name.

This was her first dinner party since returning to London, and Arabella was determined to enjoy herself. She much preferred the intimacy of a dinner party as opposed to the stifling crowd of a ball. Thinking of the ball from earlier that week, she prayed Lady Russell was not in attendance tonight to ask questions of Arabella's hasty retreat a few days prior.

Arabella wore a dress of rich royal blue velvet with an underskirt of white silk. She even had her maid style her hair into a pile of curls cascading down her shoulders and about her face in black ringlets. At her throat she wore her pearls, unwilling to ever part with their candle-glow beauty. When she stepped into the Mitchell's home, Cassandra was immediately at her side, praising her gown.

"Oh you look so beautiful. I wish I had such black hair and blue eyes. Your gown matches your eyes exactly."

"Thank you," Arabella giggled. "I admit I wanted to look my best tonight, especially after running out on the assembly a few days ago."

"No one will think you ill tonight, Arabella. You are gorgeous." Cassandra threaded her arm through her friend's and led her toward the parlor. "I am very happy you are here tonight. We have some last-minute guests who I think may interest you."

Arabella's heart lurched.

"Malcolm is here...and his brother Fredrick." Arabella stopped walking, but Cassandra urged her forward. "Fitz had met them during a card game last night and invited them to join us."

They waltzed into the parlor where several couples gathered in small groups chatting quietly. Gowns of rich velvet and satin adorned the women as the men stood by their sides in coats and breeches, some more elaborate than others, from gold embroidery to plain navy blue uniforms.

The uniformed men captured her eye when she spotted a tall man with a long queue of dark blond hair down his back.

"Commander Malcolm Thorndike," Cassandra whispered at her side. "Isn't he handsome in his uniform?"

Then, as though sensing Cassandra's regard, he turned to them.

And behind him stood Fredrick—in a naval uniform as well!

Her mouth went dry at the sight of him, and when his gaze locked with hers, she thought the floor had dropped away. She held on to Cassandra's arm for support so as not to fall.

Then he smiled and bowed slightly to her.

"Lady Mitchell—Cassie—you are beautiful as ever tonight." Malcolm strode to them and stood in front of Cassandra. Arabella recognized the heat in the man's eyes as he gazed upon her friend.

"Thank you, Commander."

"Please, we grew up together. Call me Malcolm."

Arabella turned her eyes to Fredrick, who slowly approached and stood beside his brother.

"You, of course, remember Fredrick," Malcolm said to Cassandra.

"Nice to see you home, Freddy."

Malcolm laughed.

"I don't think anyone has called me Freddy in years." Fredrick fixed his eyes upon Arabella and she lowered her gaze from his hot green glare.

"Malcolm, Freddy, meet Mrs. Thorndike. She is recently widowed and returned from Port Monmouth in the Caribbean."

"*Mrs. Thorndike?*" Fredrick mused incredulously.

Arabella couldn't bring herself to look at him.

"Tell me, *Mrs. Thorndike*, what happened to your dear, departed husband?" Fredrick prodded.

"He..." she stuttered. "He was lost at sea."

"Did you even wait to learn if this was so before leaving Port Monmouth?" His tone grew angered.

She glared up to his face, rage beginning to burn within her heart. "I stayed three months while my father ailed. When he died I didn't feel as though there was a point to remain."

"Three whole months. And tell me, *Mrs. Thorndike*, who told you that your husband was dead?"

"Well, no one exactly—" she began meekly but he interrupted hotly.

"And what of your lover? Did you even miss your lover when you heard of his death?"

"My lover?"

"Fredrick, perhaps this is not the best time," started Malcolm, quietly yet determined, grabbing his brother's arm.

"No, let her answer!" Fredrick demanded, shoving Malcolm's hand away. "Did you mourn your husband or your lover? Or did you take another to your bed that very night?"

Arabella gasped. "How dare you!" she exclaimed, forcing herself to keep her voice low.

"I do dare. Now tell me," he started in a barely restrained voice, anger bubbling just beneath the surface. "Did you truly love your husband? Or was it just the beginning of a string of lovers to taste your delights?"

Nearby guests gasped in shocked awe.

"How can you be so cruel? I never loved anyone but *you*." She inhaled deeply to try to calm herself, but she was too angry to find any measure of composure. "They said you were dead!" she yelled at him.

"And what of Captain Jacobs? Was he your lover?" he asked, his rage still only a moment away from bursting forth.

She stomped to him and slapped him across the face. "You arrogant pirate! How dare you question me like this!"

"Just answer my question—*was he your lover*?"

She didn't hesitate. "No, he was not."

He straightened and stepped closer to her. "Do you still love…your *husband*, Mrs. Thorndike?"

Seething with anger, she wanted to hurt him. He humiliated her in front of important people in London society. The scandalous fight would spread through the ranks like lightning.

Yet she realized she didn't care.

"Yes!" she spat then she swung around and marched toward the front door with her head held high.

At the entry where more guests for the evening gathered, Fredrick caught Arabella by the arm. She twisted around to slap him, but he caught her hand with his. "Don't slap me again, wench."

"Bastard!"

"Shrew!"

"Pirate!"

Then he lifted her over his shoulder. His arms wrapped about her legs as her hair fell from its perfect coif into a wild mess of black swirls.

"I demand you put me down!" she screamed at him.

"Pay us no mind, folks," he announced to those gasping in horror at the spectacle. "I am her husband, back from the dead to claim what is mine!" He marched through the door and out into the night. She wiggled and he spanked her bottom. "Arabella, you keep still like a good girl and maybe I won't punish you…much." He smacked her bottom again and she yelped.

"You brute, put me down." She hit his back and let her anger build, but in secret, her heart exploded in joy. Her body reacted to his touch and creamed in anticipation. She groaned at the power and determination of this man. Fredrick was here!

He strode out to one of the tethered horses and plopped her on top, her bottom hitting the saddle pommel. In a flash he climbed aboard behind her.

Heat from his body surrounded her, his unique scent filled her nostrils and his arms wrapped about her body possessively. As he led the horse from the others and began to ride into the night, Arabella freed her hidden emotions and she began to cry.

He rode for a few moments as she let the tears overtake her. He took them down an alley, presumably a shortcut toward his home. Then she turned in his arms and grasped his coat, her wet face rubbing against the scratchy wool of his uniform.

"I thought you were dead," she sobbed.

He dipped a hand into her hair, more pins falling away unheeded. "I went crazy without you." He kissed her forehead.

"Fredrick," she said softly and nuzzled his neck.

"I was a fool. I listened to Jacobs. He said he'd..." Fredrick blew out a frustrated breath. "Every time I thought of it, I went insane with jealousy. Even after my wounds were healed, I couldn't see beyond his boasts. Not enough to return to Port Monmouth."

"I would never have let him touch me. How could you even think I would?"

"I don't know. I was drunk most of the time, agonizing in my own pit of despair. Then we came across a British warship—and my brother Malcolm. I can't tell you what I felt when I discovered he was alive. He sobered me up and took me before Governor Woodes Rogers, the Governor of the Bahamas, to present a proposal that would change my future."

She leaned back and gazed up to his face. "You're in the British Navy."

"Aye, working for Woodes. I'm a pirate hunter now. I was pardoned, as was my crew. *Neptune's Sword* is officially in the service of the British Royal Navy tracking down pirates in the Caribbean."

She shook her head in disbelief. "But why are you here in London?"

"Looking for you."

"Really?"

"Aye, really. I sailed to Port Monmouth and we heard of the death of your father from the new governor. Then we sailed here. I lost your trail after that. Little did I know that you were using a different name."

She bowed her head. "I'm sorry. I lost everything—my father, my home—and you. I came back to England hoping to live a quiet life. As a widow there would be no whispers of my activities like that if I were an unattached lady."

"But as my widow?"

She raised her chin to meet his gaze. "You reaffirmed that you were my back-from-the-dead husband just a few minutes ago to that crowd at the Mitchell's."

"Hmm...indeed I did."

"I don't know how I can face Cassandra and that room of people after tonight."

"Cassandra will understand. As for the rest of that lot, you won't have to deal with any of them after this."

"Why?"

"Because you are coming with me back to the Caribbean—as my wife."

"They all think we're already married, including your brother and Cassandra," she said.

"Aye, as far as anyone will know, we would be merely renewing our vows. No one needs to know the truth but us—and the powers that be."

He reined in the horse, took her into his arms and kissed her. Greedy, possessive, it was a branding, and her heart soared with joy. Hunger raged beneath the surface as he tightened his arms about her. She felt completely engulfed by his kiss as he sucked upon her bottom lip and then plunged his tongue into her mouth, tasting, devouring. She opened to him, giving in to his commanding caresses and carnal desire.

His tongue sparred with hers and she moaned gently, surrendering to his mastery of her senses. It had been too long since she'd felt his arms about her body, enclosing her in his ring of sensual dominance.

His hand guided her head against his kiss as he feasted upon her flesh. The light brush of his stubble along his chin and upper lip excited her as he ground his lips along hers only to open his mouth again to duel with her tongue.

She made no move to escape, wanting him to taste all of her, mark her with his own unique taste. A hint of fine brandy spiced his mouth, and the taste was intoxicating.

He cupped her breast and she groaned at the possessiveness of his touch. His thumb rubbed across the taut peak of her nipple, and a flood of honeyed desire gathered within her sex. Even through the rich velvet of her bodice, his touch burned into her skin with searing passion.

"Arabella, say you'll marry me," he whispered against her lips. "Say you'll love me forever."

"I'll love you forever and a day." She threaded her fingers through his luscious hair, pulling it from the leather tie. "Forever and always."

"I have to make love to you. I need to be inside you."

His hand squeezed her breast and she whimpered. "Yes, oh yes."

He broke away and released his cock from his pants. The length surged and she wanted to explore his hardness further, but then he lifted her leg to encircle his body atop his horse, pulling her legs about his waist. He hiked up her skirt and burned a path with his hands up the inside of her thighs to her bare sex. His cock poised at her slick entrance and she shuddered at the contact of his length sliding along her wet folds and up into her heat.

She moaned and clutched his coat, riding the sensations now building rapidly within her. Every nerve ending sang and she lost all concept of reality. He surged up into her flesh, filling her channel, stretching her muscles to snugly embrace his sex. He growled a masculine sound as she clenched about his cock and held on to him, her body without control other than the rhythmic dance of mating. Carnal passion ignited between them as they renewed their intimacy in a fast-paced sexual reunion.

He clamped his hands about her waist and guided her hips over his cock. She threw back her head and arched her back, freeing herself from any doubts or worries and gave in to the sensations threatening to shatter her world.

"Arabella…" His voice was husky and soft, her name an endearment upon his lips.

Then he slammed into her, the head of his cock touching the deepest part of her. His cock pulsed within her, heated desire filling her so deeply, she though he touched a portal to her very soul.

The beginnings of her climax began to shake her body. She leaned into him and kissed his mouth as she exploded, quaking from the pure intensity of her emotions woven into the delights of the flesh. He returned her kiss, his arms holding her tightly as she cried into his kiss. Then he thrust into her once more, unleashing his control, spilling his essence deep into her body. A primal sound erupted from his throat, a male claiming his mate in the midst of ecstasy.

Her body rocked against his, soft curve to hard muscle, and when the climax ebbed, she shook in the glowing aftershocks. Her body quivered and she jumped in his arms, becoming aware of her surroundings.

When she giggled, he asked, "What is so funny, luv?"

"We just made love on horseback."

He pulled his shrinking length from her body and cradled her against his chest, his hands stroking her back in slow, possessive caresses. "I didn't want to take any more time in having you."

"Promise to make love to me later—somewhere more comfortable?"

He fingered the pearls at her neck. "Most definitely," he agreed with a devilish smile. Mischief lit his eyes and she shivered in anticipation.

"Take me home, Fredrick, and make love to me," she said as he helped her reposition herself on the horse.

"That and more, wench," he promised, "Much, much more."

Chapter Fifteen

છે

Once they arrived at her townhome, Fredrick escorted her through the doors and at the foot of the stairs, swept her into his arms and carried her up to her room. He climbed the stairs with ease, and she encircled his neck with her arms, burying her face into the silky length of his blond hair.

"I love you, Fredrick," she whispered to him.

His heart quaked with love for her. He paused and kissed her quickly on the lips. "I hope to hear those words from you every day of our lives together."

Once in her room, he placed her gently onto the bed. He stood gazing down at her luscious figure, soft and inviting to his touch. Her hair, black as the night, was disheveled and lay upon the pillow like waves on the stormy sea. His fingers itched to navigate through the mass—and right on down her tempting body. Then his eyes fixated upon her necklace. "Pearls become you, luv. Jewels of the sea for my most precious treasure—*you*."

Her fingertips slid over the strand about her neck. "I wear them always."

This pleased him beyond words. When he'd seen her across the room at the Mitchells', his body had flared to alertness. His cock had sprung to uncomfortable life. It had seemed as though an invisible rope had ensnared him and pulled him to her. When he'd heard her introduced as Mrs. Thorndike, anger snapped within him.

Bothered for months by Jacobs' claims, Fredrick had drunk himself into a rum-induced state of numbness for weeks. Only the appearance of Malcolm by his side shook him back to reality.

By the time Fredrick had sobered, Malcolm knew much of the story of the beautiful Arabella as hostage aboard *Neptune's Sword*. He used this to his advantage and presented a tempting deal to earn respectability in order to properly marry the governor's daughter. Fredrick consulted with the crew, and each man agreed to follow wherever he led them. Even Jeremy and Doc Bruce agreed a change of winds would do the entire crew good. With the death of Blackbeard and the capture of many other notorious pirates, life had become too dangerous for pirates in the Caribbean. And Woodes Rogers accepted nothing less than obedience. After all, the man had been a pirate himself before his position as governor.

Fredrick served at his brother's side in hunting down those ships sailing under the black flag. Eventually, Fredrick set sail for Port Monmouth in search of Arabella.

Her face had haunted his dreams, her voice echoed in his ears. The memory of her sweet flesh burned into his body, ruining any other woman's touch. Not even the simplest of pleasures like of a cup of rum could staunch the pain within his heart. Food lost its taste and drink failed to satisfy. Only Arabella could fulfill his hunger, quench his thirst—tame the desire within his groin.

Finding a new governor ruling and Arabella returned to England, Fredrick set sail immediately. He would set foot in the country he swore never to revisit. Once in town, he set eyes upon his lovely sisters, now grown and blooming with promise. Under the care of family friends, Amelia and Abigail were already the most sought-after ladies of marriageable age.

Despite the wondrous reunion with his sisters, Fredrick yearned deeply for the woman who tamed the pirate within his soul. He desired no longer to live as a rogue of the seas; he wanted to be worthy and respectable. Fredrick wanted to be a good man for his wife, to provide and comfort her—to keep her safe.

He wanted her, even when he saw her at the Mitchells'. Then her name, Mrs. Thorndike, sent his frustration and doubts to the surface. All the while, he took note of those pearls about her neck. Could he have been wrong to doubt her words when she stood there adorned in the only gift he'd ever given her?

Yet he confronted her at the party, wanting answers to put to rest any lingering doubts. He hadn't intended to grow so angered and flamboyant. A scene before Cassandra's guests was not on the menu.

However, Fredrick was inflamed, angered by her use of his name and her refusal to acknowledge him as her lover—no, *husband*.

"Fredrick," she moaned in a low, whispered voice.

He began to work at the gold buttons on his coat. "Be still, luv. Don't say anything."

She lay back and closed her eyes. Her sigh of contentment surged his cock to life once again. He flung off his coat and breeches, uncaring where they landed or in what state. All that mattered was the woman of his dreams lying in bed awaiting him to pleasure her. And he was ready to fulfill that need to the best of his ability.

Naked, he reached into his discarded boot and pulled out a knife. At the bedside, he said softly, "Don't move." He slid the cool blade into the front of her bodice and she gasped, her eyes flying open at the contact.

"What are you—?"

Her words were cut off by the resounding tear of velvet. He cut through the thick fabric like it was nothing but a scrap of linen.

"This is one of my best gowns!" she protested as he tugged the massive royal blue gown from her body.

"Get it mended later," he muttered as he cut through her chemise. "I need you naked now...and I plan on keeping you that way for a long time."

Instead of protesting again, she moaned softly.

Ripping away the barriers to her body, he straightened and drank in her nudity. Perfect in every way—from well-proportioned breasts to strong, shapely legs—Arabella was a woman made for loving.

Instinctively she opened her legs and his mouth watered. She was adorned in nothing but her pearls and a wave of possessive need flooded him. "Take off your pearls," he croaked. "Slowly."

She looked up at him questioningly, but obeyed. She lifted the tripled strand over her head. Now at its maximum length, she held the flawless string of pearls in her fingers.

"Lay back and close your eyes," he instructed.

He stepped to the bed and took the pearls from her hand. "Breathe. Take in the air about you and exhale. Relax your body. Give control over to me as I take you to the heights of pleasure."

Her answer was a low, strangled whimper.

His heart beast so fast, a heady rush of arousal pumped through his veins. Her body blushed, rosy pink coloring her skin. His pulse beat in his head as he gripped the cool pearls in his hand and then let the length drop to dangle freely at his side. His chest tightened at the thought of the pearls running across her perfect skin. His cock was so hard it hurt.

He grasped the free end of the strand and hung the pearls between his hands. Then he leaned over her chest and lightly rolled the strand across her collarbone. She inhaled sharply and her eyes flew open.

"Close your eyes," he ordered. "Or do you need a blindfold, luv?"

Her voice wavered as she panted her reply. "Blindfold me."

He searched her vanity and found some silk that he tied about her face, covering her eyes. Every breath through her parted lips sent his body into a tailspin of desire. He was almost unable to move away from her to continue his sensual exploration, almost opting to just take her.

Easing her head back into the pillow, a light pink silk scarf wrapped about her head, she was an erotic dream come to life. He picked up the pearls once more and dangled them over her breasts. Carefully, the smooth surface of the pearls rubbed exquisitely along her skin, her areolas puckering under the gentle glide.

She inhaled sharply as he teased her tight peaks, and his mouth watered to taste her pink nipples. She reached for the pearls and rubbed the beads harder against her nipples and moaned.

"I didn't say you could pleasure yourself." He liked to watch her enjoying herself, but his commands would heighten her arousal.

"My lord Captain," she moaned. "May I touch myself?" He stood mesmerized, watching her fingers trail down her abdomen to the dip of her cunt. "Please?" she asked sweetly, almost begging as her hand lay poised at her clitoris, waiting for him to approve.

"You may stroke yourself." He wanted to stroke her straining little nubbin but couldn't tear his eyes from her fingers slipping between her legs. She opened her legs a little and he watched her experiment with touch to stimulate her body. Her breathing came in rapid pants. She was a quick study to self-pleasure. "Enough. Pull your fingers away. I'll not have you coming yet."

With a whimper she obeyed, but reluctantly.

"Looks like I'll have to make sure you don't send yourself over the edge without permission." He took one arm and wrapped the strand of pearls about one wrist, and then the other. Her hands rested upon her belly and he smiled when he pulled the pearls tightly and she gasped. Holding the remaining length of pearls in his hand, he carefully laid a trail down between her legs. The pearls gently brushed over her open labia and tickled the inner lips of her sex. He lightly slipped the pearls over her clitoris and she moaned.

"Does the cool, smooth surface of your pearls feel good against the searing heat of your sex?" he asked, anxious to hear her passion-thickened voice.

"It feels…it feels very nice." She panted and thrashed her head to one side, trying to control the building need for release.

"Nice?" He pulled the pearls slowly over her nub, and she flexed her hips against the strand. "Tell me, luv. How nice is 'nice'?"

Whimpering she tossed her head to the other side, her eyes squeezed shut. "Nice." She inhaled deeply, fighting for control. "Exquisite. I want to…oh…"

He continued to draw the pearls back and forth expertly across her swollen nubbin.

"So responsive, so innocent," he murmured.

Then he increased the pressure upon the pearls, sliding them deeper through her slick folds. She writhed and widened her thighs, and with a finger, he pushed the other end of the pearls inside. She gasped and gulped down a cry as he swirled his finger into her heat, stirring the pearls deeper into her.

"Fredrick," she squeaked, her hands clutching the strand of pearls tightly, trying not to move.

He was lost in watching her sex turn a dark pink with her increasing excitement. One finger joined another inside her sheath, and she bucked her hips.

"Rock your pelvis side to side," he instructed. "Let the pearls slide around inside you."

She raised her hips to the left, and then rocked to the right. He pushed his fingers in and out of her in a torturously slow pace, all the while controlling the roll of the pearls. Her juices covered his fingers and lowering his mouth to her clitoris, he licked the surface gingerly, dipping his tongue into the creamy honey oozing from her cunt. He tasted her desire with every lap of his tongue and each pass of his lips.

When he sucked upon her little nubbin, nipping the surface with a pass of his teeth, she cried out as her orgasm overtook her restraint. He pulled at the pearls with his teeth as she came, and he continued to push in and out of her channel with his fingers. She bucked and screamed, her climax shattering any constraint upon her composure. Her inner muscles clenched about his fingers and the pearls, wetness sucking them farther into her body even as he tugged at the necklace.

Her hands lay at the top of his head, urging him to draw out the moment, and for a brief time he lost control of his senses. This strong, beautiful woman surrendered her heart and body to him. She gave of herself willingly, out of a love he neither expected nor sought. Yet, she did indeed love him.

He pulled his fingers from her cunt and moved over her body. Her fingers teased his abdomen as he positioned his hips against hers. He slid his cock into her, the pearls running along his length inside. So tight and delicious, the pearls caressed him as he started to pump into her. Her climax had subsided, but he would see another build.

It wouldn't take long to find completion as she squirmed against his body. Utterly feminine in form, she aroused him to the brink of insanity. He ached for her touch, and as her naked flesh undulated against his body, he knew this was not just a woman he made love to. Arabella was his destiny.

"Oh Fredrick," she called.

"Arabella, I love you!" he yelled as he started to explode, convulsing with climax, spurting his hot seed into her receptive core. His body shook and he howled in triumph. She squeezed his cock as she joined him in a mutual tumble into orgasmic heaven.

When the spasms began to ease in intensity, he withdrew from her heat and gently pulled out the pearls still within her body. She shuddered as each bead passed out of her, and once they were completely out, she sighed in feminine satisfaction.

He crouched on the bed beside her and then unwrapped the pearls from her wrists. "Content?" he asked, filled with male pride that he had pleasured his woman into sexual fulfillment.

She lifted her hand and pulled off the blindfold. "That was incredible!"

He lay down next to her and took her into his arms. He held her close, smelling the hint of wildflowers in her hair. She placed her hand upon his chest and for the first time in months, he felt at home. No matter where in the world his travels may lead, home was with Arabella. She completed him, fulfilled his desires and satisfied his yearning to love—and to be loved. She understood him, accepted him...loved him despite his past.

His life had changed from the moment he set eyes upon her those months ago. He'd not only gained a woman to cherish for the rest of his days, he rediscovered the family he'd lost.

"When do you sail for the Bahamas?" she asked quietly.

He squeezed her gently. "In a day or so."

"Are you sure you want me along? I've heard women onboard ship are bad luck."

"You are coming with me, luv." He gathered her head against him tightly, threading his fingers through her black hair. "I found you and I'm never letting you go."

"But we're not *officially* married. I don't think they allow—"

"You worry too much," he dismissed. "We will take care of that technicality in the morning. And before you yell at me, I intend to set about getting a special license and Malcolm can marry us as soon as we are ready. He can do that."

"Can we invite Cassandra and your sisters? I can't wait to meet them."

"Aye, we'll invite a few friends to attend."

She was silent for a moment then said, "You know, I like Cassandra Mitchell very much. Over the past few days, I've felt as if I've met a long-lost friend."

"Aye, she was one our playmates growing up. I thought she would marry Malcolm one day." He was saddened when his brother informed him of her marriage to the much-older Lord Mitchell. Malcolm had been in love with Cassandra since the day he realized she was a blooming young woman.

"I think she is still in love with him."

"I don't doubt that. Malcolm is heartbroken as well."

"Is there anything we can do?"

"Perhaps someday they will have a second chance. But for now, she is married to a powerful lord, and Malcolm is anxious to get to sea again." *Away from England...and the woman he loves.*

"I wonder sometimes if fate brought you to Port Monmouth that day. I mean, you were there to take my father as hostage, but he was away. Instead you took me, and I hated you for it. Now I am here in your arms, loving you. Strange how life works out."

"It isn't fate that brought us together." He rolled atop her, pushing his knee in between her legs, opening her slick entrance. "A Tarot card reading did." At her confused silence, he explained. "In Tortuga weeks before I met you, a gypsy said I would be defeated by a woman."

"I didn't defeat you..."

"Aye, you did, luv. I put my own desires ahead of everything just to have you. I took you that day because you excited me. And to keep you, I turned my entire life around from the lawless pirate to a respectable pirate hunter."

"What exactly did this gypsy say?"

"That a woman of love and beauty would storm into my life and ensnare my heart."

167

She wrapped her arms about his neck and smiled. "I kind of like being the one to bring down the feared pirate Thorne."

He slid his cock up into her sheath and she moaned.

"And I tamed the high-and-mighty Miss Prescott," he crooned.

"Tamed?" she laughed.

"Aye, with a few kisses...and a belaying pin." He began to move in and out of her body slowly, her juices coating his cock. "By the way, you need to be punished."

"But why?"

"You came without permission earlier—twice," he said with a chuckle as he slowly made love to her.

"Pirate," she breathed in glorious surrender.

The End

SEA HAWK'S MISTRESS

ຄ

Dedication

ೞ

In loving memory of Errol Flynn,
the greatest buccaneer to grace the silver screen.

Author's Note

ೞ

All my life I have been a huge fan of pirates in movies and literature. My all-time favorite was Errol Flynn, who romanced me at the tender age of five when I first watched *The Adventures of Robin Hood*. Granted, the character of Robin Hood was not labeled "pirate", but his penchant for robbing from the rich was a piratical act. And I loved it. Later, as I watched *Captain Blood* and *The Sea Hawk*, I was completely hooked on the swashbuckling pirate hero—and Errol Flynn.

In this book, I dropped several hints throughout for pirate lovers. For example, the island of Virgen Magra is fictional, used originally in Raphael Sabatini's book, *Captain Blood*. And of course, Captain Flint's ship, the *Sea Hawk*, is in honor of the movie, as well as the man who crossed swords in my dreams.

Chapter One

❧

"Okay folks, this is our moment of truth, the moment we've all worked for," Dr. Harvey Ford started as the search team geared up into their scuba suits. "If we're right, this will be the biggest discovery since the *Titanic*."

Nothing like the dramatic, Shelley thought while checking her oxygen tank's pressure gauge.

The *Santa Rosa* was lost at sea in 1622. It was part of a fleet of Spanish galleons that had left Havana heavy with cargo—gold, silver, indigo, copper and other treasures—and was thought to be destroyed by a violent hurricane near the Florida Keys shortly after setting sail.

Recently, thanks to radar and satellite imaging, the location of the sunken ship was discovered. Or at least, that's what they were out here to verify.

Shelley wasn't exactly part of the research team but her father, Dr. William Hanover, was head of the Maritime Society, and Shelley had been a regular on these dives ever since her junior year in high school, eight years ago. Now a graduate student at Florida State University, she'd come home for the summer and was taking advantage of the research dives. Of course, her specialization in oceanography helped secure her a slot on the dive for the entire summer. She planned on using the experience for a thesis.

Most of her friends were off visiting Hawaii or some other beach resort getaway this summer. Shelley opted to work. The thought of finding sunken treasure was too exciting to pass up.

Soon the boat came to a stop and they prepared for the dive.

"This is about where we believe the ship landed below. There is a dense reef system that could have been spawned by the sunken galleon. Be careful down there," Dr. Ford said just before diving in.

The water was a jewel-tone aquamarine—clear and clean. On the surface, it was perfection as far as the eye could see. The day was sunny and hot with a few clouds meandering in the sky above. With one last look at the boat and her watch, Shelley adjusted her scuba mask and submerged.

The current was gentle and fairly easy to swim through as she made her way deeper beneath the surface. The depths weren't too great in this area, and the reef rose from the bottom in a grand structure of coral, boulders and—the galleon.

There it was, rotted and grown over with oceanic vegetation. There was no mistaking the large ship's hull. It was on its side, supported by the rocks it landed on centuries before.

The most amazing sight was the beautiful ecosystem that spawned about the sunken ship. Yellowtail snappers, spiny lobsters, pink shrimp and King mackerel were using this underwater paradise as their home. Elkhorn coral, sea sponges, sea fans and brain coral flourished on and around the ship, practically hiding the vessel, which explained the difficulty in finding the treasure galleon.

As she neared, one of the other divers examined the coral and sea-grass-covered hull. A large hole could be seen below the ship's waterline—a circular hole? Could the ship have been sunken by a cannonball rather than a hurricane? The ships had been scattered across the Florida Keys, no central command keiping the ships together and organized when the fleet sailed from Havana. It was possible pirates picked off this straggler as easy prey.

Several of the team members entered the cargo hold and Shelley followed, anxious to see if they had indeed found the riches they all hoped for.

But the hold was empty.

As they examined the vast hull from within, it was now almost certain the ship had been victim to a sea attack, most likely pirates.

Shelley was disappointed but there was so much more this ship had to tell. The marine life that used the ship as its home was enough to keep any marine biologist in research heaven for years. As she began to formulate her request to be part of the research team, her flashlight beam caught the glimmer of metal on the floor near an empty chest, one of many that littered the hold.

Shelley swam over to the curious piece partially hidden by rotten wood and vegetation. Waving her hand over the object, clearing some of the sediment, it was apparent this was a treasure left behind—a silver bangle, possibly Aztec. She reached down and grasped it.

A sudden sensation of nausea hit her as she examined the bracelet. Yes, the silver surface was etched with Aztec designs, such as she had seen before in other pieces carried by the galleons back to Spain.

She marveled over the pristine surface of the bangle, unmarred by its time sitting at the bottom of the ocean. She turned it over and a latch on the side popped with the slightest touch, opening for the first time in centuries.

And as it opened, the world about her twisted and turned. She began to panic as the water about her seemed to pull at her body. The hull of the ship disappeared—all she saw was blackness as she felt incredible pressure wrapping around her.

Air—she needed air. In the tremendous force of the ocean, a type of whirlpool pulled her downward and she couldn't breathe. Her air hose couldn't withstand the pressure and Shelley gasped for breath. She managed to dislodge her tanks, hoping their added weight would ease the hold upon her body.

The need for oxygen won out and Shelley fell into a sea of darkness.

* * * * *

Shelley awoke, her vision blurred and her head still spinning. She felt like she'd been on an all-night beer binge and was now paying the price with one hell of a hangover.

Blinking, she saw faint light from a nearby window. She tried to move to see better, but couldn't.

Dear God, I'm tied down!

Ropes secured her wrists to the small headboard and her feet were tied to the footboard. How the hell did she end up here...tied down...and *naked*?

She was *completely naked*. A thin sheet covered her—barely—and she was very aware of the linen brushing against her sensitive skin.

Glancing about the small, dim room, she noted it was sparsely furnished with a bed, a small table and two wood chairs, all stained in the same dark hue. In the slight breeze she could smell the ocean, the salty air mixing with the scent of well-oiled wood. If she didn't know better, this seemed to be a cabin in some ancient ship.

I must be dreaming. I've been reading too many books about sunken galleons and pirates bent on plundering.

When the room rocked with a gentle motion, she realized this *was* more than a dream. She was indeed on a ship.

In bed.

Tied down.

And naked.

What the f—

The only door in the room opened and in walked a very tall figure, powerful and muscular, judging from his shadowy silhouette.

"I see you're awake," he said in a clipped British accent.

He stepped into the small cabin and the walls seemed to close in about her with his mere presence. Shutting the door behind him, this hulk of a man stood at the foot of the bed, staring down at her.

"Where am I and why am I tied down to a bed?" Her voice shook as she watched him move to the table.

Without a word he reached for a lantern—an oil lamp?—and struck a match. He lit the lamp and the gloom of the room lifted a little.

What the hell happened? Last she remembered she was on the dive with the Maritime research team. How did she get to be in this situation?

And who was this hunk of a man who gazed at her with eyes of the darkest chocolate? His dark hair was pulled back into a hasty queue and his skin glowed with a healthy tan—the mark of a man who lived and worked in the sun.

He stood silent, staring. Again.

He obviously was not going to answer her questions.

"Excuse me, but could you please say *something*?"

Instead he reached over and snatched off the sheet, revealing her naked body to his dark, alluring eyes.

"Hey! Put that back!" she ordered, wriggling in her restraints.

"Yes, keep moving like that, luv. You have fine breasts that bounce and sway with you."

She instantly stilled, and he laughed.

The vibration of his laughter tickled her skin, like a shiver running across the surface and gathering at the apex of her thighs.

He turned and pulled over one of the chairs, then sat down next to the bed. He sat in silence as he examined her with his eyes. She felt his gaze roam slowly over her exposed body. Every inch was bare and she lay still, wishing he'd cover her again. The sheet wasn't much but at least it was a barrier to those eyes.

"What do you call that…thing you wore when we found you?"

She assumed he meant her diving suit. "It's a rubber skin suit."

He cocked his head. "Skin suit?"

"Yes."

His expression was hard and she trembled beneath his gaze. Her body was alive with desire, a tangible heat that seemed to pump throughout every cell. Why did she want him to touch her skin so much? The warmth from those steely eyes made her temperature rise—and her cunt ache with a need she couldn't explain.

"How did you get to be on the *Santa Rosa*?"

Her gaze snapped to his. "What do you mean? I was on a dive."

"Dive?"

"You know…a research dive."

He shook his head in confusion.

"I was part of a team studying the *Santa Rosa*."

"How come we didn't find you aboard before it sank?"

She paused. *Before it sank?* "What do you mean?"

"We boarded the *Santa Rosa* and took all the cargo in the hold and searched all the cabins before it sank. You weren't there, yet we found you floating in the wreckage that surfaced."

The small cabin closed in about her even more. It was then she noticed his clothes. He wore tan pants that buttoned in the front, and brown leather thigh-high boots. His white linen shirt was open at the collar and he wore a brown leather vest, unbuttoned and loose. Sexy and alluring—like a swashbuckling movie hero.

What the hell was going on?

"Who are you?" she croaked.

"I am Captain Jason Flint, and you are aboard my ship, the *Sea Hawk*."

Captain Flint? Dear God, he lived almost four hundred years ago! She remembered reading about him. He was one of the more curious buccaneers that sailed the seas—born into wealth, second son of a British lord, Flint turned to a life of piracy when his father died and his brother inherited the title and the estate. It was believed that bad blood between the brothers drove Flint out of England, and fate made him a pirate. He carved his legend into history by attacking ships bound from Mexico to Spain...

Wait. The *Santa Rosa* had distinct cannon damage. Pirates—Captain Flint—had sunk the *Santa Rosa*! Well, it certainly answered *that* mystery.

But the revelation paled to another very disturbing situation—she was supposedly talking to a dead pirate captain, in his cabin, on his *ship*, while she lay naked, bound and vulnerable. This wasn't happening.

But here she was, and he was sitting close, the scent of the sea and male swirling about him, wrapping her in his sensual appeal.

"Speak, woman." His voice cut into her thoughts.

"I don't understand this at all." How could she be here with Captain Flint? Was it possible—no, it can't be. This had to be a joke. It had to be. Didn't it?

"There's nothing to understand." At her questioning look, he said, "I found you and now you are my captive."

"What do you mean, I'm your captive?" the woman asked, her temper rising as her skin blushed becomingly.

Jason had to admit, this woman was the best find from his latest victory. Sinking the *Santa Rosa* was just another notch in his pirating career but this woman, whoever she was, had a quality about her. Even if she *had* worn strange clothes and

177

spoke to him unlike any other woman of his acquaintance, she obviously had intelligence, as well as good grooming skills.

He attributed her excellent physical condition to the band of ownership she was found wearing. Her former master must have taken special care of this slave. Upon seeing her flawless skin and her shockingly perfect teeth, Jason was mesmerized. His cock had been rock-solid since he'd laid eyes on her. When the beauty opened her eyes, he was spellbound by their dark brown mystery. Who was she and how did she come to be floating in the open ocean?

Surely she will be missed. Her master would want her back. Jason could ransom her, but the thought of giving her over to another man was hard to swallow...

Since when did Captain Flint care if a woman shared her body with several men? It was a way of life on the high seas, and Jason had sampled many willing wenches in his travels. But this woman brought to the surface a forgotten sense of—dare he even think it?—*honor*.

When his crew had spotted her and dragged her aboard ship bedecked in that odd black skin, Jason felt the need to protect her. He couldn't let his crew have her, to use her body for their sexual release. No, she would only serve one master on this ship—him.

He reached out and placed a hand over the curved rise of one breast. Her little gasp was a jolt of awareness to his straining manhood. He squeezed and she closed her eyes, as though fighting the arousal his touch sparked within her.

"Stop that," she whispered.

"You're mine, luv. I can touch you."

Her body betrayed her as she arched upward, her breast thrust firmly into his palm. Her nipple was hard and pert and when he pinched at its stiffness, she whimpered.

"Please don't," she begged breathlessly.

Jason ignored her pleas, not convinced of her denials when her body reacted so deliciously to his caress. "What's your name?"

She opened her eyes and he was once again struck by their dark beauty. "Shelley."

He could easily see her atop a horse in Hyde Park, several suitors following her in hopes of a favorable glance. She brought to life a world he'd left behind. Years living by the speed of his sloop and the skill of his sword, and now he thought of rides in the park, stealing kisses in the moonlight and holidays filled with loving family. What was it about this woman that rekindled those memories from so long ago, from a life he'd rather forget?

"Please, untie me." She struggled against the ropes. He wasn't even sure why he'd tied her down to his bed. Where could she escape to? It was more for her protection. He desired her fiercely and he wanted to make sure none would sample her sweet flesh. He'd undressed her from that "skin" and took time to touch her soft curves while she lay resting in his bed. The ropes were to make sure she would stay out of trouble until he made sure she understood the rules.

"Stay here in this cabin." At her glare, he added, "My men would not think twice in ravishing you without mercy. You are safe as long as you follow my orders and stay here."

"But I can't stay in here forever."

"You can go topside, but *only* if I am with you. Do you understand?"

She seemed to consider her predicament and he hoped she'd be sensible. A pirate ship full of horny men was a dangerous place for any woman. However, his men would obey his command. The girl was not to be disturbed or touched or the pain of death would be their punishment. Pirates are ruthless and they will only follow a strong captain. If he claimed Shelley as his property, they would stay away...unless Jason met with the sharp side of a cutlass.

"I'll stay here. I won't try to run," she said in a low voice.

"There's nowhere to run but into the sea." He stood from his chair, pulled a dagger from his boot and sliced through the bonds on her wrists first, then the ones about her ankles.

Once free, she scurried for the sheet he'd pulled from her body and wrapped herself in it, hiding her creamy skin and inviting breasts.

"Know this—*you are my slave*. Whatever I want, whenever I order it..." His voice trailed off as he reached for her wrist bearing the silver slave bangle, then said, "You will obey my every command."

Chapter Two

ဆ

"Hold on…a slave? I am *not* a slave." Shelley tried to appear tough in her sheet but it was a difficult thing to do, especially when the man staring at her had such lust in his eyes. That glimmer sent shivers down her spine, ending right in her cunt. His grasp about her forearm was firm yet gentle, and the contact of his bare skin against hers was electric, adding to the wetness gathering between her legs. *Traitorous body.*

"You *are* a slave. My pleasure slave—my *sex* slave."

"And what makes you think I'll go along with this?"

Flint lifted her wrist before her eyes, fingering the bracelet. "You were *someone's* sex slave. This bangle speaks of ownership. Now you belong to me. And rule number one," he started as he grasped the sheet and gave it a tug, pulling it forcefully from her body. "Never cover yourself in my presence."

Her first reaction was to press a hand over her breasts and her crotch, but he grabbed her wrists, pulling her off the bed to stand and crushing her body to his.

Her flesh pressed against his clothed body and she couldn't ignore his hard, masculine frame. The leather brushed along her sensitive skin and she bit her bottom lip to suppress a moan.

"You're a fine-looking woman. Not too skinny and soft in all the right places." He leaned into her a little more, backing her against the wall of the cabin. The smell of leather and man filled her senses. He was driving her wild with his domination over her body—and spirit. His calm strength rendered her speechless but part of her wanted to scream her denials.

She wasn't a slave, she'd *found* the bangle. But how could she get him to believe her when she was having a hard time believing herself?

His face was a mere inch away from hers. She had the overwhelming desire to kiss him, to taste this pirate—this man who was making her blood boil with his closeness.

He leaned into her, his mouth just beside her ear, breathing warm air over the surface and sending chills across her skin. "I won't hurt you if you follow my orders. You *will* fulfill my needs—and you will enjoy every moment."

Shelley melted. As simple as it was, no man had ever promised she'd enjoy sex with him. Generally she was momentarily satisfied after sex, but nothing so earth-shattering as she imagined sex with Captain Flint could be.

He released her and moved to the door. Her body instantly missed his heat, the feel of his hard frame pressed against her. "And if you do decide to get rebellious, I will march you naked on deck for the entire crew to admire. I think they'd love to each take a crack at paddling your ripe ass for disobeying their captain. Do I make myself clear, luv?"

Images of his threat flashed through her mind. Would he really do such a thing? She wasn't in the mood to find out. She'd bide her time and be smart about her next move. She wanted to find out more intimate details about this sexy pirate.

"Well?"

She nodded. "Yes, Captain."

With a crooked smile, he opened the door and left the cabin. She quickly latched the door closed behind him.

She heard him laugh from the other side. "No lock will keep me out, luv."

Sexy as sin, devilish to the core and infuriating as hell. Damn the man. She wanted to run but couldn't, not unless she wanted to test his threats. At this point, she wasn't willing to see how far she could push the captain.

She glanced at the bangle on her arm. She didn't even remember putting it on. It had opened by itself and then she woke up here. Wherever "here" was.

Or "when" may be a better question.

Stepping over to the small porthole, she looked out the opening to see mile upon mile of sea—aquamarine water everywhere. The ship rocked gently, the wood creaking with the current. It certainly looked like waters near the Florida Keys but she couldn't tell for sure.

Shelley touched the smooth surface of the bangle. A sex slave? So this had to be some sort of Aztec slave band—and she was lucky enough to find one that transported her back in time to 1622.

Lucky? Maybe that wasn't exactly the right word she'd use in finding the bangle.

Traveling back in time seemed more like something out of an H.G. Wells novel than a tangible possibility. Shelley had grown up around science, but a technical explanation was hard to determine. She didn't even know where to begin with a hypothesis. An electrical imbalance in the atmosphere? A chemical reaction in the ocean? A magnetic anomaly from the famed Bermuda Triangle?

Science could explain practically everything, but was it that complicated? She could be lying in a hospital somewhere in a coma and just dreaming of a six-foot-three pirate stud demanding sex.

She pinched her thigh and yelped at the pain. *Nope, not dreaming.* This was no dream.

Captain Flint was *real*.

Her heart thumped faster within her chest and a knot tightened in her stomach. A real sexy-as-sin pirate, her vision of masculine perfection, wanted her to pleasure him. So what's so bad about being a sex slave to such a man?

Nothing. In fact, this could be a fantasy come true.

Marianne LaCroix

She touched the bangle again. Perhaps this was exactly why she was thrust back in time—to meet Captain Flint. Granted, it was a remote possibility, but then this entire situation was hard to believe.

Having sex with Captain Flint would probably be the most pleasure she'd ever had. *Oh yeah.* Perhaps if she just made the best of it...she could end up having a scorching affair with the pirate! Just the memory of his body pressed against hers a few moments ago made her pussy clench with need for more. God, how would it feel when they were both naked, his skin burning against hers? She definitely wanted to find out.

However, some of his demands were hard to swallow. Staying in the cabin? She needed to get out into the fresh air at some point. The small cabin would get claustrophobic quickly if she remained here all the time.

First things first, she needed clothes. He surely didn't mean to keep her naked at all times, did he? And just because he made her body vibrate with sexual awareness didn't mean she had to let him have the upper hand in everything. She was a modern woman, and weakness was not an option. Although, she had to admit, when she'd been bound to his bed and he had caressed her breast, all thoughts fled her mind and she had willingly succumbed to his skilled touch.

Eying a sea chest at the foot of the bed, she walked over and tested the lid. Sure enough, it was locked tight. Crouching down, she looked under the bed for something to help her. The entire room was so bare. She didn't see anything that could possibly help her bust the lock. She prayed there was something kicked under the bed, forgotten yet useful. In the darkness she spotted a glimmer of silver—a small, dull table knife. She reached for it and pulled it out. Yes, it was at least something she could stick in the lock to try to jimmy it open.

It took Shelley fifteen minutes of work but she managed to get the lock open. Inside the chest she found the captain's clothes, including a large cream linen shirt and tan pants. She slipped on the garments and secured them with a piece of the rope he'd used earlier. Tied around her waist, the rope prevented the too-big clothes from gapping too much.

Digging deeper into the chest, she found a sword and scabbard, elegantly carved and polished. She gripped the handle and pulled the clean steel blade from its sheath, marveling at the beauty of the piece. This was obviously an heirloom sword, and it meant something to the captain for him to hide it within his sea chest, buried at the bottom.

"Who are you really, Captain Flint?" she murmured to herself as she took the sword and set it on the small table by the lantern.

She examined the carvings on the blade, trying to decipher the design as some small piece to the puzzle of Captain Jason Flint.

* * * * *

Jason climbed the stairs to the deck. There he placed the dagger back into his boot and then reached for his cutlass and sheath and retied it to his waist. There was no way he was going down to see his female prisoner wearing his cutlass, so he had removed it and set it outside on deck. After picking up his pistol, he secured it to his belt then put on his overcoat and once again, he felt like the ruthless pirate captain.

When he strode out to the helm, his first mate, Thomas, announced, "Captain, we are in for a calm night tonight."

Calm wasn't what Jason felt. Anything but. He wanted to toss away his clothes and fuck his new captive.

Funny, she'd seemed completely surprised at being called a slave. Strange behavior. Perhaps she had hit her head and has forgotten her previous life. That must be the reason. Yet she was unlike any other pleasure slave he'd seen. Many were local women with darkly tanned skin and no knowledge of English. This woman spoke it fluently, even though she had an unusual accent, nothing like he'd ever heard before. A bump on the head might explain the bizarre words she used as well.

"She's a pretty one, Captain," Thomas said as he continued to hold the helm wheel steady.

"Indeed. But I still do not know how she came to be floating in that wreckage."

"We must have missed 'er when we searched the ship," Thomas said.

He was an intelligent lad. His father had taught him the fine points of sailing from the time he was a boy. Thomas had lost his left leg at twenty during service in the British Navy, and had fought a difficult battle to remain at sea. Jason met him in a small jail on Barbados. By then, Thomas had been discharged from the Navy and was wandering aimlessly about the Caribbean on merchant vessels. They busted free together and Jason took the young man on as his first mate, soon discovering Thomas was an excellent navigator.

"That doesn't explain…" What did she call it? A skin suit? When they fished her from the wreckage, at first they all thought the black material *was* her skin, but then it peeled away revealing her flawless flesh beneath. It was then Jason scooped her up and took her to his cabin. His men were not to be toyed with in the matter of females. Even he had been bewitched by her exposed curves and feminine allure.

"Is she awake, Captain?" Thomas asked, breaking into Jason's thoughts.

"Aye, she is." Awake and hot for his touch. It was going to be difficult to concentrate on anything else now that he'd felt her—and saw her body arch into his touch.

Women generally fell at his feet whenever he went to port. It was normal for them to fawn over him. He was rich, a powerful attraction for many of the bar wenches offering up a night of sex and companionship.

Companionship? Not really. Women never held much interest for Jason past that moment of intense need for release.

Once he came, he was done with them. It sounded crueler than it really was, for those women never stayed in his bed long after their duties were fulfilled. He was a means of money, and nothing more.

The woman in his cabin was much more than a vessel for him to use to ease his sexual needs. Hell, he couldn't remember the last time he'd gazed upon a pussy so pink and perfect, giving him a rock-hard erection. It took all his strength not to release his cock and plunge deep into her seeping core. He wanted to feel her searing heat about his length as he pumped into her. Having her tied to his bed had only added to his agony as she'd struggled against the bonds, fighting her own reactions to his touch.

No, what was he thinking? Women were nothing but trouble. It was a woman who drove him from his family, his home—a wicked woman with a taste for danger.

"Captain, yesterday when we were in port I heard that Captain Mendoza was still hunting for you. He's become obsessed in finding you—and killing you," Thomas said, concern edging his voice.

"Aye, I heard this as well. He's been hunting me for months without any luck."

"Yes, but one of these days he'll catch up with you."

Jason chuckled. "Perhaps. Mendoza is still angry for my stealing this sloop a year ago." Jason patted the helm wheel with his hand. "She's a good ship and she called to me. I couldn't ignore her call."

"Or was it the forty thousand pieces of gold on board that called to you?"

He laughed joyously. "Gold indeed calls to a pirate, 'tis our way of life."

"Aye, Captain, but now you have a dangerous man on your trail."

"He hasn't caught me yet."

It was true, Captain Lorenzo Mendoza was angered more than Jason had predicted. The Spaniard had a red-hot temper over the loss of his fortune and ship. Jason had used trickery to get the ship, attacking at night while the crew was ashore, drunk and wenching. Jason had even paid the barkeep to drug the rum served to the Spanish crew to ensure their inability to fight the bold move to capture their ship.

The *Sea Hawk* was the envy of many buccaneers sailing in these waters, and feared among merchants for its swift attack capability. Under Jason's command, the *Sea Hawk* was a true scourge of the seas. Captain Flint was feared as well as admired among his pirate brethren.

And a woman was not going to ruin his reputation. Finding this temptress was a wrinkle in his plans. He had to focus on his job, not on some alluring siren of the sea. A woman would never bring him down again.

Shelley—no, he mustn't think of her by name. The *slave* would cater to his needs then when he tired of her, he'd release her with a small bag of gold to start a new life. He'd forget her the moment she was set ashore. In the meantime, he would taste her delights to the fullest measure.

Minutes seemed to pass slowly as Jason thought of enjoying the slave in his cabin. Yet he stayed on deck at the helm, watching his crew secure the bounty from the *Santa Rosa* and get back to their regular business of caring for the ship.

Thomas tried to talk to him further of Mendoza and his latest conquests, but Jason had no interest in the other captain. If Mendoza accomplished half of the rumored conquests, he'd surely secured his slot on a pirate hunter's list as the number one menace on the sea. However, Jason suspected many of the rumors were false and spread to cause fear.

Jason wasn't afraid of Mendoza, nor any other pirate. He wasn't afraid of death, he welcomed it. Anything to ease the pain within his heart.

He had survived years in pirating, a feat in these times of death upon the sea from both rival pirates and pirate hunters. When Jason had left England for the sea, it was with a death wish. Many men died at sea and Jason figured he'd join their ranks. Alas, it was not his fate. Jason went from a common crewmember to first mate then to captain in the matter of two years. There were advantages in an education, even at sea. His former captain, Captain Stuart of the schooner the *Golden Viper*, recognized Jason's potential and quickly took him on. He later told Jason of his plans to retire from pirating and gave him the *Golden Viper*.

The schooner had served him well until they met a Spanish galleon with massive firepower. The *Golden Viper* sank to the bottom of the Caribbean Sea and Jason and his crew made for the port of Santiago. There Jason hatched his plot to steal Mendoza's ship—and spawned a reputation for pirating against his own kind. To capture a fellow pirate's ship was unheard of in the pirate ranks.

Since when did a *pirate* play by rules? The dangerous act earned Jason a reputation for cunning strength and intelligence, and his crew depended on those qualities to line their pockets with gold.

When the sun dipped into the horizon, he went to the galley and had the cook make a tray for his little captive.

Jason thought about what he wanted her to do for him tonight, and ordered Thomas to bring a brass tub and hot water to his cabin that evening. She was going to bathe her master before he used her body for his needs.

He swore emotion would never come into play with this sweet slave. It was strictly sexual. Nothing more. After all, a pirate was not to be loved—he was to be feared.

Chapter Three

ဢ

At some point during the afternoon, Shelley fell asleep on the small bed. She wasn't fully aware of how much time had passed until she heard the captain break the door lock. Despite disposing of the flimsy door latch with an effortless shove, he calmly entered the room. He placed a tray of food on the small table and pulled the entire table to the side as far as it could go. Then some men brought in a brass tub. The realization hit her as they toted in several buckets of heated water. The captain meant to take a bath!

The moment the men left, he turned on her, glaring. At the cock of his brow, she sat up in the bed.

"Rule number one, slave," he announced. "No clothes."

"You didn't expect me to stay in here naked all the time, did you?" Her ire rose.

"You either take off those clothes now or I will slice them off. Which is it, slave?"

With a loud sniff of anger, she stood and began to work the rope about her waist. "My name is Shelley, not *slave*."

"You are a slave and will be called as such." He paused then pulled the knife from his boot. "You take too long," he commented as he leaned in and sliced the rope from about her, flinging it across the room.

"Hey!" She grasped the clothes to her body but they were too big, the pants dropping to the floor. Only the loose shirt covered her, but not for long. His glare at her hands clasping the shirt about her was enough for her to succumb to his demand. It wasn't that she was weak. She could refuse. But with his powerful form and overwhelming strength, he was sure to win in the end. Besides, she wanted to see desire within his eyes—desire that she ignited.

She let the shirt fall open and it fell on top of the discarded pants.

Her body was on fire and the cool air was a welcome sensation against her warm skin. She stood straight, her breasts hardening under his heated stare. Cream gathered within her cunt as she waited for him to say something.

Peeking up at his face, she saw the raw lust sizzling in his dark brown eyes. His gaze traveled slowly over her body and she could almost feel the burn on her skin as he studied her every curve.

She fought the instant urge to cover herself as his eyes rested upon her apex. Having shaved her thatch just before the dive, she never dreamed anyone would actually *see* it.

"Tell me, did they shave you like that in the harem?" He stepped toward her and brushed his fingers over her sensitive skin. The warm touch of his fingertips across her shaven pubis made her gasp.

"No, I wasn't..." She closed her eyes and sank into the sensations he created. How could she concentrate when his fingers swirled over her apex like that? Her breathing quickened and she was lost in a world of sensual wonder.

Then he pulled away. She snapped open her eyes, questioning his absence. But there before her, he stripped out of his clothes and—

Oh, holy cow! Were there men built like that *before* steroids?

Muscles rippled and flexed beneath tanned skin, his chest was perfectly smooth and when he turned his back to her, she saw faint healed scars across his toned back from what she assumed was a lash. He was whipped? She gasped in spite of herself and he turned to face her for a moment.

"Life's tough on the seas."

"But it looks so—"

"It *was* painful, but according to the code, I deserved my punishment." He turned away from her once again and unbuckled his pants, allowing them to drop to the floor.

Shelley saw the most luscious male ass flex enticingly as he stepped into the brass tub. Damn, he was an impressive figure of a man. What was his cock like? Sadly she hadn't seen it before he lowered into the tub and sighed.

"What did you do to deserve getting whipped?"

He chuckled low. "I punched the second mate of the *Golden Viper*. I was but a mere seaman. The sentence for striking a crewmember is forty lashes but Captain Stuart had ordered only twenty. Later he told me the second mate was a no-good bastard who deserved a knock to the jaw. The captain took me under his wing after that, and I took over his command later. But it took me two months to fully recover from the lashing."

The water splashed gently as he moved in the tub.

Her heart ached for him. A man whipped—

"What are you waiting for? Bathe me now, slave."

Son of a bitch. He deserved to be whipped—*right now*. A full forty.

Then she had an evil idea. What if she could arouse him then deny him completion? She smiled as she stepped over to the tub and crouched down. Reaching for the washcloth and soap, she brushed her body against his wet skin. He inhaled sharply, and she knew he was much more affected by her than he wished to admit.

Oh yes, this could be fun.

"What do you wish for me to wash first...Captain?" She added the last to give the impression that she was aware of her status as a slave serving her captain. There was a hint of erotic excitement in the idea of having this sexy man be her master and commander.

"You may start with my back," he instructed, the smallest glimmer of passion edging his voice. "Then move down from there."

He leaned forward in the tub to allow her better access to his back and she was struck by the sheer beauty of the power that lay beneath the tanned skin and the lighter-colored scars from the whip. Well-developed sinew moved in a fluid grace of strength, and she ached to touch him.

Shelley lathered the washcloth and at the first touch upon his back, her body reacted in acute awareness of his virile masculinity. She tried to gulp back her moans and concentrate on lathering his skin, washing away the grime and sweat, but the slippery consistency of the soap only added to the sensual seduction. He didn't have to actively try to arouse her, just looking at him made her juices gather between her legs. In her crouching position, naked and vulnerable, she was sure he could smell the scent of her excitement.

Did she actually think she could deny this man anything he asked? It seemed impossible, his affect upon her too keen. Her building desire to offer herself without a fight seemed the only course to find some sort of relief.

Her pussy swelled with need and her clit throbbed with a growing passion to be stroked into oblivion by the captain.

She set her cloth over the side of the tub and reached for a jug nearby filled with clean water. She picked it up and rinsed his back.

"Mmm, that feels good, slave."

That word made her body jolt up a notch in anticipation. Good God, how can the idea of being a slave to this man, any man, be so sexually appealing?

"I'm glad you approve, Captain."

He leaned back in the tub and closed his eyes with a sigh. "In the privacy of our cabin, you may call me Jason."

"Will you call me Shelley then, *Jason*?" She picked up the washcloth and lathered it again.

He cracked an eye at her. "We'll see."

Well, it was better than, "You are a slave and will be called as such".

She began to wash his chest and marveled over the male beauty of his form as she touched him through the cloth. The heat from his body seemed to call to her, beckoning to her.

He caught her wrist and when she turned her gaze to his, she gasped at the intense storm of emotions raging within their dark depths. "Touch me with your hands," he softly commanded.

Nodding absently, she dropped the cloth and placed a hand upon his upper chest. Sure enough, the heat seared her.

As she leaned toward him, her breasts hanging just above the water, he reached up with a gentle splash and caressed one hard peak. She closed her eyes and struggled to breathe as he ran a thumb across her tight nipple, sending shivers of delight down her spine. Her clit ached with need and she was tempted to ask him to help her.

She wanted him. More than anything, she needed him—his touch, his strength, his power over her.

"You're such a beauty, luv. So ripe and ready for the taking," he said, giving her nipple a slight pinch. "Tell me…was your former master good to you? Did he teach you the ways to seduce and please a man?"

Silence seemed to be her best answer. She couldn't bring herself to lie, knowing sooner or later he'd discover she had no master. She was a victim of magic, a time traveler, a woman discovering desire seemingly for the first time in her life. Besides, how would he react to her claim of being from the future? He'd probably think she was suffering from some tropical jungle fever and crazed delusions. It was entirely possible. However, the man beneath her palms was *very* real.

He watched her with those eyes, so aware of her every movement, every reaction. She slid her hand over his chest to his nipple and pinched the taut point. He inhaled sharply then chuckled. Grasping her wandering hand, he led it slowly beneath the bathwater, down his abdomen to the large shaft straining between his legs.

Instinctively she encircled her hand about its girth and squeezed slightly.

"Oh fuck," he murmured.

She began to move her hand up and down his cock. Heat pulsed from it, driving her to continue her slow, torturous seduction. Up, down, pause. Up. Down. Pause. Squeeze.

His breathing was ragged as he fought for control.

Power over this mountain of a man was drugging her sensibilities.

Just when she though she was the one with the upper hand, so to speak, he moved with a flash, pulling her into the water. Atop him, her body vibrated as it came into contact with his entire length.

The urge to kiss him was overpowering but he pulled her head down and nibbled at her neck. Whispering promises of ecstasy, he nudged her legs open, pulling her knees up to either side of his hips and slipping his cock right between her legs.

All conscious though fled her mind as her body took on a rhythm of rubbing against him. Water splashed out of the tub but she didn't care. The added slippery surface on his skin and hers only drove her further, her needs outweighing any concerns of how she came to the past or how she'd ever return to her own time.

All that mattered was Jason and the sensation of him pressed against her. His cock rubbed against her labia and she moaned as she positioned herself to take him into her.

Then the searing heat of his steel-like erection pushed into her. Shelley saw stars behind her eyelids as he filled her exquisitely to the hilt. Her body paused in its movements just to enjoy the sensation of him inside her.

"Sweetheart, come on, fuck me," he croaked, his hands upon her hips.

She leaned back, straightening her body while keeping him buried safely within her. He groaned and reached up to cup her breasts. She moved her hips slightly, the glorious thrill of his cock well within her pussy surging with each passing second.

Lifting her body up with her thighs, supporting her weight and direction with her hands upon the sides of the tub, she began to move with him inside her hungry cunt. She found a tempo as she used him for her own pleasure. He thrust up into her each time she came down upon his cock, groaning his satisfaction.

Water continued to splash wildly out of the tub as she fucked the captain. There was going to be quite a mess to clean up afterward but he didn't seem to care. And neither did Shelley. She was having the ride of her life.

He stroking the pointed, aching tips of her nipples and she moaned as she lost herself in the moment.

The climax built within her, beginning at the point of their joining and radiating throughout her body, into every muscle, every nerve. Her clit slammed against his pelvis, driving her higher into ecstasy, out of her mind with complete rapture.

He grew larger within her as he approached his own breaking point. It was just enough to send her reeling over the edge. Her orgasm slammed into her like a cannon blast, every limb vibrating with the sheer force of pleasure. She cried out in her newfound euphoria, a place she'd never experienced before this. But now, tossed into the past and into the life of this pirate, Shelley came alive and screamed as her body shook with glorious spasms. From the top of her head to the tips of her toes, she rode out the elation of her climax as her pirate lover found his own completion and spilled his seed deep within her body.

As her spasms began to calm, her body still surfed upon the aftershocks of this amazing experience. She'd had lovers before, but none had ever brought her to such heights of bliss. The captain left all her past lovers in the dust.

Shelley relaxed against him, turning around to lie back against his hard chest. He wrapped his arms around her and breathed warmly against her ear. His chest moved with each breath as he found his natural rhythm once again.

The water was low and it cooled their skin. He played with a stray tendril of hair pasted against her neck. She breathed deeply, taking in the normalcy of the moment, of being so close to this man who showed her such pleasure.

"You are well trained, slave," he breathed against her neck before kissing the sensitive skin there.

It was like a bucket of ice water dumped over her.

She was still a slave to him. Nothing more.

And why the hell did that hurt so much? Why did she care?

"Slave," she whispered in disbelief, tears threatening to spill from her eyes.

He stilled. "*My* slave." He tightened his arms about her. "*Mine.*"

Somehow his possessiveness was strangely comforting. She wasn't just any slave, he had claimed her.

"No man will ever have you again. You belong to me." His voice was unwavering, and a jolt of renewed desire shot through her veins.

She turned her head to him, one side of her face pressed lightly to his shoulder, and she sighed.

If she was to be a slave to any man, she wanted it to be her pirate captain.

He reached down between her legs and touched her clit with his fingertips. She moaned and opened her legs farther. His touch was hot and she was on fire once again. At one light

197

stroke of his finger against her nubbin, she was ready for more.

Even now, just moments after they'd fucked, she felt his cock harden against her backside. Just this simple reaction to her made the juices flow from her cunt. She was hungry for him to be inside her again.

"Jason," she whispered as she arched into his touch.

"Yes, luv," he gasped as he continued his gentle assault. "I want to hear my little slave come again."

"Oh God," she cried, and bucked when he carefully pinched her clit between his finger and thumb.

Her mind was unable to think clearly. Not as he held her small organ so intimately. He tested its sensitivity as he teased her clit by moving it in small circles.

"Bet you love getting your pussy licked, don't you?" he asked with a groan.

Her only answer was a nod and a moan. She couldn't arch up high enough to encourage him to increase the pressure upon her clit. Just a little more, just a slight increase in his touch would send her shattering.

But he chuckled and refused to let her come. "Not yet." He pressed his free hand against her middle, easing her back down into the tub and against his hard body—a body she was going insane for in want of exploration.

She burned to map his body, to learn every line, every crease, every muscle. If only he'd stop this torment and let her find release.

And she knew what would send her over. She wanted that huge cock up her ass.

She shifted in the tub, rising again over his cock. When she felt he was properly positioned, she sat very slowly, taking him into her anus.

"Bloody hell," he croaked as she gave herself a moment to adjust to his size. Her anal muscles clenched about him, and she loved it as the pain ebbed and the ecstasy built once again.

She wiggled her ass with him inside her, and he steadied her with his hand upon her hips.

"Touch yourself," he commanded.

Oh yes.

She knew just what she needed.

In control over her clit, she thrummed it as he moved within her. She felt filled, stretched, and as she passed her fingers over the sensitive surface of her nubbin, she was lost in rising passion.

He grunted behind her as he pumped into her tight hole and she rubbed herself faster, her body moving in abandon as she climbed higher and higher.

She wanted to push herself further, to prolong the moments of sheer bliss. Just as her body seemed on the edge of climax, she paused to let her body calm for a few seconds before caressing her clit once again. Meanwhile Jason seemed lost within her, thrusting, groaning with each squeeze about his cock.

He grasped her breasts, one in each hand and squeezed them roughly. She loved it.

Shelley strummed her clit with a frenzied pace and brought herself to a mind-blowing climax, and Jason wasn't far behind as he pumped into her, climaxing with a triumphant yell.

Chapter Four

ℬ

Pirates are to be feared. He had no room in his life for love. However, he could take on this temptress as his personal slave—his mistress. She'd never know the touch of another man after tonight. He'd make sure of that. There was no chance of him letting her go as he'd planned just hours ago. That was before he'd tasted her skin, sampled her skills and reveled within her body.

But he'd never love her. No, love would be a curse. He'd never want her to suffer because of him. It was better to keep her as his mistress. Love would never become part of the equation.

Love had taken a toll upon his soul once already. He'd lost a brother because of love. He'd become an outlaw to his country because of love.

"Are you all right?" she asked, breaking the silence that had fallen over the room. Only a few moments ago their screams of ecstasy drowned out the gentle beat of the waves breaking against the wooden hull.

"I was just thinking of home."

"Would it help to talk about it?" She grasped his hand and pulled his arm about her, enclosing herself in his embrace.

He sighed. "I haven't been home in seven years."

"Why don't you go back?"

"I can't. I'd be arrested the moment I set foot on British soil."

"Why?" She paused as he chuckled softly behind her. "No, dumb question. You're a pirate. Of course you would be arrested."

"It is nice to know someone forgot I was a pirate, even if it was only for a moment. I wasn't always a pirate. I was a respectable man until…"

"Until?" she pressed.

"Until the day I killed my brother's wife."

She turned quickly, water splashing out of the tub at her movement. "You killed your brother's wife?"

He nodded solemnly, still unsure how much to tell her. Shelley was the first person in whom he felt the need to confide his story. But could he truly trust her? "I really don't–"

"Were you having an affair with her?" she guessed.

"Aye, I was. She was a beauty and I was young, impressionable. She lured me into her bed and I followed like a naïve schoolboy."

"How old were you?"

"Fifteen." He paused. "It was wrong and I knew it. But it was hard to deny myself the touch of her skin once I had her."

"And how long did it take your brother to find out?"

"About three months. He was in France for business during the affair. When he returned, he found us together in bed." He stopped, thinking back to the day when James burst through the bedroom door in a rage after obviously hearing the sounds of sex from the other side.

"Go on." She laid a comforting hand upon his arm and her genuine concern warmed him.

"He pulled out his sword and challenged me so he could defend his honor. As the new Earl of Essex, he demanded satisfaction. He was upset and very angry as he loved Claire immensely. I knew this and yet I was drawn in by her beauty and sexual prowess. She was a lonely creature, longing for her husband but choosing to find her satisfaction elsewhere when James failed to fulfill her needs.

"As James and I fought in the bedchambers, and eventually out into the vast hallway of the castle, Claire chose to announce to the entire household her husband's...*difficulty* in bed. I guess she was trying to help by taking the focus off me and onto herself. Only when I turned to her, James struck. My sword flew from my hand—and into Claire."

"Oh God," she murmured.

"Claire lay dying, proclaiming her love for James—and me. When she died, James banished me from the estate, claiming I was a murderer. He told me to leave England, never to return. I'm sure James reported Claire's death to the authorities as murder."

"But it was an accident!"

"No, I killed her."

"It was an accident, Jason. You couldn't have controlled where the sword would land."

"I killed her the moment I entered her bed." He touched her cheek and felt her cooling skin. "Come, let's get out of this cold water and into bed. We're not through for the night."

As Jason helped her from the tub and dried her cool skin, he felt a surge of tenderness. No one had ever heard his side of the tale that drove him from his home. And this mysterious woman seemed to ease his fears with the gentle curve of her lips. She listened to his horror without fainting or striking out at him with accusations of murder.

A strange feeling began to fill his heart toward this woman that appeared from nowhere into his life.

He carefully toweled her goose-bumpy skin, and at her small smile as he wrapped a towel about her body, an achy tug at his insides made him pause.

She stepped across the small room to the bed, her wet blonde hair stuck to her neck and upper shoulders. Cocooned in a pale, threadbare towel, Shelley was the portrait of a woman of class and distinction. This was not a peasant or a bar wench, she was much more. She may not be dressed in elegant gowns and her hair wasn't coiffed into the latest style, but she was the most beautiful female he had ever encountered.

And she belonged to him.

He smiled and approached her. "I want to sample you again, but in bed this time."

Her unmistakable desire flushed her cheeks in a becoming blush. She licked her lips, her tongue swiping over her top lip and he was caught mesmerized. This couldn't be anything more than fascination that made him want her. But having been inside her twice, it seemed to only whet his appetite for more.

He was serious when he'd said she belonged to him. No other man would ever have her. As he moved to the bed, he pulled the towel from her grasp in one slow, fluid tug. She let it fall away and he couldn't wait to taste her again.

"How do you feel about being my slave now, luv?" He reached out to run her hair between his fingertips, soft and smooth like fine silk from the Orient.

Without a word, she turned her head to his hand and took his index finger into her mouth. He nearly came unglued as she sucked upon his finger, her tongue swirling sweetly about its length.

The urge to kiss her overwhelmed him.

Then she leaned into him and the feel of her cooling skin against him drove him insane with need.

He captured her within his arms and lowered her to the bed.

"Jason," she moaned. It sounded like a plea.

He sank onto her, her softness a welcoming cushion for his harder body. A groan of longing passed his lips as he felt her hips thrust upward. But her satisfaction would not be met...not until he mapped her body with his hands and studied every peak and valley of her luscious flesh.

Starting at her neck, he licked the sensitive skin and felt her erratic pulse. She clung to his shoulders with her hands and wrapped one of her legs around his thigh. She wriggled beneath him and the smooth contact of skin against skin cranked his libido higher.

He took a hard nipple into his mouth and she cried out. She gripped the back of his head to her breast as he suckled her stiffened nipple deep into his mouth. She clawed his back but the slight pain only drove him onward to taste more of this little wildcat.

He released one nipple only to capture the other and suckle upon its delectable texture. Her nipples were like ripened raspberries sweetened by the sunshine, and he lost himself in feasting upon her delights.

She rubbed her leg along his thigh and he relished the silky texture of her. Such a beauty—a true treasure to be cherished. And Jason intended to lose himself in this greatest of treasures night after night.

He continued on, licking the sweet skin around the curve of a breast, down one side of her torso and to the center of her navel. When he dipped his tongue into her belly button, she whimpered. She ran her hands through his hair, pulling its length from the queue to fall loose about his shoulders. The sensation of his hair against her responsive flesh caused her to toss her head back.

"Open your eyes and look at me," he commanded.

She lay there lost in her own moaning.

"Shelley…look at me."

The use of her name shocked him, but it felt right—and it was just the thing to bring her back from her ecstasy. She lifted her head and looked down at him crouched over her navel.

Her eyes struck him to the core, the depth of her desire reflecting in the dark brown pools. Who was this woman and how did she get on the *Santa Rosa*? Her clothes were as strange as her accent, yet her passionate freedom with a stranger was the trademark of a well-trained sex slave. She'd taken him into her body with a yearning to please—again, typical of a trained slave. But it also seemed she wanted him for *her* pleasure. That was *not* his experience with a sex slave.

"Please, Jason," she pleaded as she opened her legs wider.

It was too much a temptation to ignore. He moved lower to gaze at the open folds of her sex and inhaled her natural feminine scent—one laced with desire as her cream dripped about the opening. Her pink, moist pussy called to him to feast upon its sweet nectar.

He touched the little bud that tempted him with a soft brush of his finger. She sighed, a throaty groan, as she grasped the sheet with her hands, and he watched her cunt turn a darker shade of pink. Another pass of his finger over her clit and she bucked her hips upward.

As he began to trace his finger through her folds, coating it with the thick cream of her sex, he watched her react to the increase and decrease of pressure, learning exactly what excited her further.

It filled his being with a sense of sexual gratification at every sound of passion he coaxed from her. And something else...pleasure within his *soul* to give her such moments of bliss with the merest touch of his fingers upon her body.

He was not a man who pleasured women for his own fulfillment. He was to be pleasured, not the other way around. What caused such a change with this strange woman? She was different from the others of his acquaintance...even Claire.

"Jason," Shelley moaned.

Her voice was heavy with desire and he could hold off tasting her no longer. He lowered his mouth to her clit and kissed the hot bud. It strained between his lips to a hard point. Her scent filled his nostrils as he flicked his tongue over her clit, and she cried out in blissful agony.

Trailing his tongue lazily over her throbbing nubbin, he dipped the tip of his forefinger into her slick passage.

"Oh...*yes*," she whimpered in abandon.

When he grazed his teeth against her clit she yelped, but not in pain. She grasped the sheet beneath her tighter as she kept a close rein on her excitement, prolonging fulfillment.

He slowly pushed two fingers deep into her cunt and sucked upon her clit. She climaxed, no longer able to hold back, and he moved his fingers within her, her muscles clenching down upon them in rhythmic contractions. She screamed in unison with her spasms and he increased the pressure of his mouth upon her nubbin.

In and out and in again, he worked her orgasm with his fingers, drawing out her pleasure. And when she began to come down from her euphoria, he pulled his fingers from her and drank the juices flowing from her pussy.

Sweet and delicious, it was a taste uniquely Shelley—like the finest French wine. He licked her like a man deprived of sustenance, her honeyed cream the elixir of his very existence. He rubbed her tender clit with his thumb as he continued to lap up her juices and she tumbled into a second climax. Sticking his tongue well into her channel, her cum flowed into his mouth with each squeeze of her muscles.

Cries of her joyful submission filled the room as Shelley rode out her orgasm.

Jason backed away from her wet, pink cunt and just gazed upon its feminine beauty—well loved and flushed with spent passion.

Her breathing was labored as she lie back trying to recover from her climactic spasms. But he wasn't through, not yet. His cock was rock-hard and aching to plunge into the depths of Shelley's cunt.

He knelt on the bed looking down upon her. Her hair was wild and splayed across the pillows, her chest rose and fell as her breathing began to calm and a light pink glow colored her skin as a sign of passionate exercise.

She opened her eyes and gazed up at him towering over her. "That was amazing."

A glimmer at her wrist caught his eye. The slave band.

Was she taught to compliment her partners in bed?

The thought of her performing for another man enraged him. Could he wipe clean her memories of any past lovers with one night of sexual delights? He wanted her to think only of him, to want only *him* to fulfill her desires. Even if he had to keep her tied to his bed to get his way!

He reached for the ropes that had been left on the floor, and in a flash he bound one of her wrists to the bed frame.

"Wait! What's going on?" she asked in a confused frenzy as she fought against his grip.

"You're mine and I intend to make sure you remember that fact."

As he caught her free wrist to secure it to the bed, she struggled. "What do you hope to accomplish by tying me down again?"

"By keeping you here at my whim, I will make you depend on me for everything. Only through your surrender can I be sure you are my obedient slave."

She stilled. Her dark eyes filled with tears. "I thought what we just shared was special."

Jason leaned over her body, her breasts brushing along his chest. "It *was* special, luv. And now I am going to make you submit your body...and *heart* to me."

"How?"

"By making you beg me to fuck you. To take you and make you mine alone."

She gasped and he smiled down at her. He ran his gaze over her perfect body, soft and inviting, and he took hold of his cock and began to stroke its hardness.

She squirmed on the bed as she watched in amazement at his member growing before her eyes.

"You're cruel," she whimpered.

"Not cruel, just determined. I want all of you."

She stilled her struggles and relaxed. "But you have me as your captive slave."

He covered her body with his, gasping at the heat of their flesh touching—an inferno circling about them both at the contact. "Aye, I have your body, but I want much more than your flesh." He nudged open her legs and his cock ran along the slippery folds of her sex.

He glanced up at her hands holding onto the ropes with all her strength as he slowly entered her body. Her head tossed back on the pillow, her eyes closed and her breathing increased, and he felt her succumb to passion once again.

His cock moved deeper into her channel.

"*Oh…*" she breathed when he pushed in farther, his balls flush against her buttocks.

He paused, savoring the simple ecstasy of his cock buried within the wet core of her…his slave…his mistress. Emotion flooded his senses at the physical bliss of their connection. No port wench ever felt so good.

When he began to move within her sheath, she grasped her bonds tightly and thrust up her hips to encourage his pace to quicken. He was approaching his breaking point, finding it difficult to hold back his climax. As he pushed in and out of her, she wriggled and moaned in complete abandon and it was more than he could tolerate.

"Tell me, who is your master, luv?" he asked as he thrust into her cunt with an powerful expert's skill.

"You," she whispered.

"Shout the name of your master. Tell me who owns you…desires you." He retreated then thrust inside once again, more forceful and controlled.

"Jason…oh Jason!" she cried as her muscles began to clench about his cock, sucking his length deeply into her body.

He shouted with his release, his heated essence pouring in waves of ecstasy as he joined her in the heights of passion and desire in a shattering climax.

Grunting with each spasm, Jason emptied himself into his slave lover.

As their bodies began to calm, Jason reached over, untied Shelley's wrists and lay down on the bed, gathering her close to his side. She wrapped her arms about him without hesitation. When she sighed in contentment, his heart ached.

Maybe a pirate needed more than to be feared. Perhaps a pirate needed to be loved after all.

Chapter Five

Shelley awoke alone the next morning. Her body ached but felt wonderful. Never had anyone loved her as completely as Jason. He must be the reason she'd been thrust into the past.

A knock at the door announced his entrance as he carried in a pitcher of water.

"I see you are awake, luv." He placed the pitcher on the table. "Thought you'd like to clean up and come topside today."

She sat up quickly, forgetting the sheet as it fell to her waist. "You mean it?"

He stood unmoving, his eyes raking over her breasts. "You'd best cover up, luv, or you will never see daylight this day." His voice was thick with desire and goose bumps rose on her arms under his intense gaze.

He grabbed a wash basin from under the bed and poured water into it. "But first I will leave you to wash and dress. Then I will take you on deck to meet my men." He opened the door and, with his hand upon the knob, turned to her. "On deck you will call me 'sir' out of respect. My men must know without doubt that you belong to me. Do you understand?"

"Aye, Captain, sir," she said with a low laugh.

A small smile curled his lips. "Perhaps you should call me 'sir' in bed as well."

She stood and let the sheet fall away from her body, exposing herself to her lover. "I am here for you to command, sir." She lifted her hands and cupped her breasts, teasing her nipples with a few pinches between her fingers.

She had no control over her wants as she offered herself to him once again. Her cream gathered between her legs, lubricating her passage.

Without a word he bolted the door and shed his vest. "Vixen," he whispered as he took her into his arms and kissed her neck. Shelley melted into his embrace and the roughness of his clothes excited her further as they brushed against her naked flesh.

He released her to shed his shirt. She moaned, wishing to prolong the moment but quickly realizing this was not going to be a slow mating as she ran her hands over the toned surface of his chest. She passed over his nipples with her fingertips and he ripped open his breeches, pulling out his powerful cock.

She instinctively wrapped her fingers about his length and shuddered at the heated strength within. He paused as she gripped his thickness, letting out a ragged breath while holding on to his last thread of control.

She was mesmerized by his organ and her mouth watered to taste its magnificence. "I want to please you," she said in a husky voice as she moved her hand slowly up and down his rod.

His answer was a groan. "You please me well."

She lowered to her knees and admired the masculine beauty of his sex. Full, purplish and shiny, the bulbous head of his cock was like a ripe plum, inviting her mouth to encircle it and take a savory taste of its sweet flesh. She licked the tip gently with one swipe.

He growled and splayed his fingers through her hair, silently guiding her to continue. But she pulled back slightly, wanting to admire his powerful cock further. It was thick and hard, and when she held it and squeezed, he moaned.

She felt a surge of feminine power over her lover, a man that commanded so much about him, but was rendered weak with a touch of her hand.

With her other hand, she tested the size and weight of his balls. He tightened his fingers in her hair, trying to control his urge to come a little longer.

She licked at a glistening bead that gathered on the tip of his cock and then closed her mouth about the head. Instinctual need and desire to please overtook her actions as she began to take his cock deeper into her mouth. She continued to hold his sac in one hand as she guided his length with the other. Closing her eyes, she gave Jason her heart by pleasuring him into orgasm.

Shelley needed to taste him upon her tongue. She wanted to drink him, know she brought about his surrender. The captain was a master of men, but she wanted to give him escape from his duties and experience freedom within sexual release.

Moving up and down his cock, she lost herself in blissful ecstasy. He had claimed her body as his last night, and now, Shelley claimed him. She knew why she'd come back in time. It was for Jason. He was the reason she was there. And she'd make sure she'd enjoy every moment. Who knew when—or if—she'd ever return to her time?

She hummed as she devoured him and he began to cry out as his balls tightened within her hand. Warm spurts of salty liquid filled her mouth as he came. His hands held her head to his groin, guiding her with each thrust of his cock and every burst of the essence of his climax.

As his orgasm calmed, she pulled her mouth from about his length then licked away any stray droplets from her lips.

His grip on her hair eased and he wavered on his feet.

She remained crouched on the floor. Sitting back on her heels, she waited for him to recover. He sat down on the bed and closed his eyes, his breathing beginning to calm.

"You please me *very* well, luv," he finally said breathlessly.

She giggled. "As I said, I'm here to please, am I not, Captain?"

"Aye, you perform your duties well."

She paused in silence. "I don't consider being with you a duty."

He peeked open an eye. "If you were not my slave, would you still wish to share my bed?"

"I am *not* your slave." She crawled closer to him and laid her hands upon his thighs. "I am your lover."

He reached for her face, tracing the curve of her cheek with his fingertips. "Do you give of yourself freely to me?"

She nodded. Her eyes searched his face and she saw the intensity of his thoughts racing through his mind. She was sure many women gave their bodies to him, but did any offer their heart?

He reached for her hand and laid it within his own. He fingered the slave bangle at her wrist for a few moments then said, "You must be anxious to get some fresh air. I will step out while you relieve yourself, bathe and dress. Just knock on the door when you are dressed and ready."

Their gazes locked and for a moment, she hoped he would kiss her. Instead he lifted her hand to his mouth and placed a kiss on the back.

As she remained crouched on the floor, watching him leave her alone in the cabin, a tear ran down her face.

He wanted her body but he didn't want her love. Or was he afraid to love?

Maybe it was for the best. She was heading into stormy seas tampering with the past. The captain disappeared from history, killed during a sea battle according to her research. If he was supposed to die in a sea attack, what significance would her presence have on his fate?

Shelley took a deep breath and exhaled slowly. Fate played a cruel part in this saga. Heartache and pain were sure to play a part in this eventually. She just had to remain strong and keep a stronger grip on her heartstrings.

However, she knew it was too late for that.

After relieving her bladder in a chamber pot, Shelly went about her toilette.

She splashed water on her face and cleaned her body as best she could in the bedside basin. The water was cold but refreshing. After drying off, she slipped on the pants she'd found in his chest along with the white linen shirt and secured the waist with some rope. A small smile curled her lips as she thought of Jason using that rope to tie her to the bed, then showing her complete ecstasy in her surrender.

She combed her long hair with a brush from his chest and tried to plait the length to keep it from tangling. She tucked it into the back of her shirt and then donned a plain black tricorne hat. When she was done, she tapped on the door and Jason opened it.

"You look like a captain's wench, luv."

"I was trying for cabin boy." She smiled up into his face. With the sun at his back, his brown hair glowed with a hint of copper.

His eyes grazed her figure and lingered upon her loose breasts. "No, luv. No man in his right mind could ever mistake you for a boy."

Her cheeks heated and he laughed softly. He offered his hand and said, "Come, wench. You need some fresh air to fill your lungs."

She climbed the stairs and emerged on deck to sunshine and salty air. The crewmembers were busy at work tidying the rigging or scrubbing the wooden deck with brushes. Some paused in their duties to look up at her. Jason stood behind her and placed a hand upon her shoulder, and her tense muscles eased.

One man ordered the others who had stopped cleaning the deck. "Get back to work, ye mangy dogs!" The men jumped at his voice and hurried back to their task.

"Come." Jason gently directed Shelley to move aft and climb more stairs to the quarterdeck.

There above the main deck, Shelley took in the beauty of the ship at sea. The sails caught the breeze and powered the craft through the aquamarine waters. The sun's rays danced on the waves as the ship cut through the sea with an awe-inspiring power.

In an enchanted daze, she moved to the railing and gazed out over the jewel-toned waters, spotting a school of dolphins frolicking alongside the hull.

"Dolphins like to race the ship. Amazing, isn't it?" He stood behind her and she could feel the welcoming heat from his body wrap about her. He laid his hands on her shoulders, and she closed her eyes and sighed.

"Amazing isn't the right word," she said in a dreamy voice. Her heart began to thud faster within her chest. Tender emotions encircled her heart as his breath kissed her exposed neck, sending tingles of joy down her spine.

"How do you feel, luv?" His voice wavered.

"Happy."

He exhaled and gently squeezed her shoulders with his hands. "Good."

Their words were simple but the emotional turmoil beneath the surface was almost palpable. She leaned back into his chest and relaxed her body. He slipped a hand into her shirt and cupped a bare breast. The contact of his warm hand to her cool skin made her shiver with a renewed need. She couldn't get enough of his touch. It was like heady wine, addictive and enticing.

He removed her hat and pulled her blonde hair free from her shirt. She welcomed the refreshing breeze through her hair.

Should she be feeling such tenderness toward this man, a pirate who claimed her as his slave? She hated the term but somehow liked his possessiveness, his complete domination over her mind and body. It would be easy to fall in love with him. So easy.

"Shelley?"

"Yes?" she answered dreamily.

"I'm not entirely inexperienced with women. I've had more than I can remember. One was pretty much like the next. But you..."

She stood frozen, holding her breath, her heart hanging on his words.

"You are not like the others." He squeezed her breast tenderly and she shivered as she slowly exhaled. He ran his free hand through her hair and she closed her eyes, savoring his caress.

They stood in silence as he continued to tantalize her with his loving touch. She melted into him, absorbed by his presence.

"Who are you? Are you a sea witch come to enchant me with your magic?"

"I'm not a witch," she whispered.

"But how did you get to be here?"

She turned toward him and he wrapped his arms around her waist. She laid her hands about his neck and gazed up into his face. "If I told you how I really came to be floating in the open ocean, you wouldn't believe me."

He touched her chin and tilted his head. "Tell me." His voice was commanding yet gentle.

"I—"

Chaos erupted below.

"All hands on deck! A ship to southern! A ship to southern!" The lookout called the warning to the ship's crew members.

"Shelley," he started as he grabbed her arm and pulled her along to the entrance to his cabin below deck. "Get below. Stay out of sight."

Then the lookout yelled, "'Tis the *Corazón Negro*. And it flies the skull and crossed swords—Captain Mendoza's flag!"

"Damn it," Jason muttered as he turned and raced to the quarterdeck. "He finally caught up with me."

Chapter Six

ഐ

The *Corazón Negro,* the *Black Heart.* His nemesis, Captain Lorenzo Mendoza, had acquired the famed brigantine as his vessel for revenge. Jason was sure the Spaniard had customized the ship to its best advantage, which meant Jason's best defense was speed. He should try to avoid hand-to-hand combat as his crew would surely be outmanned by that of the bigger ship.

"There are about twelve cannon, Captain," Thomas announced as he peered through the spyglass.

"Mendoza wouldn't risk weighing her down with much more." The cannons were only meant to cripple the opponent, preparing for the swoop and slash pillaging of the pirate crew. "However, let's not take any chances in underestimating."

Thomas lowered the spyglass. "What shall we do? Attack?"

Jason studied Mendoza's new ship. She was sure to be loaded with swivel guns on the rails and the crew probably outnumbered his four to one. Trying to make a break for it seemed the most intelligent thing to do. It would be what Mendoza anticipated. However, he didn't want to run. He never backed down from a challenge. The Spaniard was hot for revenge and perhaps it was time to face his wrath.

Without a word, he took the spyglass from Thomas and lifted it to his eye. There he saw the activity buzzing on the *Corazón Negro.* They surely intended to board the *Sea Hawk.* Perhaps if he turned to fight, it would confuse not only Mendoza but his men as well.

"Well, Captain?" Thomas prodded. Nearby there stood more of his crew, all waiting with bated breath. A gaze at the hungry faces of his crew and Jason knew their hearts' desire.

"To arms, me lads!"

A cheer rang out over the deck as the men scrambled for their cutlasses and flintlocks.

"Avast ye dogs! Prepare for battle!" The quartermaster yelled out orders as the ship turned to meet with Mendoza and his *Corazón Negro*.

Just then, Shelley emerged on deck.

"Damn the woman!" Jason fumed as he began to stomp over to her, standing by the stairs to the cabin. Dressed in his pants and a white linen shirt, her hair wildly blowing in the sea wind, she was the most beautiful creature he'd ever seen. However, she was even lovelier when in complete surrender within his arms.

"Get below!" he bellowed, angry with his own brief fantasy of moments ago, the image of her panting with pleasure beneath his touch.

"No."

"Aboard ship is no place for a woman, let alone during a battle. Now do as I tell you and get below."

"No, I don't want to—"

He grasped her upper arm roughly. "Look here. What did I tell you about defying me? You want Mendoza to see your pretty blonde hair? I assure you, he'd want you. But he'd tire of you eventually and then sell you to a brothel in some remote pirate town. Do you want to have smelly seadogs between your legs?"

"I can't..." Her voice shook.

Gazing into her eyes, he realized his mistake. She wasn't defying him out of stubbornness. "You're scared." His voice softened.

She nodded. "Please, let me stay up here."

He wished he could but danger was now bearing down upon him. Having her so close affected his senses and his thoughts scattered for a brief moment.

"Come." He eased his hold on her arm and led her below, back inside the cabin.

"I can't stay in here with all this going on."

He closed the door behind him then caught her face between his hands. "Shelley, you have to stay here. And whatever you do, don't open the door for anyone but me. Bolt it, barricade it." At her fearful eyes he leaned into her. "There's a sword in my sea chest under the clothes. And under the floorboard beneath the bed, I have a set of pistols. Get them out and don't be afraid to use them if someone tries to come through the door."

Cannon fired in the distance. The battle had begun.

He kissed her forehead and turned away, opening the door. Before he closed it behind him, he said, "Shoot anyone who tries to get in."

As he headed topside, he cursed himself for growing soft toward a woman.

Then he cursed the day he ever stole from Captain Mendoza.

* * * * *

"Great." Shelley stood staring at the bolted door. That little lock wasn't going to keep anyone out. She definitely didn't feel safe here. Where the hell would she feel safe on a ship engaging in a sea battle with pirates?

The only place she felt secure was at Jason's side. That's where she wanted to be.

Cannon fire cracked again, this time closer. She stepped to the porthole and saw the brigantine bearing down on them. Noise of the crew running and working the rigging above echoed through the small cabin. It sounded like a war was raging already on deck.

Jason had the reputation of an intelligent pirate, a man who had sunk and plundered numerous ships in the Caribbean and Atlantic. Certainly he'd be able to outwit the other pirate. If this sloop could take down the gigantic *Santa Rosa*, a brigantine shouldn't be hard.

She hoped.

As cannon fire erupted from the *Sea Hawk*, she began moving the furniture in front of the cabin door.

"It's time to wake up, Shell. The sex was good...okay, better than good. It was earthshaking, but this is just *not* part of the fantasy." Cannons fired from both ships and she fell to the floor as the ship rocked to one side.

Were they hit?

A cheer rang out from the men but she wasn't sure why.

She shoved the chest against the bed that blocked the door. Taking out the sword she'd examined earlier, she still didn't feel safe. What good was a sword if you didn't know how to use it?

Next she tested the floorboards, and sure enough, they were loose where the bed used to sit. She pulled out a few shorter boards to uncover a polished box. She clicked open the silver latch to reveal two dueling flintlocks. They were exquisitely crafted of silver with deep, intricate engravings of vines around the barrels. The ivory handles also echoed the vine carvings on their smooth surfaces.

She had a little knowledge of this type of firearm, having a father who collected pistols as a personal hobby. He preferred Civil War weapons, but also had a set of dueling pistols said to have settled many disagreements before dawn.

The cannon fire stopped and the movement above stilled. She picked up one of the guns and went to the porthole.

They were about to come alongside the brigantine! The smell of gun powder and salt filled her nostrils as the entire scene outside seemed to move in slow motion. Then with a yell, grappling hooks were tossed over to the other ship. The crew pulled the ropes tight and heaved, bringing the ships closer.

Then all hell broke loose as gunfire erupted between the ships. Shelly ducked from the open porthole as the musket balls flew rampant.

Clutching the sword in one hand and a pistol in the other, she crouched in a corner, praying she'd live through this horror. Noise from above roared unlike anything she'd ever experienced. Men screaming, pistols firing at will and brutal hand-to-hand battles raged like an unrelenting thunderstorm upon the stormy sea.

She didn't want to risk looking out the porthole to see what was happening, she didn't even want to move from her corner.

She wanted out of this dream-turned-nightmare.

The bangle. Maybe if she worked the clasp, it would take her out of this place as fast as she got here. She hesitated for a moment, thinking of Jason, not wanting to leave him behind.

Despite his piratical ways, including his insistence that she was his sex slave, Shelley couldn't help but like Captain Flint.

Like? Maybe that word wasn't strong enough for how she felt. But she wasn't ready to admit much beyond that.

She was attracted to Jason and had experienced sex unlike any she'd ever had before. Past lovers couldn't compare to his sensual skills or invoke the instant burning desire that enflamed her body with his mere presence. Just a glance at his soft brown eyes filled with lust made her want to fall back on the bed, panting for his touch. She could easily spend hours— no, days—just letting him fuck her over and over.

In truth, being Captain Flint's sex slave was not a bad position to be in. She enjoyed it, in fact. He expected nothing more than her willingness to please him, and in turn, pleasured her in the process. There were no expectations beyond that. Perhaps it was her years of advanced schooling and hard studying that made her wish to throw responsibility to the wind in favor of stolen moments of pleasure within the pirate captain's bed. It wasn't torturous to be his sex slave in the least.

Yes, she *liked* him very much, and she was certain that he liked her too. Sex was fabulous and they seemed to possess compatible personalities—even if he was a roguish pirate.

Another crash of explosions sounded, pulling her thoughts back to the battle and shaking her to the core.

Boom! Boom! Ka-boom! The ship quaked violently around her with each discharge. How long would this go on?

Okay, great sex or no, she wanted *out*. She'd go back and live happily knowing she'd had the greatest sex of her life— with the sexiest man to ever walk the Earth.

She tried the clasp. It wouldn't budge. She tugged at it with all her might.

Nothing.

"Damn it."

Just then, the wall beside her was blown open by a cannonball that flew through the cabin. With her arms, she covered herself from the flying wood splinters, silently thankful it wasn't her head that had been blown away.

Tears began to spill from her eyes as she huddled in the corner. "Make it stop. Oh God, if you hear me, make it stop!" she cried.

The pounding in her ears was so loud, she couldn't think straight.

No. The pounding wasn't in her head.

She glanced up and saw the bed moving. They were at the door, forcing their way in.

She grasped the pistol tightly in her hand. Her heart beat wildly in her chest and she gulped down the fear. Her breath caught as she saw the lock break away from the door before a grimy-faced man leered at her.

"Aye, here she is," he called out.

He wasn't alone.

She lifted the pistol, taking her best aim at his face. "Get out of here or I'll blast you into Davy Jones' locker!"

He laughed along with the two other men she estimated were standing behind him. "Poppet, don't be cross. Cap'n Mendoza wants to meet you." He pushed against the door and the bed moved against the chest. It wasn't going to keep him or his friends out.

"I'm warning you one last time, you bloody pirate! Push that door again and you'll regret it." She cocked back the hammer and the man paused.

"You never shot a man before," he said.

"There's always a first time, asshole."

Another explosion rocked the ship and she found the strength to not waver from her stand. However, the bed and chest slipped a few inches away from the door. The men pushed hard with a loud yell.

Shelly squeezed the trigger and the moment took on an eerie slow motion as the grimy pirate fell to the floor in a heap. She sat amazed, staring at the pool of blood forming on the floor, and the remaining two pirates took advantage of her shock.

They grabbed her and cursed as they yanked her off the floor. She snapped back to the situation at hand but not fast enough to swing at her attackers before they strengthened their grips. The sword she held in her other hand clattered to the floor in the struggle.

One of the men, tall, blond and fair, looked like a Viking misplaced in time—and about as nasty as one of those brutal barbarians. He swung back one hand and slapped her across the face hard, startling her into stilling her fight. "Bitch, you'll pay for killin' Higgins."

"Yeah, hope the cap'n punishes her by givin' 'er to us for some fun," said the other pirate, a dark-haired man with a face brown and rough like old cracked leather.

"I'd kill myself first before letting one of you dirty pirates touch me!" She pulled her shoulders against their grip but they were much too strong.

The Viking leaned in and said, "Alive or dead, we won't care, poppet."

She gasped. Good God, how did she ever get into this mess?

They pulled her up the stairs. She tried to drag her feet but was rewarded with another slap across her cheek. It burned at the contact, the blood throbbing beneath her skin.

On deck, she got a full view of the battle. Maimed corpses lie at their feet, spilling deep red blood across the wooden planks. Pirates battled each other, cutlasses slicing the air with aimed purpose to cut down their foes. Blood spurted everywhere as blades sliced through flesh. Gunfire and battle cries filled the air along with the stench of burning wood and sulfuric discharges from the cannon gunpowder.

It was amid the carnage that she spotted Jason dueling with another man, a dark, tall man with a large navy blue hat and plume, a white linen shirt, navy breeches and long tail coat, and high black leather boots. He was the classic vision of a successful pirate captain and she recognized him immediately—Captain Mendoza.

She'd read of him in her volumes of text, but never thought she'd be kidnapped by his crew. Mendoza had a taste for gold—and women.

"Come on, wench," the Viking hissed.

At their pushing, she renewed her struggle. There was no way in hell she was going with them without a fight. She kicked at their shins and Leather-face screamed.

"Jason!" she cried out when the men changed tactics and lifted her off her feet. Viking took her shoulders and Leather-face took her feet, literally carrying her as she wiggled to get free. "Jason! Help!"

Tears burned her eyes as the thunderous noise of gunfire, men yelling and the clanging of swords clashed about her. Jason surely would never hear her calls.

They carried her across a makeshift plank onto the rival ship, where more fighting took place.

There was no holding back her flood of emotions as reality hit her full force. She was now the prisoner of a pirate— a man that wasn't Jason.

Chapter Seven

ॐ

"You bastard," Jason yelled at Mendoza as he spotted Shelley being carried off the *Sea Hawk*.

"Ah, but *amigo*, when I saw her golden hair and your obvious attention to her, I knew she was a prize beyond all others." Mendoza laughed as he poised his sword in readiness.

Jason swung and Mendoza parried with expert skill. Jason was blind with rage at seeing her struggle with her captors. He had to get her back.

Mendoza attacked and Jason deflected his blade's sharp edge. The Spaniard was one of the most dangerous swordsmen in the Caribbean, and Jason found himself challenged by his expert skills.

Their blades struck and Jason threw his weight into the sword, tossing his body close to Mendoza's. Swords crossed, Mendoza chuckled, enjoying his triumphant attack upon the *Sea Hawk* and capture of Shelley.

"I won't let you keep her," Jason ground out between clenched teeth.

"You'll have to take her from me, *amigo*."

Jason pushed against the Spaniard and he stumbled backward. Instead of charging into the duel again, Mendoza laughed and turned, signaling to his crew with a wave.

Enraged, Jason charged—then fire burst into his shoulder, making him fall forward onto the deck. He glanced up and saw Mendoza holding his cutlass in one hand—and a smoking flintlock in the other.

"Forgive me but I have a hostage I am anxious to meet. I came to reclaim the *Sea Hawk*, but I think a beautiful blonde that has captured the attention of my enemy, Captain Flint, is much more rewarding." Mendoza pushed the barrel of the flintlock into his belt and smiled. "Consider our debt paid."

Mendoza was a handsome rogue with exotic dark skin and jet black hair. He had a sensual air that seduced many willing—and unwilling—females.

Images of Shelley with Mendoza tortured Jason. He'd never let that Spanish bastard touch her creamy skin.

Jason tried to move but his shoulder burned with pain and he groaned in agony. Mendoza sauntered back to his ship and Jason lay in a puddle of his own blood, helpless to save...

What was she to him? A slave? He swore she'd become nothing more than that, a servant to his desires and passions. Somehow, that had changed. His heart ached as he watched Mendoza's men leave the *Sea Hawk*, cutting away the ropes.

"Captain, they got your woman." Thomas crouched next to him to examine the wound.

Your woman. The words struck true to the core. Shelley belonged to Jason. She was his slave, his property—his mistress.

"You're in love with her," Thomas said quietly, cutting into Jason's thoughts while trying to stanch the blood flow.

Jason looked up into his friend's face. The world was wavering and his strength was draining. The urge to close his eyes and fall into the welcoming darkness of oblivion was tempting.

"Is it possible?" he whispered. *Love.* He swore never to love another again. After the painful affair with Claire and losing not only her but his brother as well, could he risk his heart with Shelly?

"Possible? Captain...*Jason*...I've known you throughout all your pirating days. I've never seen you look at a woman like you have at *her*. I can see it in your face—and hers."

The will to live crept over his soul. "Aye, she's unlike any other woman I've ever met."

The ship's surgeon ran to his side and gave Jason a weak smile.

"Report, Doc? How many dead?"

"More injuries than deaths, but I estimate ten dead with fifteen or so severely wounded—including you," the older man said, his creased face smeared with blood and grime. He quickly washed his hands in some clean water and proceeded to remove the makeshift dressing.

Jason gave orders for them to weigh anchor to repair the ship and tend to the wounded. As the surgeon probed for the ball in Jason's shoulder, he ordered the captain to drink healthy doses of rum.

"He stole my woman," Jason said in a slurred voice as the surgeon pulled out the metal lodged in his flesh.

"Yes, Captain." Thomas nodded as he held a bowl of water for the surgeon.

"My mistress. He stole *my* mistress. I swear, if he harms her—no, if he so much as *touches* her, I'll carve out his heart and feed it to the sharks." Jason took another gulp of rum, letting it ease his pain.

Thomas stood silent.

"You think he'll try to seduce her?" Jason's words were more incoherent with each passing moment.

"Aye, Captain. I believe so."

"Fucking son of a bitch." He took another gulp. "I'll kill him. I'll hunt him down across the sea, across the world if…I…have…to…"

The surgeon pulled out the last of the debris in his captain's shoulder as Jason surrendered to unconsciousness.

"The cap'n means to chase down a girl?" asked the surgeon. He took the rum bottle from Jason's limp hand and poured some of the alcohol over the wound.

Thomas nodded. "Aye. Mendoza didn't just steal a girl— he stole Captain Flint's treasure."

* * * * *

Leather-face and Viking took her below deck. The brigantine was much larger and roomier compared to Jason's sloop. The captain's cabin was vast, decked out for a man of wealth and riches. Decorated in fine velvet and brocade, it gave the impression of a chamber fit for a successful pirate captain. The several chests about the room, each bursting with gold, proved that fact beyond any doubt.

"You wait here, poppet. The cap'n will be here as soon as he takes care of that filthy Flint." Viking laughed before bolting the door closed behind him.

Alone in the cabin, she sighed, rubbing her temples. The noise outside was thundering, yet more distant. The fight was primarily on the *Sea Hawk*.

She certainly wasn't going to just sit here and wait for Mendoza to come and rape her. She began to rummage through the chests for some sort of weapon, and soon enough found a jewel-encrusted dagger. She pulled the blade from the gold sheath, and it shone flawless in the sunlight filtering in from the large windows behind the captain's desk.

Stepping over to the grand windows, she saw burning wreckage and men falling overboard the *Sea Hawk*. Shelley felt the bile rise as the men floated unmoving within the water, and then a dorsal fin broke the surface—sharks. She gasped as the bodies were pulled under by the feasting sharks now circling the carnage.

Shelley turned away, squeezing her eyes shut. Blood and gore filled her mind as the fighting continued.

Another cannon blast shook the ship and Shelley ran to the captain's elaborately decorated bed—an oasis for seduction. She pulled her body into a ball and covered her ears from the horrors outside.

What will happen to her? Will she ever see Jason again? Would she live to see tomorrow's dawn?

A cheer rang out above on deck, yet she lay still, unwilling to move from the bed.

Then she was aware of the ship lurching in the water, pulling away from the *Sea Hawk*.

They were leaving. Was Jason dead? Would Mendoza leave without killing him first? Fear coursed through her as her heart raced. She gripped the dagger's handle for courage as she waited. The pirate was sure to check on his captive soon.

She remembered her reading of the infamous Captain Mendoza, a Spaniard with a taste for wine, women and gold, not unlike any other brigand of the sea. He knew no loyalty, attacking ships of all countries, plundering their goods for his own benefit. It was thought the captain started his career in piracy with the death of his wife. She'd been raped and murdered when a ship of pirates attacked the small island village in Jamaica where they resided. Mendoza, an officer of the Royal Spanish Navy, swore vengeance and carved his way into history as he hunted down the men responsible for killing his beloved wife. Once his thirst for revenge was quenched, Mendoza continued his pirating career, opting for high-seas adventure over law-abiding respectability.

Another cheer from above, followed by the sound of men running, filled the cabin. Shelley rose from the bed and hurried to the window. They were indeed pulling away from the *Sea Hawk*.

Just then, the door to the cabin opened and Shelley spun around to face her captor. The knife in her hand gave her the confidence to endure this unforeseen twist of events.

Captain Mendoza filled the doorway with confidence and power. His tanned skin shone dark against his smile. Midnight black waves fell about his head and down over his shoulders. His body was lean and strong, filling his tight breeches with toned muscle. Mendoza was the picture of a sexy pirate straight from a cliché "bodice ripper" romance novel from the 1980s.

He closed the door behind him with a click of the lock and then whipped off his dark navy coat, revealing a white linen shirt loosely fitting over a perfectly sculpted chest.

"Welcome to my ship, *senorita*," he said in a thick Spanish accent, a sound that caressed her skin and sent shivers down her arms. "You, no doubt, know who I am." His dark brown eyes were full of gleeful mischief as he raked his gaze up and down her form.

"I know who you are, Captain Mendoza. Your reputation precedes you."

"*Excelente.*"

Her heart pounded in her chest but she refused to let her fear show to this pirate. "What of Captain Flint?"

Mendoza strode to a side table where a decanter of wine sat with several glasses. As he picked up a glass and poured the deep red wine, he replied, "He is on his ship."

"Is he dead?"

He turned and stepped toward her, reaching out to her wrist and the bangle. "What is your interest in *Capitán* Flint?"

"He...he is..."

"Your former master. You have a new master now, *querida*. You belong to me, payment for *Capitán* Flint stealing my ship."

"He gave me as payment for a ship?"

Mendoza smiled, a devilish curve of his sensuous lips. "Not exactly. I wanted the prize most cherished by Flint, so I stole you." He traced her jaw with a fingertip and Shelley stilled, unprepared for her reaction to this Spanish seducer. He leaned into her and whispered against her cheek, "However, I have not collected on my debt in full—yet."

That snapped her back to reality. Yes, Mendoza was handsome, alluring and seductive, but he was not Jason. Angered, she brought the point of her knife to his abdomen.

"There will be no collecting from me, unless you have a death wish, *Capitán*."

With a laugh he stepped backward. "The sea witch has talons, I see."

"Best you mind my talons and keep your hands to yourself."

His answer was another laugh.

Her ire rose as he casually walked back to the decanter to refill his glass. "Now tell me. Is Captain Flint dead, pirate?"

He took a large swallow of his wine as he made her wait for his answer. The glass empty, he placed it upon the table.

"Well?"

"He lives still, *querida*. At least he was alive when I left him clutching his shoulder after I shot him."

"Bastard!" she yelled and charged at the Spaniard.

He anticipated her move and effortlessly knocked the blade from her hand. They struggled but the captain was stronger. He held her within his grasp, yet Shelley refused to surrender.

"Wildcat!" He swore in Spanish and maneuvered her to the bed.

She fell back upon the rich coverlet and before she could escape, Mendoza threw himself down upon her. His weight pressed her into the soft mattress, trapping her body. She was very aware of his hard body dominating the situation. He was aroused but she didn't feel excitement over the heated cock rubbing against her thigh. Not even his thick breeches could hide his erection.

Shelley couldn't think beyond Jason lying wounded on the deck of the *Sea Hawk*. Mendoza clasped her wrists with his hands, exerting control over her struggles. His power over her drained her strength as she caved into her fears.

"Please don't," she pleaded as tears burned her eyes. *Is Jason dead?* The question repeated over and over in her mind.

"*Dulce*, I must taste you."

"No...*please*. Stop!"

He stopped and pulled back from her. "You best forget *Capitán* Flint, *querida*. You belong to me now."

"No—" He kissed her roughly, his mouth crushing hers. His tongue demanded entrance to her mouth, dominating her senses as well as her responses. Her mind raced. Was this her fate, to find love only to be ripped away and brutalized by another man?

He whispered endearments to her against her lips then plunged his tongue back into her mouth, forcing her to meet his kiss. He was an expert in driving a response from an unwilling lover—a man used to taking what he wanted regardless of the circumstances.

"Give yourself to me," he said in a husky voice.

"Never," she gasped.

"I want you willing."

She stilled. Could she ever be willing to surrender to the man who possibly killed Jason? Was he even alive? The question would haunt her forever. She realized regret and guilt would pain her if she were ever to give in to Mendoza without making sure Jason was alive and safe. She could surrender to Jason, but not to Mendoza—not to the man who had stolen her from the arms of her lover.

"I can't. I'll never give myself to you."

He drew back to gaze down upon her face. "I do not have to give you a choice, *querida*. You are mine to do with as I please."

"And you always take what you want."

"Precisely."

"You may force my body to surrender...but my heart belongs to Jason." She waited a moment as the dark embers of his eyes flared with rage. "I love him," she said quietly. "And he loves me."

Then he caressed her upper arms gently, a touch so loving, her heart skipped. "I can love you, *querida*," he said softly, vulnerability echoing in his voice. Mendoza was desperate for love, she realized—and wanted *her* to give him what he required.

She closed her eyes as tears now ran down her face and onto the pillow. She could never betray Jason. "No."

Instead of Mendoza retreating as she had hoped, the top she wore was ripped from her body. She screamed and tried to fight against him but he held her wrists securely. Then he dipped his head down to her chest and began to lave a nipple. She gasped as his skilled tongue circled the taut flesh, and then he gently grazed his teeth over the very tip, driving her body into a frenzied response beneath him.

Cream gathered between her legs as he took her nipple into his mouth and suckled.

Within her mind the man loving her wasn't the pirate Mendoza—it was Jason. And in her building excitement, she called out his name. "Jason!"

The name of Mendoza's enemy upon her lips in a moment of pleasure was like a wave of arctic water crashing over his libido. The Spaniard jumped off the bed in anger and Shelly scrambled to cover herself with the coverlet.

"Witch," he spat. "When you come to my bed, I will have you begging for me. And it will be *my* name upon your lips as you take my cock into your body."

"I will *never* give myself to you willingly," she declared angrily.

He grabbed his coat and shoved his arms through the sleeves. "We shall see about that."

And a moment later, he left the cabin with a slam of the door.

"No we won't, *Capitán*. I promise you to my last breath— you will never have my heart."

Chapter Eight

ॐ

"You'll not take her as I live!" Mendoza yelled as Jason approached with sword in hand.

Behind Mendoza stood Shelley, held captive by two other pirates. His blood boiled as the men held her to their sides. Her blonde hair was loose and blowing in the sea winds like a carpet of spun gold. The scene angered him further as her eyes pleaded with him across the deck.

She loved him. He felt it as sure as if she had spoken the words aloud for all to hear.

"Then I'll take her when you're dead!" he called back to the captain.

Aboard the **Corazón Negro,** *Jason moved with lightning speed and attacked the Spanish captain. He had chased the black-hearted pirate across the stormy Caribbean for this very moment. The most violent hurricane couldn't keep Jason from his revenge.*

The blades clashed with a clang of metal against metal and Jason fought for the life of the woman he loved. No sacrifice was too great. No price too steep. He would give his life to protect her.

"Shelley!" the fevered captain cried out as he thrashed within his bed.

"How much longer will his body be able to withstand this?" Thomas asked the surgeon evaluating the unconscious Jason.

"The cap'n has a strong heart and a thirst for revenge. He'll survive this fever," Will Pitt, the surgeon, said as he spooned some water between Jason's lips.

"It's been two days since—"

"Don't ye worry, Thomas," the older man said as he stood at Jason's bedside. "Once the fever breaks, the cap'n will be at the helm leading us on a vendetta against Mendoza."

* * * * *

Shelley lay in Mendoza's cabin alone. While she slept, food and water appeared regularly on a bedside table, assumingly brought by the pirate captain. She hadn't spoken to him since he stormed out two days ago. She took advantage of his angry avoidance to rest. So much had happened in the several days since she'd been whisked back in time. She still wondered if it was all a dream. However, being kidnapped by a rival sea captain was not part of any fantasy.

She sighed and sank into the lavish luxury of Mendoza's bed. At least the pirate had rich tastes for comfort. The bed was heavenly and she welcomed the soft warmth.

Then the bed mattress dipped to her side and a warm body slipped in under the covers. His hands upon her body, she sighed again. He reached around her and cupped a breast in his palm and moved closer to her naked body. She felt the hot, searing heat from his hard cock pressing against her backside and the hypnotizing sensation of his toned body along her back.

He squeezed a nipple and she moaned his name.

"Jason."

"I'm here, Shelley," he whispered into her ear. His warm breath against her skin created goose bumps along her arms and she shivered.

She turned toward him, welcoming his heated body slipping along hers. "Is this a dream?" she asked drowsily.

His answer was a kiss, and Shelley lost all sense of her surroundings as his lips mastered hers with skill and passion. She threaded her fingers through his long hair and drank in his closeness, letting her desire reign over her body. His tongue darted in and out of her mouth, tasting her with each pass, and she moaned.

"I was so afraid you were dead," she panted against his mouth.

"You gave me the will to live, luv," he declared breathlessly.

"But...he said he shot you."

"Mendoza is a terrible marksman. Now shut up, wench, and let me love you."

His body, muscled and powerful, seemed to engulf her as he kissed her deeply. He moved atop her and his weight was a welcome sensation as he pressed her down into the luxurious bed. His hand in her hair, his kisses turned frenzied and hungry, devouring her very being. She held onto his broad shoulders, losing herself in the moment.

Her breathing came quick and uncontrolled when he spread her legs and slipped his cock into her channel. She was slick and ready, and the entry was a delightful ecstasy. She came immediately as his size filled and stretched her walls.

It was pure need driving them. Shelley needed to have Jason within her. She'd thought he was dead, but here he was in her bed, making love to her. Hot passion unlike anything she'd ever experienced threatened to consume her as his body molded to hers in a perfect fit.

Her breasts flattened against his chest and her tight nipples strained against his body in painful points. As he moved, they rubbed along his sweat-slicked body, and she arched farther into him, wanting more. It was an unconscious reaction, and she willingly gave herself over to instinct and lust.

Jason pumped in and out of her body, his cock growing within her with each thrust. Shelley wept as she gave herself to him. It was not out of physical need but out of the love within her heart. She cried out with each push of his length deep into her body, like the perfect puzzle piece to her life. He grunted above her as his pace quickened and she floated on sexual euphoria when he spilled his seed into her.

Colors bust behind her eyes as another orgasm crashed over her body. Her muscles clenched and released about his cock, sucking his essence into her. Every nerve exploded in a climactic blast of passion, need, lust and love. From her toes to the roots of her hair, she felt the completion of her sexual bonding with the pirate of her heart, her sea hawk.

"I love you, Jason." Shelley wept as her body convulsed and her control deserted her. Nothing could have held back the words upon her lips—and in her heart.

"My love, my treasure." He kissed her face with heated lips. "I could never lose you."

A crack in the distance startled her, and it took Shelley a moment to realize the waves crashing about her were more than ecstasy.

Her eyes snapped open and Shelley scooted back in the bed in a startled fright. About her the chests of gold and jewels swayed with the rise and fall of the ocean, and chairs fell over and slid back and forth across the floor.

Mendoza slammed open and closed the door behind him. He stood for a moment then went about the cabin securing the chests.

"Prepare for a rough night. A hurricane is coming in fast upon us."

She sat silent, clutching a blanket against her chest. She had dreamed of Jason. She made love to Jason in a dream. It was only a dream! Tears burned her eyes as reality hit her like a slash of icy water.

"Do not fear, *querida*. I have taken this ship through many a storm here in the Caribbean."

She shook her head, wishing this adventure was at an end. Crying seemed the only outlet for her frustration and heartache.

Mendoza sat down on the bed and took her into his arms. She welcomed his comfort despite her anger with the Spaniard.

Jason is alive. She knew it in her heart. He was alive.

"It will be over soon. And once we clear this hurricane, I will take you ashore to a nearby island. My men will make repairs and...we can get better acquainted. How does that sound?"

She was numb as he held her. He read her silence as agreement and he dipped his head, kissing her.

His kiss was warm and tender and not completely unwelcome. She was shocked at the change in his manner from strength and control to gentle lover. Shelley found herself kissing him back with a shy flick of her tongue along his.

"Sweet sea witch," he murmured against her lips.

The storm raged closer with each moment outside—yet the one within her was much more dangerous as she clutched Mendoza and kissed him. His kisses were like spiced rum—exotic and intoxicating. Her hands grasped at his coat, pulling him closer. Pain, loneliness and heartache flooded her, and she gave in to the sexy Spanish captain for a few moments of human contact and tenderness.

He moaned into their kiss. "*Querida*, I must leave you. My men need me to command the ship through the storm."

She released his coat and let her hands fall to her lap.

"Stay here and rest. Don't wander out of the cabin. I do not want you to be washed overboard in the storm."

She nodded absently, confused at her neediness for his company. Was it only two days ago she swore to never let him melt her icy heart? Yet, after two days of solitude on Mendoza's ship, her resolve wavered.

She lay back in the bed and wept. Her dream of Jason loving her with such urgency and Mendoza's sweet tenderness confused her. She loved Jason, yearned for his presence, ached for his touch to ease her fears and torments, yet it was her new captor's voice that soothed her. He whispered to her in Spanish, words she didn't know, but his meaning was clear with his soft tones—he wished to comfort and reassure.

His voice wrapped about her in a loving caress amid the growing danger threatening outside. The room's rocking increased and she squeezed her eyes shut.

"It is best you shut out the swells. In case you feel ill, there is a pot for you to vomit into on the floor."

"Swell," she croaked.

A bang on the door and a crewman yelled in heated Spanish through the door for the captain. Mendoza answered and then turned back to her. "*Querida*, I must go. Stay safe, and I will be back when it is over." He leaned over and kissed her forehead.

She opened her eyes and peered up at his face. "Thank you, Captain Mendoza."

"Please, call me Lorenzo."

She smiled weakly. "Thank you…Lorenzo."

"And what is the name of my beautiful hostage?" he asked with a light tone. The remark was teasing and she smiled.

"Shelley."

He rose and buttoned his coat to face the hurricane that tossed the ship. For a man responsible for the lives of the hundred men aboard, Lorenzo appeared serene and unworried.

"Shelley…" he started. "I shall return during the night to make sure you are faring well."

He opened the door and for an instant, the wind and rain poured into the room. With a slam of the door behind him, Shelley was alone once again.

She lay in the bed and closed her eyes tightly, as though the simple act would protect her from the storm outside—and the one raging within her heart.

The dream gave her hope. He was out there, calling for her. She felt the tug within her soul to seek out her true love. He loved her, she was sure of that. He had never spoken of love, but her heart knew the truth.

And what of her attraction to Lorenzo? He was the man who had injured Jason, yet she wanted him to caress her, comfort her. He'd fought Jason out of revenge and she was his prize. However, kidnapping her from Jason was a beneficial twist of fate, saving the crew of the *Sea Hawk*. The battle was shortened and had not ended in the sinking of the *Sea Hawk*. Fewer lives were lost because she was kidnapped, and Shelley latched onto that small piece of information to find solace in her current situation.

The room swayed and Shelley realized this must be the hurricane thought to have sunk the *Santa Rosa*. Instead pirates—Captain Jason Flint—had sunk the *Santa Rosa* days before the storm.

She tried to think about her reading on Captain Mendoza. The attack on the *Sea Hawk* probably happened regardless of her traveling back in time. However, the battle's outcome was altered with her kidnapping. What had changed? Should the *Sea Hawk* have been lost? Was Jason supposed to be dead?

She couldn't remember the fate of Mendoza. Perhaps it was for the best. She hated the idea of affecting history—disturbing the natural course of time—with her time hop.

Clasping the silver bangle at her wrist, she took comfort in its presence. Putting it on brought her here—and to Jason. And somehow she would find her way back to him.

* * * * *

The hurricane hit the *Sea Hawk* with a vengeance, and the crew secured the rigging and managed to survive the worst of the storm. The seas began to calm and the winds died down as the injured Captain Flint's fever broke.

"Where are we?" he demanded, rising from his bed. "Have we spotted Mendoza's ship?"

"We lost the *Corazón Negro* three days ago, Captain. Right after he kidnapped your woman."

"Damn it, three days?" Jason bellowed. "I've been out for three days?"

"Fever. You were out of your head," Thomas said as he stood by the bed. "You passed out after Will removed the musket ball."

Jason nodded. "He has three days' head start on us."

"I believe I know where he is heading."

Jason cocked a brow. "To the island of Virgen Magra?"

"He will put in to make repairs from the storm, if they sustained any. It is the closest island to make such repairs and take on provisions," Thomas reasoned.

His arm in a sling, Jason pulled his coat over his good arm and draped the other side to hide his injury—his sword arm. "Set a course for the island of Virgen Magra."

He opened the door and slowly climbed the stairs to the deck.

"Captain, are you well enough to move about?" Thomas asked from behind him.

Jason peered out over the sea to the horizon. "I must be ready. I must regain my strength."

Out there in the Caribbean, Shelley was the hostage of his nemesis. Mendoza had kidnapped his woman, and for that, Jason intended to seek revenge.

During his illness Jason dreamed of Shelley. Her warm body wrapped about him, her heart welcoming him with a love that shone brightly within her eyes and the tenderness of her touch. He made love to her, his body demanding to join with hers, a union of souls and bodies.

But it had only been a dream.

He reached for the spyglass and gazed out into the distance. The sun began its decent into the horizon, gold and red colored the waves, casting an ethereal aura across the surface.

"Shelley," he whispered into the wind. "My love, my treasure."

* * * * *

In two days the *Sea Hawk* sailed into sight of Virgen Magra. The small island stood alone with a fine sand beach surrounding the rich, thick vegetation within. The *Corazón Negro* sat at anchor in the inlet on the eastern side.

"Sail about the island and set us on the western beach. I will take a landing party to meet Mendoza on the eastern inlet."

Jason stood ready on deck. He'd removed his sling the day before to work his sore muscles in preparation for his encounter with Mendoza. His shoulder ached but the wound was healing well. However, Jason knew it severely put him at a disadvantage.

"You will have to fight Mendoza with intelligence rather than might," Thomas said at his side.

"Aye, I do not believe my arm will hold out for long against him in a duel."

"Mendoza will not give her up willingly," Thomas said in a low voice. "She is his prize."

"She is *mine*, and I will do whatever it takes to get her back." Anger roared through his veins at the thought of Mendoza sullying his woman. "And if that black-hearted Spanish bastard even touched her, I will make sure he pays with his life."

Thomas sighed. "Captain, you have to think clearly. If she is alive—"

Jason suddenly turned on his first mate. "She *is* alive," he broke in. There was no doubt in Jason's mind, she was alive. He could almost feel the connection between them strengthen with every mile he sailed closer to her, and knew she felt his pain and longing.

"Concentrate on getting her back. Anger makes even the most seasoned fighter grow careless." Thomas laid a reassuring hand upon his friend's good shoulder. "Forget revenge. Save the life of the woman you love."

Chapter Nine

ꙅ

The *Sea Hawk* anchored at the small island of Virgen Magra in the dark hours of the morning. As they approached, Jason could make out the main mast of the *Corazón Negro* as it floated in the small inlet. He hoped the element of surprise would fool Mendoza and his crew and give Jason the advantage.

At dawn, Jason led a small landing party ashore. Anchored on the other side of the island, he left little to chance.

The party happened upon one of Mendoza's scouts—asleep with a rum bottle in hand. They secured the drunken man to a nearby tree so as not to give away the surprise too soon.

When they arrived just outside the pirate's camp on the beach, Jason's nerves were on edge. He scanned the tents but saw no evidence of Shelley anywhere.

Then from one tent, Jason spotted Mendoza emerging, stretching his arms, his shirt rumpled and unkempt. Since when did the properly dressed captain sport such wrinkled clothes?

Then from the same tent, Shelley stepped outside. She appeared sleepy and when Mendoza spoke to her, Jason spotted tenderness between them. Had the Spanish scoundrel seduced her into his bed?

Jason's blood boiled as he watched his nemesis and his mistress exchange smiles and pleasantries.

"Fickle wench," Jason muttered.

"Looks can be deceiving, Captain," Thomas said in a low voice. "I see sadness in her smile."

Jason answered with a grunt. He looked closer at her face. Was she truly unhappy? He noticed the dark smudges under her eyes and the downward curve of her lips when Mendoza walked away. Was her smile merely an act for her captor?

She stood outside the tent and gazed at the thick jungle foliage inland. When her eyes paused over the area where he sat and observed, his heart leapt. Upon her face was the hope and longing he felt within his heart.

"See, Captain—she awaits you."

Jason smiled as he handed his looking glass to Thomas. "I think it is time we pay Captain Mendoza and his crew a morning visit."

* * * * *

Last evening Mendoza's *Corazón Negro* anchored in the inlet of a small island. According to Shelley's estimation, they were amid the Bahaman islands.

Mendoza set about a seduction that night. Shelley was tempted to give in to his strong body and alluring voice. A man speaking words of sexual promise in a Spanish accent was extremely hard to resist, however, she held to her heart. A few kisses were all she shared with the captain, along with a few gentle hours lying in his arms. He remained a gentleman to her wishes—wanting her to accept him of her own free will. It was hardly what she expected from him, or any pirate for that matter, but Captain Lorenzo Mendoza was a man longing for love—more than he was willing to admit.

As Shelley emerged from the tent where she slept with Lorenzo, she had the feeling of being watched. She scanned the trees just off the beach but saw nothing. Perhaps it was wishful thinking that Jason had found her so quickly.

Would he even come after her? She prayed he would. But how would he know where Lorenzo would set ashore to make necessary repairs to the *Corazón Negro*? This island seemed much like any other—uninhabited and desolate.

"Would you care for a cup of tea, *querida*?" Lorenzo asked her.

"Oh yes, that would be lovely."

"I may be a pirate, but I do have a taste for the civilized." He laughed. It was a sound that made her smile. The woman who truly held his heart one day would be a lucky woman indeed.

Then a commotion by the trees drew her attention.

Out of the green foliage walked a group of men—led by Jason!

His face was hard, his mouth drawn in a grim line. His eyes were like stone and he walked past her without a glimmer of recognition.

"Mendoza, I believe you have something of mine," Jason said commandingly.

Lorenzo laughed and waved Jason to come and sit outside his tent, where there sat a few chairs and a small table set for morning refreshments.

"I do not recall having anything belonging to you, *Capitán*," Lorenzo said as he sat. "You had stolen my ship and I collected on that debt. We are even."

Jason refused to sit and stood glaring at the Spaniard. "We are *not* even."

Lorenzo thought for a moment. "Yes, perhaps it was not an even trade. She is worth much more to me than any ship."

"The girl is mine. I'm here to take her back."

Lorenzo clucked his tongue. "No, *Capitán*, she is mine. You have a fine ship and I have a beautiful woman. My hunt for revenge is over. Now leave this island before I grow angry and teach you another lesson."

Shelley stood stunned, watching the exchange. Jason acted as though she was invisible, yet he demanded her return. A shiver of anticipation skittered down her spine at the thought of his naked body sliding along hers. She almost moaned at the mental image of being tied to his bed, ass in the air, ripe for a paddling. Cream gathered between her legs and her cunt clenched in want for his touch.

Her reaction to Jason was so much deeper than that to Mendoza. She was attracted to Lorenzo, but she was *in love* with Jason. Her pirate lover awakened the woman inside who yearned to emerge and experience sexual pleasure—and love.

"Careful, Captain, I am not feeling forgiving this morning."

Lorenzo leaned forward in his chair. "Don't threaten me, *Capitán*. The *senorita* remains as my lovely hostage."

Jason laid a hand upon the hilt of his sword. "She comes with me. The woman is my slave, and as such, she is my property." He drew his sword and pointed the tip at Lorenzo. Jason's command faltered for a split second before he fought down the outward sign of weakness.

Shelley took note of the painful wince upon Jason's face. She wanted to go to his side and help him. But his countenance was firm—his heart was ice. He wouldn't even spare a glance in her direction.

"I fear you take your life into your own hands. You are not well enough to face my blade."

"Afraid to find out, Mendoza?"

Lorenzo's face turned angry. "You are a fool, *Capitán*." He stood and pulled his blade from the sheath at his side. "You see her as only a slave. I see her as my future wife. I will fight for what I claim as mine."

Wife? Shelley glanced from Lorenzo to Jason as they stripped away their side arms and began to circle each other on the beach.

Lorenzo wanted to marry her. Jason wanted to possess her. What did *she* want?

When Jason pealed away his coat, the strips of a bandage shone beneath his white linen shirt. Her breath caught as the men faced each other—anger, resentment and revenge filling the air with a thick aura of negativity.

Someone was not going to walk away from this confrontation. Someone was going to die. Could she live with the consequences of this battle?

It was like watching a scene from a movie as the two powerful men faced off with their sword skills as their only defense.

"Perhaps we should end this feud today," Lorenzo quipped as he slashed his sword through the air. "To the winner go the lady and the ship."

Shelley's heart beat wildly as Jason swung his sword at his foe.

"So be it!" The crash of metal against metal filled the air as the two pirate captains battled upon the beach—fighting for their very lives.

Her chest tightened as her breath came quicker, anxiety pumping through her veins with each beat of her heart. How could she stand here watching Jason and Lorenzo fight over her like wild beasts over a mate? To the winner go her body— and all the rights of a male over his woman.

Lorenzo cut and slashed and Jason parried each attack. However, strain etched Jason's face with each cut of his sword. His prior wound was draining his strength quickly and Lorenzo used it to his advantage. Instinctively, she moved forward when Jason fell backward onto the sand. She was promptly grabbed by Jason's first mate, held back from interfering in the battle.

"It is between them now," he whispered.

Lorenzo motioned to Jason to rise before continuing the fight.

"This is insane!" She pulled her arm from the man's grasp. "Jason is injured. He can't last much longer against Lorenzo."

"He knew that before he even challenged Mendoza." He paused then said as they watched Jason attack Mendoza once again with his sword, "He loves you more than his own life."

"What good will that do me if he gets himself killed?" She turned to the pirate and pleaded with him. "Let me go. I must stop this."

"Do you love him?"

Tears streaked down her face as her heart's longing ate at her soul. "More than anything."

They turned back to the men fighting for the right to own her, and when Mendoza slashed open a wound on Jason's right arm, Shelley screamed.

She broke away from her captor and ran across the soft sand, yelling, "Stop!"

Jason grabbed at the wound with his left hand, pausing a moment to stanch the blood. Lorenzo lowered his sword at her approach. She ran to Jason's side and threw herself at him. She clung to his body crying and he wrapped his right forearm about her waist weakly.

"Jason…please stop. I can't take anymore," she wept.

"Shh, luv." Jason nuzzled her hair and her tears flowed harder.

From behind her, Lorenzo breathed heavily. "Go. Take her. And the *Sea Hawk*."

She turned in Jason's arms. "You're letting me go?"

He closed the distance between them. Touching her face with gentle fingertips, he said in a low voice, "I stole a few moments with you, *querdia*. You will always carry with you a part of my heart…but I see your heart belongs to him." He looked up and gazed at Jason. "Gold and jewels buy a warm companion for your bed, but there is no treasure as precious as the love and devotion of a true lady."

She reached up and touched his tanned face. "Thank you, Lorenzo. You are a true gentleman."

He leaned in and whispered, "Do not say that too loudly. I don't want to ruin my reputation as a bloodthirsty pirate."

"You will find your true love, Lorenzo. She's out there waiting for you."

He straightened and sheathed his sword at his side. "Perhaps. Until then, I carry the image of you within my heart." He bowed gallantly, turned toward his ship, waved to his crew to prepare for their departure and in a few strides, he was gone.

"He is a good man," she whispered.

Jason smirked. "He is a pirate."

* * * * *

Mendoza's crew had broke camp on the island, but Mendoza ordered the main tent be left behind for Jason to recover from his wound. Shelley helped Jason to the tent to bandage his arm.

"I thought I had lost you," Jason said as she helped him lay back on the pillows piled on the rug-covered sand floor of the tent.

Shelley had been swept into a dream. In slow motion, she began bandaging Jason's wound. Luckily the cut was superficial and had merely oozed a small amount of blood, which was staunched fairy quickly.

"You could never lose me, Jason." Her fingers worked to secure some cloth about his arm and her body hummed with awareness at his closeness.

He reached for her hand. His skin was warm and inviting. "When I saw them take you, I wanted to chase them but—"

"I know," she reassured. "You came as soon as you could. I know that."

"I dreamed of you. Crazed musings from a mind riddled with fever and a heart struggling with feelings I have never known before."

She gazed into his eyes and was struck by their intensity. She gingerly touched his face. "I love you, Jason. I don't know how I came to be here, but I do know you are the reason."

Confusion wrinkled his brow. "What do you mean?"

"I can't explain it without sounding completely insane." A tear fell down her cheek as the tender love for this man overwhelmed her. "I just want to love you for as long as I can," she sobbed. Her tears tasted salty against her tongue as she licked away the wetness upon her lips.

He reached for her, burying his face into the length of her hair. She loved his command over her senses—his needs demanding her body's compliance. She wanted to give him everything she had to offer.

"I need to make love to you," he whispered against her ear. He tucked her body beneath his and began to touch her. He reacquainted his hands with her curves, covering a breast with his hand and testing its reaction to his skill. He pinched her nipple through the fabric of her dress and she whimpered in response. Between her legs, cream gathered and the ache for his touch intensified. Her cunt quivered in its emptiness, demanding to be filled.

He pulled up the hem of her dress and the warm air kissed her sex. She couldn't find her voice as his fingertips grazed over the sensitive skin of her thigh. She shivered despite the tropical heat within the tent. A fine sheen of sweat covered her skin and Jason seemed determined to taste every slick inch of her body. He moved down her body, his hands mastering her responses and his mouth testing her submission. Not even the fabric of her dress could mask the hot demands of his lips.

He spread her legs farther as he lowered his body between her legs. He brushed his thumbs slowly over the smooth skin framing her labia, and she shuddered as the lips parted and her juices seeped from the opening.

"Ah, luv, you are so perfect," he said. He continued to trace her nether lips with the pads of his thumbs, driving her anticipation higher.

He parted the wet folds and her clit seemed to vibrate with excitement as his warm breath caressed its sensitive surface.

When he tentatively passed the tip of his tongue over the straining nubbin she cried out, her body overwhelmed with the building sensations caused by the rhythm he set with his licks.

Shelley panted and rode the path to climax quickly. She arched her body as Jason continued to tempt the small nub with his talented tongue. She reached down and spread her fingers through the thick length of his hair, holding his head to her crotch. She cried out with every pass of his tongue over her clit, and when she could no longer take the sensual assault, she came.

When her orgasm crashed over her senses, it was as though every cell within her exploded into ecstasy. Heated joy washed over her with each squeeze of her muscles, but the emptiness of her sheath left her whimpering with unfulfilled need. She needed Jason's cock inside her, pumping to the beat of her body's sexual rhythm.

Her body sang in the euphoria of the moment. Brought to the pinnacle by the man she loved—it was worth more than any pirate's gold coins or gem-encrusted treasure.

Chapter Ten

ಬಿ

Breathing rapidly after her trip to paradise, Shelley reclined upon the lavish pillows, trying to recover from Jason's mastery over her body. As she relaxed and calmed, Jason removed the dress she wore, given to her by Lorenzo. Unbuttoning her bodice was much too time-consuming, apparently. Jason opted for the knife, cutting the fabric away with swift strokes.

"Rule number one, luv," he said at her askance expression.

She simply smiled. "No clothes."

He disposed of the dress, throwing the tattered fabric aside. "It is good you remember that, because I intend to keep you naked as much as possible."

"I think I'm going to enjoy that, Captain."

"My mistress of the sea shall wear only the finest dresses obtained by me."

"Mistress?" Her joy was damped. Was that all he wanted from her, to be his mistress?

"Would you rather I refer to you as my sex slave?" he asked with laughter in his voice as he playfully nipped her earlobe.

She couldn't help but join in his sexy playfulness. "Ah, but being *your* sex slave is not such a bad position to be in. I've never had so much pleasure until I was captured by you, Captain."

He stilled. "How many masters pleasured you?"

She met his gaze. "No man mastered my body, or my heart, until you."

For a second she thought he'd kiss her, something she longed for him to do. She'd sampled his body but he'd never given her the simplest gesture of love—a kiss.

Instead he murmured against her skin, "You shall have no other."

Her eyes rolled back as Jason kissed a trail from her ear to her breasts, his hands molding her body to his.

Jason lavished attention upon one breast and then the other. As he suckled upon her aching nipples, he whispered, "Touch yourself. Show me how much you love me."

She reached down to her sex and dipped her fingers through her wet folds. With one pass of her fingers over the sensitive tip of her clit, she moaned loudly.

"Jason," she whispered.

"You are so beautiful, Shelley," he said in a low, husky voice.

She stretched and moaned as he traced his hands over her body. She felt cherished, worshipped and loved.

She wrapped an arm about Jason's head and groaned. He nuzzled her breasts, his face buried between the two mounds. He licked and kissed them as he gently squeezed them together with his hands.

Her body moved against him, urging him on.

"Tell me how you want me. Tell me you want to fuck me," he said as he reached between her legs to her clit, juices sluicing over his fingers. She guided his fingers with her own to show him the spot that drove her wild.

"I want you, Jason. I want you inside me. I want to fuck you long and hard."

"Mount me…ride me, luv."

They rolled on the pillows and then Shelley straddled his hips. As she placed her legs about Jason, her labia gaped open and she became overly aware of how empty she felt. There within a few inches was Jason's cock, thickly veined and hard.

He placed his hands on her knees, moving his palms slowly to her waist before grasping his cock and sliding it through the slick cream of her pussy. "Fuck me, Shelley. Now."

She lifted herself with her thighs, slowly guiding her hips over his length. As his size filled her, she moaned in joy. Pleasure wrapped about her as she moved slowly down onto his cock.

She slid her body up and down on Jason's cock, lost in the sensations building within her. His hands lay upon her hips, guiding her, slowing her pace. She fought his control but he cooed to her soft commands and promises of unending passion.

Jason mapped her torso with his hands, studying her curves with each thrust. His fingertips were warm and hungry. When he cupped her breasts, she gasped at the heat of his skin against her sensitive flesh. Her nipples ripened at his touch and her cunt quivered when he gently pinched her taut nipples. She thought she'd climax just then, but more was to come. Every inch of him coursed through her body with each beat of her heart.

She relished the leisurely skill with which he made love to her. When he reached for her clit and circled his thumb over the surface, euphoria hit her. A powerful orgasm pulsed through her like an explosion, igniting every cell in her body.

Jason! Oh how I love you! She managed to peek at him as she came and his intense need to please her was written upon his face. She wanted to scream out her heart's truth to him again, but instead bit her lip.

She was a woman here by strange magic, a twist of fate that couldn't be explained. How could she have let her heart be touched by a man who lived as a pirate—in 1622!

She moved her hips slightly, gaining a moan from her pirate lover from the past. She smiled when her body jolted and her heart skipped a beat as another climax washed over her.

Jason became more insistent in his thrusts and she felt stretched to the brink, and loved it. But she wanted more. She needed his confession of love.

"Jason," she whispered breathlessly. "Tell me you love me."

At that instant he came, wrapping his arm about her, bringing her face close to his. His warm seed pumped into her and he kissed her hair. He confessed in a husky voice, "I love you. Only you...forever...my love."

It was too much. Shelley came a third time as her lover awaited her on the summit of mutual sexual ecstasy. Her spasms vibrated throughout her body as Jason's cock pulsed inside her.

Held on the precipice of sexual paradise, Shelley was overcome by sensation and staying awake became difficult. She relaxed into Jason and whispered, "Forever." Then darkness swirled about her senses, and Shelley eased into a content unconsciousness.

When Shelley came to, she was lying on her side with Jason kissing her face.

"Are you all right, luv?" Jason asked anxiously.

"Yes, I'm okay. Just blacked out there for a few moments."

Jason brushed her hair and kissed her temple. "I love you so much. I do not think I could stand losing you ever again."

She gazed into his eyes. "I love you more than anything, Jason." But how could she ever say she'd never leave him? She was a time traveler, a woman living in a place she didn't belong.

"What is it? You seem troubled." He paused then asked, "Is it Mendoza?"

She cocked a brow. "Nothing happened between Captain Mendoza and me. I couldn't give him what he wanted."

"Why?"

She giggled. "There's room for only *one* pirate in my heart."

"Anyone I know?" His voice was lighter, but sleepy.

"Aye. I believe so, Captain." She lightly kissed his cheek. "You."

"Good, otherwise I would have had my rival shot in the morning."

"I thought punishment was to walk the plank?"

He laughed. "If you don't be quiet and let me get some sleep for a few hours, I will make *you* walk the plank."

She snuggled into his arms, cherishing the welcoming warmth of his body next to hers. "Pirate."

* * * * *

Shelley and Jason didn't leave the tent the rest of the day or evening. As the sun rose in the sky the next morning, the couple walked on the beach together, the waves lapping along the shoreline in a rhythmic dance while seagulls swooped out over the water for their early morning meal.

"I have something I want to talk to you about." Jason's voice broke into her thoughts.

"Yes?"

He appeared troubled, or possibly unsure. "I want to quit pirating."

She stopped and looked at him in surprise. "Quit? But how?"

He turned to her and placed his hands upon her shoulders. "I actually thought to give back the *Sea Hawk* to Mendoza. He can pass the command on to someone he feels worthy."

"But what would you do?"

He folded her hands within his. The gesture was tender and her heart skipped a beat. "Get married and build a mansion for my beloved wife and have lots of children."

Could she even hope he meant to marry her? "I thought you said you wanted me as your mistress."

"I want to build a new life for myself, and I want a wife by my side, not a mistress."

"But—"

"Do not worry about your slave band. I grant you your freedom. I will make sure it is removed."

Her breath caught. What about her life in the future? If the band was removed, what would happen?

He dropped to one knee. "Would you marry me, Shelley?"

"I..." She wanted, more than anything, to say yes. But she was from another time, brought back across the centuries by an unknown magic. To agree without thought would be so easy. But she couldn't honestly agree to a marriage. Not without knowing if she would stay. Not without telling him her story. "Jason, I have to tell you something."

He stood up. "What is it? Are you already married? I thought you were only a—"

She placed a finger over his lips. "Please. Just let me talk. It's going to be hard to believe. I'm not sure *I* even believe it."

Questions and confusion reflected in his eyes, but she pressed on. "I'm not really a slave. I am not even from this time. I was on a research dive for the newly discovered galleon, the *Santa Rosa*, thought to be sunk by a hurricane in 1622. However, by examining the hull, it was apparent the galleon sank during a sea battle—probably pirates."

He dropped her hands and gazed at her face with dawning fear.

"As I swam through the wreckage, I came across a trinket left behind — this bangle." Shelley lifted her arm and fingered the silver band. "When I picked it up, the latch unhooked and I was sucked through some sort of time vortex. I can't really explain it beyond that it was unlike anything I've ever experienced. When I woke up, I was in your cabin on the *Sea Hawk*." She paused and reached for him. "I'm from the future, Jason. I was brought here by magic…and I don't know if I will remain here or one day suddenly get pulled back to my own time."

She stepped closer and laid her head against his chest. "But I met *you*, and now I never want to go back. If you remove this band, I don't know what will happen."

He reached for her arm and touched the bangle that had brought her across time. "Can it be true?"

She nodded, her tears wetting his linen shirt. She sank into his embrace, his body heat welcoming and soothing to her fears.

"I knew you were different, luv. But this is…quite unbelievable."

She backed away from him and saw the skepticism written on his face. "You think I'd make up something like this?"

"I think you have been at sea for a long time and the sun may have gotten to your mind," he said gently. "We can stay here for a few days until you get to feeling better before moving on to Tortuga."

He thought she was nuts. "I am *not* making this up. You have to believe me! I'm not crazy."

He stepped toward her but she backed out of his reach.

"Do you believe me?" she asked in painful sorrow.

"Shelley—"

He reached for her but she pulled away, shaking her head as she continued backing away, putting more distance between them. "No. Don't touch me," she said, tears falling freely. She grasped the bangle and tugged at the clasp. "I've been through too much—traveling back in time, falling in love with a pirate, getting kidnapped…I can't take any more. I just want to go home and end this."

The bangle opened and fell from her wrist onto the sand.

She stared at the silver band glittering in the sand for a brief moment then looked up at Jason, who ran toward her—then faded into nothingness.

The sunny island darkened before her eyes and the ground shifted beneath her feet. She fell to the sand and water ran over her legs. She shivered and closed her eyes to the bright flashes blinding her, sending her mind reeling in confusion. Dizziness engulfed her and when she finally felt the warm rays of the sun upon her skin, she blinked away the disorientation.

She was alone on the beach.

What happened? The bangle! Her eyes searched the tropical forest just beyond the beach—and realized the foliage was much more overgrown than she remembered.

She rose to her feet and staggered off in the direction of the tent. But it was nowhere to be found.

With sadness in her heart, she fell to the sand and tears burst from her eyes as she sobbed.

Her time in the past was over.

Chapter Eleven

ဢ

Shelley sat staring out at the sea at her father's beach house. That's where she'd stayed for the entire summer, each day looking out over the ocean — pining for her pirate lover.

Had it really been two months ago since she'd been aboard the *Sea Hawk*? Two months since she had been blasted into the past and into the arms of a sexy pirate? And oh, how she wished that's where she was today.

However, the moment she removed the bangle from her wrist, Shelley had been thrust back to the future and he was out of her life forever. How could the fates be so cruel as to let her find love and passion only to rip it away?

As the waves crashed against the Florida beach, Shelley sighed. A tear ran down her cheek as she let sadness eat at her soul.

"Honey, are you okay?" she heard her father ask as he stepped out onto the deck.

She couldn't answer.

"You haven't been the same since...since the accident." He took a seat next her in a lounge chair.

That was what the dive had become known as, "the accident". According to the divers, she literally disappeared that day during the expedition. Vanished into the depths of the ocean. Search parties combed the area for her, but to no avail. A week later, she had been found alone and crying by the Coast Guard, hundreds of miles away on a small uninhabited island in the Bahamas.

She couldn't bring herself to tell them the truth. Who would believe that she'd traveled back in time? She didn't even tell her father, fearing he would think she was insane. So, when everyone asked what had happened, she claimed amnesia. Considering the circumstances, no one questioned her further about "the accident".

"I think it's time you talk to me about what happened out there two months ago," he said in a solemn voice. "Enough is enough. I can't stand seeing you like this."

"Dad, you wouldn't believe it if I told you." She was sure he'd ship her off to a mental hospital the instant she told him. As a scientist, he'd never believe it. Or would he?

"So there *is* something. I knew it. Now…out with it. Time to reveal your secrets, honey. It's the only way you can find peace."

She turned on him. "I don't want to find peace, I want Jason!"

His face crinkled with confusion. "Jason? Who's Jason?"

"Captain Jason Flint."

Shelley spent the next hour spilling the events that haunted her heart. Of course, she skipped over the sexual escapades she'd shared with Jason. No sense in telling her father that she had liked it when Jason tied her to his bed.

When she was through, he sat silent for a few moments, digesting her tale. It was hard to believe, even to her.

"Time travel." He sat staring out over the water, shock written upon his face.

"Yes. If I didn't actually experience it, I would say it was a load of bullshit."

His gaze slid to her face. "Well, it *is* very hard to digest, honey."

"Then why I am sitting here without a clue as to how to move on with my life? I feel like I left my life back in 1622 with Jason."

"If it was anyone else, I'd say it was impossible. Time travel is fiction, an H.G. Wells novel, not something that actually happens."

"But I'm telling you, it *did* happen. I'm not crazy. This is not some story I made up. I went back in time and fell in love with a pirate captain. I lived through a sea battle, was kidnapped by a rival captain only to be a prize in a duel. It all happened. I swear." Shelley's heart hammered in her chest. He *had* to believe her.

"You say a bangle was the key to this whole strange adventure?"

"Yes. I found it in the wreckage on the dive."

"Honey, it wasn't with you when they found you on the island."

She sighed. "I know. It was left behind, back in time."

"The questions that remain are, what happened to the bangle after it came off, and where is it now?"

"I don't know. I assume Jason has it."

She turned to stare back out at the ocean.

"Maybe we ought to do our own treasure hunt, Shelley."

Turning her gaze to his, she asked, "What do you mean?"

"I mean, if this happened as you say, wouldn't your captain have left the bangle somewhere for you to find on that island, the last place he was with his love?"

She shook her head. "Dad, you don't believe me, so why pretend otherwise. I told you that you wouldn't believe it."

"*You* believe you went back in time. I don't know what to think about it." Then he sighed and added, "However, if it *is* true…"

"What?" Her heart pounded harder.

"If it truly happened, your captain would certainly try to reach you."

"And?"

He hesitated then said, "Maybe your captain buried the bangle on the island, hoping you'd find it in the future."

Could it be possible? "To return to him in the past?"

He reached over and squeezed her hand. "It's entirely possible."

For the first time in months, Shelley had hope. "When can we go to the island?"

"Tomorrow. We'll take the Marine Society's boat. On the way to the docks, we can pick up a couple metal detectors and supplies. Right now, let's go download a map of the island and see if we can pinpoint where to look first."

She gave him a crooked smile. "You don't really believe that Jason left the bangle there on the island for me to find, do you?"

He sighed. "Not really. But I'll help you no matter what I think. I just love you and hate seeing you in pain. Maybe you can find peace if we look for any sign of your pirate captain."

"Thanks, Dad."

* * * * *

The next day on the island, Shelley and her father searched, but with no luck. In fact, all they found was a rummaged hole in the floor of the tropical forest. Someone had been there just recently and cleaned out whatever had been hidden there. Shelley realized other pirates had probably anchored on the island, just as Jason and Mendoza had. Could it have been treasure left behind?

"Look, a piece of eight," her father said as he picked up a silver coin from the sand. "There was definitely *something* buried here. Whoever dug this up probably made off with a fortune," he said, eying the size of the hole. He scanned the area around it, lined with wood and dried leaves. "And they knew exactly where to look too. I didn't find signs of a search anywhere else."

"Maybe they were using metal detectors," she said as she sat on a small pile of sand.

Her father stood silent, gazing out toward the beach.

"Dad? Did you hear me?"

He just stood there, shock written on his face.

Shelley dropped her metal detector and ran to his side. "Dad, are you okay?"

He pointed toward the beach. "I don't think *he* needed to use metal detectors."

"He? Who's *he*?" she asked as she turned her head toward the beach.

"The captain."

She gasped at the vision. Surely it was something brought on by the heat. Or island fever.

No, it was *him*.

"Jason," she whispered.

Her father stuttered in disbelief.

Jason strode up from the beach toward them. She sank to the sand, her legs giving out beneath her. Stunned, she was unable to believe her own eyes.

He stopped and stood before her. He was dressed in modern clothes—khaki shorts, a light green T-shirt with "Key Largo" silk-screened across the front and dark sunglasses. As different as he appeared, she recognized him by the confident stride, the span of his shoulders and the sexy-as-sin smile.

"Captain Jason Flint. As I live and breathe," her father said in awe.

Jason reached out to her and offered his hand—and she noticed the bangle about his wrist! He'd used it to find her!

She placed her hand in his, comforted by the gentle warmth of his skin. She rose from the sand and leaned into him. His hard body was welcoming as he wrapped his arms about her.

Broken from his daze, her father cleared his throat. "Well, you two seem to need some time to, er…talk. I'm going back to the ship, Shelley. See you back there in a while. I have a bottle of whiskey I need to open." Her father made a hasty exit and left them alone on the beach.

"You're here," was all she could say before Jason captured her lips with his.

Nothing needed to be said. His kiss expressed the longing—and the love.

His lips were commanding and firm. She melted into his kiss as he urged open her mouth with a swipe of his tongue. She moaned against him and he deepened his kiss. His tongue danced against hers as his hand splayed across her back. One hand cupped the back of her head, holding her steady as he increased the pressure against her mouth. It was raw and primal, and she loved it. She answered his desire with a fire of her own. Her pussy creamed and her clit ached for his touch—for him to claim it as his own once again.

Jason continued his assault upon her mouth. Like a pirate deprived of his most cherished treasure, he plundered her lips with hungry kisses. He demanded from her, and she answered. There was nothing she'd hold back from him—she wanted to give him everything.

Her hips moved against his thigh in an instinctive motion. He grasped her thigh and lifted it, and she curled her leg about him, holding onto him for balance. He lifted the hem of her skirt and pushed aside the moist crotch of her panties. Her labia gaped open in a wet invitation and Jason moaned when his hand found her ready for him. As his thumb passed over her clit, she whimpered in sheer delight.

"Shelley," he breathed against her lips as he continued to tease her nubbin.

"Jason. I missed you!" She began to cry tears of joy as her climax built quickly throughout her.

"I went insane when you left, Shelley. I needed you. I didn't want to be without you." He whispered close to her ear and his warm breath sparked the rise of goose bumps across her skin.

"You believe me now?"

"Without a doubt."

She sighed in relaxed ecstasy. He lowered her to the warm sand and pulled her T-shirt over her head, then removed her skirt and panties before pulling off his own shirt and shorts.

"I have to make love to you. I need you," he whispered.

Her heart beat wildly as his hands glided over her body. He squeezed her nipples to tight buds, ripe for suckling. As his mouth enclosed over one straining crest, she whimpered.

He reached down with one hand and gently massaged her clit, fingers gliding thorough her slick juices. She moaned and opened her legs wider, inviting him to touch her further.

When he slid one finger into her channel, she gasped and came. He continued to suck upon her breast as he pumped his finger in and out of her body.

Her muscles clenched about his finger and she was gloriously aware of the man covering her body with his own. She dug her fingernails into his muscular shoulders as she rode out the waves of her climax.

Her hips increased their rhythm in time with his gentle thrusting as he dipped two fingers into her seeping cunt. She cried out as another orgasm crashed over her body. Convulsions ravaged her senses as she succumbed to the expert touch of her pirate lover.

And just when she thought she'd die of pleasure, he adjusted his hips over her sex and entered her.

"Oh Jason!" she yelled when yet another wave of orgasm hit her.

He filled her, stretched her vaginal walls to capacity. A woman deprived, she bucked wildly against his hips, wanting to take him deeper. When he came within her, he grunted and yelled in surrender to the ecstasy.

"I love you! I love you," he said over and over as he pumped his warm seed into her.

She grasped his hair and pulled his lips down to hers forcibly. Before she kissed him, she breathed against his lips, "My pirate love."

* * * * *

"But I don't understand. How did you come to be dressed this way?" she asked later as they walked together, the sun setting over the ocean, painting the sky bright orange and red hues an artist would envy.

"When you disappeared, I was lost. It took me weeks to think clearly." He paused and then cleared his throat. "I admit I turned to rum to help with the pain."

"Of course," she said understandingly. She had been tempted to drown her sorrow as well when she returned to the future.

"Once the haze ebbed, I had a plan. I buried most of my treasure here. Then I gave back the *Sea Hawk* to Mendoza, along with forty thousand pieces of gold."

She trembled at the memory of the dark, alluring captain. "What was his reaction?"

"I think he understood my sorrow. I asked him to leave me here on the island." Jason paused and added, "Eventually, I tried on the band, more as a way to be close to you than anything else."

"You left your time for me," she mused aloud.

"The life of a pirate is short, my sweet. I had nothing left there." He reached for her cheek and stroked her skin delicately. "My future is with you, no matter where—or when."

"But how did you know it would take you to my time?"

"I didn't. I thought perhaps you'd come back to the past, though I didn't know how. Then I put on the band and things got *really* strange—as though I'd been drinking spiced rum all night in Barbados and my mind couldn't think a single thought clearly. When the feeling eased, I knew *something* had happened. I realized time had passed judging from the overgrown plants on the island. I took some coins and hoped to find a ride to the nearest port." He stopped and turned her in his arms. "The Coast Guard found me and took me to Key Largo. There I sold the coins, and used the money to buy some clothes and a boat."

"Then you returned to the island for the rest of the treasure," she concluded.

"Well, yes. But not before looking for you in Key Largo. No one seemed to know anything. I kind of got lost a few times. So many strange things! It's a lot to take in for a man from the past."

"But how come you came back to the island *today*?"

He smiled. "I've been living on the boat I bought on the other side of the island. I saw your boat come in and the fastest way I could get here was to go around. I had to row because the water is too shallow here to bring my ship."

"Your ship?"

"I bought a ship and named her the *Sea Hawk's Mistress*. I can't stay away from the sea. She has been my only love for so long—until you came into my life. I hope you don't mind."

"Of course not, but what about...I mean, won't you be missed in the past?"

He shook his head. "There was nothing left for me there. I will have simply vanished—like I fell into the sea, never to be seen again."

She looked down at his right wrist, at the bangle shining in the setting sunlight. She reached out to touch it gingerly...

It popped open.

Nothing happened. No vortex. No disappearing act.

"I don't understand it," she said as she examined the bangle in her hand. "Why didn't you disappear?"

"I don't know." He reached for the bracelet and tentatively secured it on her left wrist, where it had been the day he met her.

Still, nothing happened.

"Perhaps it is fate, Shelley."

"You think love was the key to its power?"

He nodded. "Like a curse broken with a kiss."

Love's first kiss. With all they had done together—on the ship in his cabin, on the beach—*Jason had never kissed her lips*! Until today.

"I promise, luv, that I will kiss you every morning and every night, until the day I die." He got down on one knee and held her hand in his. His eyes, so full of love, looked upon her with genuine tenderness. "Marry me."

She tugged on his arm and he rose from the sand. "Yes! *Yes!*"

He took her into his arms and she began to cry.

"Now, now, luv, this is no time for tears. We have our whole lives ahead of us," he said as he brushed away the moisture from her face.

"So...what will a transplanted pirate from the 1600s do in the twenty-first century?"

"Well, I certainly can't sail the Caribbean Sea attacking ships, can I?" He smirked down at her.

"Certainly not," she laughed.

He held her tightly, tucking her head beneath his chin. "Then I'll have to settle for sailing around the world in my yacht with my beautiful and feisty wife."

"You know," she laughed as she hugged him, "nothing sounds lovelier than a life on the sea." She soaked in his presence, cherishing the simple closeness of his body. Never again would she shed a tear in heartache for her lost pirate love. He had come for her, and he was there to stay.

He pulled away from her, his mouth grim. "I must warn you. The rules will still apply aboard ship here as they did back in my time."

Confused by the sudden loss of light humor, she wrinkled her eyebrows. "What do you mean?"

"You are my sex slave, and rule number one—"

"No clothes," she interrupted with a chuckle.

He laughed, breaking the mock seriousness of his mood. "Think you'll be able to sail under the command of a pirate?"

"Only if you promise to have your wicked way with me night after night."

"Aye, luv. Of that you can be sure."

Why an electronic book?

We live in the Information Age—an exciting time in the history of human civilization, in which technology rules supreme and continues to progress in leaps and bounds every minute of every day. For a multitude of reasons, more and more avid literary fans are opting to purchase e-books instead of paper books. The question from those not yet initiated into the world of electronic reading is simply: *Why?*

1. *Price.* An electronic title at Ellora's Cave Publishing and Cerridwen Press runs anywhere from 40% to 75% less than the cover price of the exact same title in paperback format. Why? Basic mathematics and cost. It is less expensive to publish an e-book (no paper and printing, no warehousing and shipping) than it is to publish a paperback, so the savings are passed along to the consumer.

2. *Space.* Running out of room in your house for your books? That is one worry you will never have with electronic books. For a low one-time cost, you can purchase a handheld device specifically designed for e-reading. Many e-readers have large, convenient screens for viewing. Better yet, hundreds of titles can be stored within your new library—on a single microchip. There are a variety of e-readers from different manufacturers. You can also read e-books on your PC or laptop computer. (Please note that Ellora's Cave does not endorse any specific brands.

You can check our websites at www.ellorascave.com or www.cerridwenpress.com for information we make available to new consumers.)

3. *Mobility.* Because your new e-library consists of only a microchip within a small, easily transportable e-reader, your entire cache of books can be taken with you wherever you go.

4. *Personal Viewing Preferences.* Are the words you are currently reading too small? Too large? Too... ANNOYING? Paperback books cannot be modified according to personal preferences, but e-books can.

5. *Instant Gratification.* Is it the middle of the night and all the bookstores near you are closed? Are you tired of waiting days, sometimes weeks, for bookstores to ship the novels you bought? Ellora's Cave Publishing sells instantaneous downloads twenty-four hours a day, seven days a week, every day of the year. Our webstore is never closed. Our e-book delivery system is 100% automated, meaning your order is filled as soon as you pay for it.

Those are a few of the top reasons why electronic books are replacing paperbacks for many avid readers.

As always, Ellora's Cave and Cerridwen Press welcome your questions and comments. We invite you to email us at Comments@ellorascave.com or write to us directly at Ellora's Cave Publishing Inc., 1056 Home Avenue, Akron, OH 44310-3502.

erridwen, the Celtic Goddess of wisdom, was the muse who brought inspiration to storytellers and those in the creative arts. Cerridwen Press encompasses the best and most innovative stories in all genres of today's fiction. Visit our site and discover the newest titles by talented authors who still get inspired - much like the ancient storytellers did, once upon a time.

Discover for yourself why readers can't get enough
of the multiple award-winning publisher

Ellora's Cave.

Whether you prefer e-books or paperbacks,

be sure to visit EC on the web at
www.ellorascave.com

for an erotic reading experience that will leave you
breathless.

Made in the USA